What people are saying about …

# Stretch Marks

"The novel to buy alongside *What to Expect When You're Expecting*! Funny, poignant, and cleverly written, Kimberly Stuart's *Stretch Marks* reminded me of all the misadventures, challenges, and joys of being pregnant—and the surprises that come with motherhood. A delightful read from an author who tells it like it is!"

**Susan May Warren,** award-winning
author of *Nothing but Trouble*

"*Stretch Marks* is an absolute gem! Funny, authentic characters live out their messed-up lives and experience the deepest graces of life and spirit. Bravo, Kimberly Stuart!"

**Ginger Garrett,** author of *Chosen:
The Lost Diaries of Queen Esther* and
Chronicles of the Scribe series

"What a sparkling, sassy—with the word twirled in gold sequins—hilarious, brave, and smart romantic comedy. The characters in *Stretch Marks* are so engaging I want to take yoga and color my hair with them! This is Kimberly Stuart at her finest, a soaring triumph for Christian fiction."

**Claudia Mair Burney,** author of
*ɪ* and *Wounded*

# Stretch Marks

A NOVEL

# Stretch Marks

## KIMBERLY STUART

David C Cook®
*transforming lives together*

STRETCH MARKS
Published by David C. Cook
4050 Lee Vance View
Colorado Springs, CO 80918 U.S.A.

David C. Cook Distribution Canada
55 Woodslee Avenue, Paris, Ontario, Canada N3L 3E5

David C. Cook U.K., Kingsway Communications
Eastbourne, East Sussex BN23 6NT, England

David C. Cook and the graphic circle C logo
are registered trademarks of Cook Communications Ministries.

The Web site addresses recommended throughout this book are offered as a
resource to you. These Web sites are not intended in any way to be or imply an
endorsement on the part of David C. Cook, nor do we vouch for their content.

This story is a work of fiction. All characters and events are the product of the author's
imagination. Any resemblance to any person, living or dead, is coincidental.

All Scripture quotations taken from the King James
Version of the Bible. (Public Domain.)

LCCN 2009929974
ISBN 978-0-7814-4892-5
eISBN 978-0-7814-0348-1

© 2009 Kimberly Stuart
The author is represented by MacGregor Literary

The Team: Andrea Christian, Jamie Chavez, Sarah
Schultz, Jaci Schneider, and Karen Athen
Cover Design: Amy Kiechlin
Cover Photos: iStockphoto, royalty-free

Printed in the United States of America
First Edition 2009

1 2 3 4 5 6 7 8 9 10

062509

For my little ones

# Acknowledgments

The team at David C. Cook makes me love my job. I send wild applause to Don Pape, Terry Behimer, Andrea Christian, Amy Quicksall, Ingrid Beck, and Jaci Schneider for their persistent and creative hard work on my behalf.

Jamie Chavez is the answer to most of my problems, at least those of the literary nature. This book would be pathetic without her intervention.

Jennifer Ruisch is a brilliant editor and writer. It is nothing short of a coup for me that she happens to be a friend and sister as well.

I am indebted to Adam and Rachel Andrews for their friendship and for their thoughtful help on the Chicago end. Come in, Peoria?

My writing group has endured many versions of these chapters. Thanks go to Dawn, Kali, Mia, Wendy, Chantal, and Murl for their kindness and consistent hard work.

Rachel Maassen, MD, provided me with sound medical counsel, some of which I probably messed up anyway. After thirty-two years of friendship, she remains the truest of true.

Ginger Garrett knows how to write, laugh, parent, and do

speaking gigs, and all before nine a.m. I've witnessed it! Ginger, you are one of my favorite perks of getting into this bih-nuss.

Many laughter-and-tears-drenched thanks to Amy from Minnesota, Amy from Iowa, and Kristen from 52nd Street, for always hoping, always praying, always assuming I could do it with God's help.

The Beach brood deserves its own catalog of thanks. You are dear to me, every one.

God has created an amazing cocktail of friendship for me in Julie David. Sass, spunk, hearty laughter, and a heart bursting with love for Jesus. Plus she sells lots of books for me. My gratitude goes to her and to Kevin, who sends us along with Godspeed and great support.

Chip MacGregor deserves more money than he's paid. There, Chip Chip. It's in print.

Thanks and much love go to Jocie, Barry, Scott, and Laura, readers all and an in-law girl's great blessing.

Randy, Patti, Ry, Jen, Linds, and Jimmy love me, love my husband, love my kids, and never seem to complain about it. Thanks to them for knowing about the indicting family videos, proof of my snotty stage(s), and loving me anyway.

Welcome and auntie blessings go to Skyler Jayden. Love me best, love me best, love me best.

Ani, Mitch, and Thea are entirely unimpressed by their mother's profession but still manage to inspire so much of it. You three are gifts to the most undeserving, but good gravy, am I grateful.

And to Marc, I send effusive, embarrassingly weepy thanks for making the cheesecake and never turning back. Life is ever sweeter with you.

# I

# Under the Weather

Mia's nose was stuck in her own armpit. Not a lot of glamour there, but she was working toward a higher purpose.

"Think of how your organs are thanking you for acknowledging *them*, for being considerate enough to stretch *them*." Delia's voice floated from the front of the room where, Mia knew without looking, she joined the class in a binding pose that could make most grown men cry like little girls.

Mia breathed an audible breath, collecting a healthy whiff of deodorant-infused sweat. In the nose, out the nose, throat relaxed. She closed her eyes, feeling the ends of her fingers beginning to slip out of the bind. *Liver, pancreas, you're welcome*, she thought and felt her stomach make an uncharacteristic lurch. The radiator kicked in beside where she stood, infusing heat and a bass hum to the room. Mia focused on an unmoving spot on the floor and not on the spandexed and heaving tush of the woman on the mat in front of her.

"And now using the muscles in your core, slooowly release and come back to mountain pose." Delia manipulated her voice and cadence to stretch like honey. On any other day, her instructor's voice sounded like a lullaby to Mia, a quiet but persistent reminder to breathe deeply and recycle paper and plastic. Today, though, Mia felt an urge to ask Delia to speak up. She wanted concrete sounds, solid sounds; the feathery intonations landing lightly around the room made her insides itch. She pulled out of the bind and stood at the top of her mat, feet planted, palms outturned.

"Feel better yet?" Frankie whispered to Mia from the mat next to her.

Mia sighed. "Not yet."

"Let's move into our warrior sequence." Delia modeled the correct form on her lime-green mat and the class obediently followed suit.

Four poses later Mia hadn't shaken the bug she'd hoped was just an out-of-sorts feeling to be shed with a good workout. She felt elderly, cranky. Not even downward-facing dog had brought any relief. She lay on her back during the last minutes of class, trying to melt into the floor, *be* the floor. The spandexed woman was snoring. This final pose, savasana, was intended to provide participants final moments to recover, to be still and let their minds quiet before reentering the chaos of the outside world. Most yoga aficionados soaked up the pose. In Mia's class she'd spotted a plump, permed woman wearing a sweatshirt that declared in stark black print *I'm just here for the savasana.*

Today, though, Mia couldn't keep her eyes shut. She curled and flexed her toes, wishing Delia would crank up some Stones or Black Crowes instead of the Tibetan chimes lilting out of the stereo. Her impatience with a woman who freely quoted Mr. Rogers was beginning to worry her. Even in the hush of the room, her thoughts continued in an unruly spin, and when Delia brought everyone back to lotus, Mia glimpsed a scowl on her reflection in the mirror.

"Let's just enjoy the long, strong feeling of our bodies," Delia said. Her eggplant yoga gear revealed taut muscles. "Our organs are thanking us for a good massage."

*Right. Organs. Mission accomplished,* Mia thought, trying to concentrate on the gratitude her body owed her. But her mind crowded with images of bloody, squishy masses, pulsating or writhing in the way organs must do, and she found herself springing from her mat and bolting to the back of the studio. She threw open the door to the ladies' room and gripped the toilet bowl in a new pose, aptly christened Riotous and Unexplained Retching.

* * * * *

"Mia?" Frankie's voice was subdued, even though a postclass din was making its way through the restroom door.

Mia emerged from the stall. "I guess sun salutations weren't such a good idea." She washed her face and hands at the sink, trying not to inhale too deeply the scent of eucalyptus rising from the soap. She watched her face in the mirror, noting the pale purple circles under her eyes that persisted even with the extra sleep she'd indulged in that week. Mia smoothed her eyebrows with clammy fingers, taking care not to tug the small silver piercing, and glimpsed Frankie's concerned expression in the mirror. "Don't worry," Mia said. "I feel much better now. Must just be a virus."

Frankie handed over Mia's coat and a hemp bag proclaiming *Save the Seals*. "I'll walk you home. Let's stop at Gerry's store for soup and crackers."

Mia made a face. "Crackers, yes. Soup, definitely not."

Outside the studio, weak February sunshine played hide-and-seek with wispy cloud cover. Frankie planted her arm around Mia's waist.

Mia glanced at her friend. "I like the blue."

Frankie turned her head to showcase the full effect. "Do you? I meant for it to be more baby blue, less sapphire, but I got distracted with this crazy woman on the Home Shopping Network and left the dye on too long."

In the two years Mia had known her, Frankie had demonstrated a keen affection for adventurous hair coloring. Magenta (advent of spring), emerald green (popular in March), black and white stripes (reflecting doldrums after a breakup), now blue. The rainbow tendency endeared Frankie to Mia, who'd braved an extended though unsuccessful flirtation with dreadlocks during college, but otherwise had settled for a comparatively conformist 'do of patchouli-scented chestnut curls.

"How did this change go over with Frau Leiderhosen?"

Frankie whistled. "She *loved* it. In fact she wondered if we could have a girls' night out this weekend and take turns trading beauty secrets."

Mia snorted, which was an unfortunate and unavoidable

byproduct of her laughter. The snorts only encouraged Frankie.

"'But, Esteemed Employer,' I said, 'I can't possibly instruct the master! A mere mortal such as I? It'd be like a Chihuahua taking over the dressing room of J-Lo! Or Sophia Loren! Or Gisele Bundchen, a woman who shares with you, dear boss, an impressive German name and an uncanny sense of style!'"

"Stop it." Mia clutched her stomach and groaned. "Yoga and laughter are off limits until further notification from my digestive tract."

Frankie sighed. "I do feel sorry for her. I never should have shown up with a mousy blonde bob cut for the initial interview. I was *so* average librarian." She shook her head as they slowed near Gerry's Grocery. "Only to turn on her the first week on the job."

It had occurred to Mia more than once how much she could have benefited from a green-haired librarian in the small Nebraska town where she'd grown up. Not until she was well into adulthood did she realize that not all librarians were employed to scare children, like the dreaded circulation director at Cedar Ridge Municipal Branch with the spidery braid and hairy mole. Mia had cowered behind the legs of her father when he would stop in to check out an eight-track or the latest release by Louis L'Amour. The moled woman had snapped at Mia once when she'd fingered a book on a stand, announcing down her nose that the book of Mia's interest was for display only and could not be checked out. Never mind that *Bird Calls of the Northeast* had not exactly beckoned to eight-year-old Mia anyway, but the chastisement was enough to keep books at an arm's length for years. How different Mia's interest in reading could have been had a spitfire like Frankie been the one behind the desk!

Frankie's supervisor, Ms. Nachtmusik, with her impossible surname that changed with each conversation, didn't know the gift Frankie was to her patrons.

"Hello, ladies." Gerry looked over his glasses. He stopped pecking madly at a calculator on the front counter. "How are things with you?"

"Mia's sick, Gerry." Frankie patted Mia on the head. "We need sick stuff."

Gerry pushed back on his stool and stood. He clucked like an unusually tall occupant of a henhouse. "Sick, Miss Mia? Headache? Stomach? Fever?"

Mia shook her head. "Stomach, I guess. I think crackers will be enough."

Gerry looked disgusted. "This is not your duty to decide. Miss Frankie and I will take care of the illness. Sit." He pointed to his stool and waved at her impatiently when she didn't jump at his command. Gerry shuffled off, muttering about the tragedy of young people living in cities without their parents.

Mia slipped Frankie a rolled-up reusable shopping bag and whispered, "Make sure to steer him away from pesticides."

Frankie winked at Mia and skipped behind the man on his mission.

Mia greeted the next few patrons entering the store. She tried watching the game show on Gerry's small black-and-white, but she couldn't seem to follow the rules. *I'll just lay my head here for a moment*, she thought, pushing Gerry's calculator aside.

● ● ● ● ●

"Oh, good heavenly gracious, we need to call an ambulance!" Gerry's words seeped like molasses through Mia's subconscious. She wondered who was injured and if it had anything to do with the impossible rules on that game show.

"Mia, honey, are you okay?" Frankie was tugging on her shoulder.

"Hmm?" Mia pulled her eyelids open into the glare of fluorescent lights. Her head was, indeed, on the front counter, but so was the rest of her body. She turned her head slowly to face Frankie, who had crouched down beside her and was inches from her face. "I'm lying on the conveyer belt."

"Yes, yes, you are," Frankie said while guiding Mia to a sitting position. She gauged her tone of voice to fit a three-year-old on Sudafed. "Gerry and I left to get some groceries and when we returned," she enunciated, "you were lying on the counter." She nodded up and down, up and down.

Mia shook her head. "I was really tired. I needed to sleep." Her voice trailed off. She kept her hands on her face for a moment, fingers brushing past a stud in her right nostril and the ring in her eyebrow. Eyes open, she peeked through the cracks in her fingers. Behind Gerry, who was patting his pockets frantically for cigarettes that hadn't been there since he'd quit a decade before, stood his son, Adam. Mia tried running her fingers through her yoga-tangle of hair.

Adam cleared his throat and smiled.

Mia realized she'd dropped her hands and had commenced a creepy stare session. "Hi, Adam," she said too loudly. "How are you?"

Adam bit his cheek in an attempt to take seriously a question coming from a woman sprawled next to a cash register. "I'm great, Mia. You?"

"Fantastic," she said and swung her legs to the side of her perch. Gerry rushed forward to offer her his arm, Adam close behind. Mia held up her hands in protest. "I'm fine, really," she said. "Just a little tired, apparently." She walked slowly to the front door and turned to wave. "Thanks, Gerry. You're a great host. Adam, good to see you. Frankie, are you ready?" She opened the door without waiting for a response and stepped out onto the sidewalk.

Gerry pushed away Frankie's twenty-dollar bill and handed her the sack of sick stuff as she fell in behind her friend.

●  ●  ●  ●  ●

They walked five minutes in silence. Dusk was long gone, the sun having set early in the February evening. Mia was from the Midwest and didn't much mind Chicago winters; Frankie, however, hailed from Southern California and moaned every few steps as wind from the lake found its way through coats and mittens and headed straight for skin.

"I will never know why we have chosen this misery." Frankie held Mia at the crook of her arm like a geriatric patient. Mia felt too exhausted to protest. At the foot of the stairs leading to her apartment building, she stopped. She watched a dapper older gentleman with mocha skin descend the steps and allow his eyes to fall on her.

"Hey, Silas," she said.

"Evening, girls," Silas said. He dropped his keys in the side pocket of his suit and tipped his hat, a soft brown fedora trimmed in striped black ribbon. He cocked his head slightly and narrowed his gaze at Mia. "Girl, you don't look so hot." Silas furrowed his brow and looked at Frankie. "What's the story, Francesca?"

"We're not sure," Frankie said. "But don't worry. I'm taking her straight upstairs before she can toss her cookies again."

Silas took a nimble step back, sidestepping puddles in his retreat. "Honey, I'm sorry. Ain't no fun getting sick."

"Thanks," Mia said. She handed him a box of Lorna Doones from her stash of groceries. "Brought your favorites. Goodness knows I won't be needing a visit with Miss Lorna this evening," she said, wrinkling her nose at the thought.

Silas clucked and shook his head. "Your mama raised you right, girl. I thank God for you, Mia, and I know my dear Bonnie is happy to look down from glory and see me so well taken care of." He patted her gloved hand. "I couldn't ask for a better neighbor. You get better now, you hear?"

The girls took the steps slowly. When they reached the front door and waited for Mia to fish keys out of her bag, Frankie cleared her throat.

"So, um, what was that business at Gerry's all about?"

Mia shook her head. She dug deeper in her purse. "This is one bizarre virus. I don't even remember making the decision to go to sleep."

"Yes, right. I didn't mean the counter episode. I meant the eye-lock with Gerry's son."

"Found them," Mia said and pushed her key into the lock. "Sorry, what were you saying?"

"Hair-fixing, googly-eye thing with Fig Leaf."

Mia tried to look disapproving. "You and your nicknames. I like the name Adam. I cringe to think of what you call me behind my back."

"Hmm," Frankie said. "Today would be a toss-up between Vomitronica and Queen of Feigned Emotional Distancing."

"I'm not feigning anything, for those of us who've read too much Jane Austen," Mia said. She led the way into the lobby elevator and pushed the button for the fourth floor. The door closed with a shudder and Mia shrugged. "It's really nothing."

Frankie crossed her arms and positioned her finger above the emergency stop button.

"All right." Mia sighed. "When I first moved to my apartment, I was momentarily single and also in need of a neighborhood grocery. I found Gerry's, and Adam was always there with his perfect smile and impeccable Persian manners." She sighed and watched the numbers light up on their ascent.

"Oh, my gosh. This is so *Rear Window*."

"Isn't that the one where the woman is paralyzed?"

"No," Frankie said with labored patience. "That's *An Affair to Remember*. I'm hinting less at paralysis, more at love at first sight."

Mia rolled her eyes as the elevator door opened. "I noticed him, he noticed me, we flirted, and then I was no longer single." Mia stepped into the hallway. "It was nothing. Seriously. As you might remember, I'm happily in love with another man. End of story." She led the way to her apartment door. "Sorry to disappoint. I *was* recovering from an episode, remember."

"Exactly!" Frankie was triumphant. "Your defenses were down, you were caught off guard and didn't have time to censor what was and wasn't socially appropriate—"

"Shh. He might be home." Mia paused at her apartment door and ignored Frankie's dramatic jab of her finger down her throat.

"That would be *so* unusual," Frankie said, *sotto voce*. "You can't mean he would be eating your food and smashing organic potato chips under his rear as he watches *Baywatch* reruns on *your* couch?"

Mia called into the room, "Anybody here?"

Frankie muttered, "Because we wouldn't expect you to be anywhere else."

Mia pinched Frankie's arm when she heard rustling in the living room. "Lars?"

He stepped into the entryway, blond hair tousled, mouth opened in a wide yawn. "Hey, babe," he said around his yawn. "Hey, Frankie."

"Hi, Lars," Frankie said sweetly. Mia avoided eye contact with her friend and instead pulled her arms around Lars and gave him her cheek to kiss.

"Don't exchange any of my germs," she said. "I think I'm sick."

Lars stepped back, nudging Mia out of the embrace. "Really?" He wrinkled his nose. "Like puking sick?"

Mia unbuttoned her coat. Frankie tugged her friend's arms out of the sleeves and unwrapped her from a bulky crocheted scarf. "Like, *totally* puking sick," she said, watching Lars for any recognition of her mocking tone. None detected, she rambled on. "She, like, ralphed after yoga and then at Gerry's she *totally* fell asleep under the scanner."

Lars had turned and was heading for the fridge. Mia shot a pleading look at Frankie, who sighed and nodded a momentary truce.

"You should have called and told me you were going to the store. We're almost out of soy milk," he said, nose in the fridge. "And I ate the last Carob Joy after lunch."

Mia filled a glass with water. Lars had piled his dishes in the sink, and it occurred to her to thank him, as this was a marked improvement from finding them all over the apartment, crusty, molding, and sometimes neglected until they smelled of rot. Determined not to conjure up any more detail of those images and too tired to explain to Frankie later why dirty dishes piled in the sink was a step upward, she sipped her water and shuffled toward the bedroom.

"Thanks, Frankie, for taking care of me," she said. "I owe you. But I can't think about it right now, okay?"

Frankie followed her into the bedroom. She turned the covers down as Mia undressed and placed a saucer of crackers on the bedside table. "You take care of yourself, do you hear me?" For a woman with blue hair, Frankie could command the maternal authority of Olivia Walton when summoned. "Call me tomorrow morning. Or before if you need me. Not that Lars isn't the nurturing, restorative type ..."

Mia moaned. She lowered herself into bed and curled up into a fetal position.

"All right, all right." Frankie spoke softly. She turned out the light. "Sleep well, Mimi." She waited a moment for an answer from under the down comforter but Mia was already drifting toward sleep.

# The System

When Mia woke, inky black had settled in the room. She raised herself up on one elbow and made her eyes focus on the dresser clock. Nine twenty-four. She'd slept for two and a half hours. She kicked off the covers and was pleased the action didn't make her want to run to the restroom. Her fuzzy slippers peeked out from under the bed. They murmured a soft-shoe on the wood as she padded out to the living room. Lars was reading in the papasan chair by the window. The open pages of his book shone unnaturally in the only light illuminating the room. He looked up.

"How's your tummy?" he said, shutting his book. He stood and led her to the couch where they could sit together.

"Better," Mia said. She yawned. "I'm still really tired, but I think I'm hungry."

Lars pulled a soft green blanket from the back of the couch and draped it around Mia's lap and legs. "How about some pho? I stopped at Hanoi Market for some noodles."

Mia closed her eyes and smiled. "Perfect."

She let her head rest on a pillow while Lars heated her dinner in the kitchen. *See?* she told an internal Frankie. *This is how he is, not the mooch you think you see in him.*

When Mia closed her eyes, she could see Lars when they'd first met. They'd registered for the same senior seminar their final semester of college, "Patriarchy, Famine, and Genocide in Twenty-First-Century Africa." Seven students and one prof met weekly to discuss painfully long and depressing research articles on the state of African politics, economy, geography, and sociology. Mia had noticed Lars for his thoughtful comments, or at least that's how she told the story now. She left out that she first was drawn to Lars because of his lips. They were full, always pink, and seemed to encourage mind-wandering. The thought still made her blush, as she was not typically one to objectify men, certainly not while intending to concentrate on the effects of tribal patriarchy on modern African elections. But the lips were what got her attention. The thoughtful comments were just an excuse to watch the lips move.

"Here we go," Lars said. He set a steaming bowl of soup on the coffee table and tugged the table toward the couch. "Hold on," he said and returned to the kitchen. Mia could hear him rummaging around in a paper bag. He turned slowly into the family room, brow furrowed with the task of holding a wide mug of tea, chopsticks, and a saucer dotted with slices of lime.

"Such great service in this place," Mia said, laying her head on

Lars's shoulder when he settled into the couch. "I should definitely eat here more often."

Lars kissed the top of Mia's dark curls. "I'm happy you're happy. My dad would so not believe how enlightened I am, male partner serving female and all that. You're one lucky girl, you know?"

Mia could hear the smile in Lars's voice and tried her best to exude her luckiness. "Absolutely I do. Neither of my parents was very good at the partnership thing either, so we're both renegades." Her first slurp of broth sank, one pampering centimeter after another, down her throat and into her body. She hummed her approval.

"Good?" Lars said. He rose from the couch to snap up his cell phone, which was trumpeting a wild dance tune by his favorite world music group, HealPeace. He checked to see who was calling and shut the ringer off. "Bryan," he said to himself.

"Really?" Mia squeezed a lime wedge over her soup. "That's great. Does he need you for a job?" She cleared her throat after the question, regretting how eager she'd sounded.

"Probably," Lars muttered. He scrolled through a text message. "I'm kind of busy, though, so I don't know if it will work out."

Mia kept her eyes on her noodles. When asked about his profession, Lars said he was a freelance writer. This translated mostly to the odd short piece here and there, usually contracted by Lars's high-school buddy, Bryan, a magazine editor who was kind enough to pass along work when it was available. The relationship was tenuous, as Lars felt Bryan stifled his creative spirit with the extensive editing he did on each piece before publication. Mia had seen some of Lars's rough work, however, and felt Bryan was a literary savior. *Irregardless* and *satisfication*, for example, were not the best ways to use the English language, try as Lars might to convince. Neither was opening a piece with a two-hundred-word quotation by Engels a foolproof device to engage the reader.

"You're too busy?" Mia asked. "What are you so busy with?"

Lars looked up from his phone. "Did I pay half our rent this month?"

"Yes," Mia said. She avoided his gaze by the tip of her mug.

"And the three months before that?"

"Yes, you did," Mia said. She groaned into her tea, the voice of her mother admonishing her (again) for having a "live-in" outside the bounds of marriage.

"What's to gain?" her mother would say in her best Dr. Laura voice. "Why *should* he propose when he has all the benefits without the risk?"

Not that Mia's mom was one to talk about marital success, Mia tried to remind herself. But eighteen years of brainwashing had to have repercussions on a girl's thought life.

"Okay, then," Lars said, flipping his phone shut and tossing it onto the chair by the window. "You can feel confident that my decision not to work will not adversely affect our *arrangement*." He strode back toward the kitchen and Mia let him go. She could barely keep her eyes open and was finding it increasingly difficult to enjoy the act of eating. This left little reserve for entering into an argument with Lars. Lars, who could crush an otherwise bright person in a debate. Lars, whose tenacity wearied Mia to the point that she was always the first to forget the original point of discussion and the first to give up and give in. Having witnessed many of these "conversations," Frankie had developed a disgust for what she saw as Lars's unwillingness to lose a battle.

"Stop letting him do that!" she would say to Mia later. "He is not always right." Mia would shrug. "I know, and he probably does, too, on some level. But it's so much easier to let those things go. I just don't care enough and he does, so we both come out ahead, right?"

Mia shuffled to the kitchen. She covered her bowl with plastic wrap and put the leftovers in the fridge. On her way out of the room, she met Lars in the hallway near the front door. He was pulling on his coat.

"I'm meeting Dan at the Dive. He needs a little cheering up."

Mia leaned against the door frame. "What's wrong? Something with Avery?"

Lars snorted. "You could say that. She's threatening to dump him if they don't get engaged."

Mia nodded slowly. "An interesting way to resolve the marriage question. Spend the rest of your lives together or dump each other. It seems like there should be some middle ground there, doesn't it?"

Lars moved to her and enveloped her in his arms. "See? That's exactly why I'm with you and not someone like Avery. You acknowledge the ridiculousness of convention. You see through marriage as an antiquated system left over from—"

"—the unequal and barbaric days of class wars, dowries, and institutionalized sexism." Mia looked up and smiled. "I agree completely."

He kissed her. "I know. And knowing that makes me risk getting your plague by kissing your lips." He kissed her again. "You rest. Don't wait up." He turned and locked the door on his way out.

He hadn't apologized, but Mia thought there must be lots of ways to communicate one was sorry, and maybe not always with a penance of words.

● ● ● ● ●

A week later Mia sat with her head in her hands. Her desk phone was ringing and she was summoning the strength to answer it. "Urban Hope," she said, resting her forehead in her palm.

"You sound horrible. Are you still feeling like excrement?" Frankie's voice was inappropriately loud but there was no volume control on Mia's ancient phone.

"I would appreciate you not mentioning anything remotely related to an unpleasant image, smell, or taste. I cannot be held accountable with what I might do with such information." Mia swiveled in her chair and leaned her head against her office window. She told herself the cool of the glass was soothing.

"Have you gone to the doctor yet?"

"Not exactly."

"Mia, this is your big chance to stick it to the Man, just like you and Lars connive to do. You work for the system, the system is broken, the system pays peanuts and keeps the downtrodden down while the wealthy thrive. *But* the system gives great insurance benefits, so get your rear to the doctor's office and start cashing in, for once."

"Are you chewing on something?" Mia watched a little girl cross the alley below, holding with a death grip to the fingers of her father.

Even from two stories up, Mia could see the red patent leather shine on the girl's shoes.

"Yep," Frankie said, "and it is so stinking good. I've always wondered what those lamb things taste like. You know, those cute kabobs impaled on their little skewers at that place on Fullerton?"

Mia groaned. "All right. I'll make an appointment with a doctor."

"Excellent," Frankie said, so loudly that Mia had to pull the phone away from her ear. "Tell them it's an emergency and that you work for the government. Maybe they'll squeeze you in this afternoon."

"You have definitely inflated my job to mean something it doesn't."

"Love ya, kid. Call me later."

Mia let the phone drop to its cradle. She lugged a phone book from her bottom desk drawer and set about searching for a board-certified answer to her problem.

# 3

# Breaking News

The waiting room at Brookview Medical Clinic brimmed to overflowing with runny-nosed children, sneezing elderly people, and harried staff. One by one, patients were called back by a nurse who looked young enough to be violating child labor laws. She wore purple scrubs with a cheerily decorated name tag reading "Carrie Lynn!" Care Bear stickers floated around her name and a big smiley face covered the *a* in Carrie. She flipped papers anchored into a clipboard and cleared her throat. "Mr. Hoffman," she said and looked up hopefully from arms laden with identical folders.

Mia sat near the girl and was the only one who heard her announcement. She smiled at her encouragingly. "Maybe try it again."

Carrie Lynn nodded and took a deep breath. "Mr. Hoffman?" The change in volume was incremental. "Sid Hoffman?"

Mia scanned the room and saw a bevy of older gentlemen

chatting in the corner. She rose and walked to their group. "Excuse me, Mr. Hoffman?"

A man in a three-piece pinstriped suit looked up with sparkling eyes. "Yes, miss?"

Mia smiled. "The nurse is calling for you." She nodded toward Carrie Lynn, who looked like she might kiss Mia out of gratitude.

"Thank you, dear." Mr. Hoffman stood slowly and walked with Mia toward the nurse. "I'm afraid I didn't hear you," he said to Carrie Lynn and shuffled past her down the hall. Carrie Lynn sighed. "I still can't get used to the yelling," she said to Mia and rushed after her patient.

Mia settled back into her chair and paged through a year-old issue of *InStyle*. The room was spinning slowly after her sudden burst of physical activity. *I won't be able to be the megaphone again*, she thought. *That girl is on her own unless she wants to deal with a dramatic demonstration of the stomach flu in her waiting room.*

Mia was the next to be summoned. Carrie Lynn had said only the first syllable of Mia's last name before her patient was at her side. The nurse bit her lower lip and looked so grateful that Mia worried about the emotional stability of her caregiver.

"We just never had to do that part in nursing school." Carrie Lynn spoke as if she and Mia were Chi Omega sisters meeting for lattes and biscotti. "I mean, I love the one-on-one, talking to Mrs. Jones and putting her at ease before the doctor comes in. But *that* room?" She shuddered and gestured for Mia to step onto the scale. "It is *always* that busy. And people are *always* staring like that."

Mia was having one of her more profound waves of nausea and therefore felt exempt from reciprocal communication. Carrie Lynn didn't seem to notice. She fiddled with the calibration of the scale when Mia stepped up to be weighed.

"One forty-five. How tall are you?"

Mia cleared her throat and gathered all her concentration into the Don't Lose It box in her head. "Five-six."

"Room eight, this way." Carrie Lynn padded down the hall in purple Crocs. They passed through an area recently cleaned with bleach. Synthetic pine scent weighed heavily in the air. Mia breathed through her mouth and scanned the room numbers for eight.

The door shut and Mia obediently seated herself on the crinkly papered table. Carrie Lynn began her inquisition.

"And why are we seeing you today, Miss Rathbun?"

"I can't seem to shake this flu."

"Influenza? You've been feverish? Cold symptoms?" Carrie Lynn wrote in loopy letters, dotting each *i* with carefully inked purple hearts.

"No, not that kind of flu. I feel nauseous. And unusually tired." She took a deep breath. "I'm thinking it's mono. A colleague at work had mono last month. She must have sneezed on me or something."

"Let's leave the diagnosing to Dr. Rivas," Carrie Lynn said, lips pursed in disapproval. "So no cold symptoms, right?" She drew the word out as she carefully crossed out *influenza*. "Nausea and fatigue. Any vomiting?"

"Yes, probably twice a week for the last three weeks."

"That's when the symptoms first began?"

"Yes." Mia paused. Carrie Lynn wrote. "Maybe four. Yes, four. I felt sick and tired for a while before I actually started throwing up."

Carrie Lynn passed a deliberate purple line through more

markings. Mia thought there would be less stress associated with Carrie Lynn's dictation practices if she'd give up the hearts.

Left alone to wait for the doctor, Mia lay back on the exam table. She rolled over to a fetal position and tried to fake her body out to think it was relaxed instead of lying prone in a sterile and uncomfortably cold medical clinic. In the room next to hers, a baby cried with reckless abandon. Mia could hear the frantic pleas of the mother to calm down. Insistent *shhhh*s, sounding nearly like a hum so forced were they, filtered through the plaster between the two rooms. The baby continued to scream.

A brisk knock shook the door a nanosecond before it flew open.

"Miss Rathbun, I'm Dr. Rivas. Good to meet you."

Mia scrambled to a sitting position. She shook the hand he offered. "Nice to meet you as well."

Dr. Rivas strode to the sink and commenced a splashy hand washing. He cranked the paper towel dispenser, hard, three times. Nodding toward the screams in the next room, he said, "Quite the set of lungs in that one. 'Course they all do. Poor mama can't get any sleep with crying like that."

Mia mumbled an appropriately sympathetic response but continued watching with wide eyes Dr. Rivas's flurry of activity. He flipped open the metal trash receptacle with his foot and slammed the dirty paper towels into the bag. "Whoosh!" he said to no one in particular. Carrie Lynn entered quietly and took up the corner farthest from Mia, purple pen in hand and poised above her chart.

"So." Dr. Rivas came to a sliding stop on his rolling stool and sat at an awkward height just below Mia's knees. "Nausea, fatigue. No headaches?"

Mia shook her head.

"Fever? Loose stools?"

Mia closed her eyes and shook her head.

He perused the chart offered by Carrie Lynn. "Date of last menstrual period?"

"Um." Mia had to concentrate on this new question. "I'm not exactly sure. I switched birth control because I was gaining weight—"

Dr. Rivas's head snapped up to Mia's patella. "Different oral contraceptive?"

Mia told him the prescription name.

He slammed shut the folder. "There you have it. A switch like that can make your GI tract go through a rebellious stage. A lot like my two teenaged sons." He snorted. "The oldest one just got a tattoo that says *Viva la revolución*." He shook his head and scrawled a series of marks on Mia's chart. "What a joke. He drives a Volvo and thinks a revolution would be cool? He's clueless." Dr. Rivas thrust the papers to the nurse and rose from his stool. "Carrie Lynn will draw some blood to rule out anything serious. But you should be back to feeling peachy keen in no time."

Mia and Carrie Lynn both jumped when the door slammed behind him.

"*That* must have been an adjustment too," Mia ventured.

"You have no idea," Carrie Lynn muttered. She withdrew a syringe, cotton swab, and bandage from the cupboard over the sink. "Dr. Rivas has asked for a broad screen of tests. Anemia, diabetes, thyroid. I'll need you to put up both sleeves so I can check for a good vein."

Concerned that vein probing and bloodletting might put her

over the edge, Mia shut her eyes and concentrated instead on her cell phone ringing within her purse. It was a peppy Latin number, one she suspected Dr. Rivas's son might appreciate, particularly when blasting through the speakers of a Volvo.

●  ●  ●  ●  ●

By the time she pushed through the door to her apartment, Mia was laden with three burgeoning *Save the Seals* bags, the day's mail, and Lars's dry cleaning. She found it a mystery why a freelance writer needed to professionally launder his clothes when she was usually the only one who saw him in the act of writing. The pollutants and toxins released during the cleaning cycle of one dress shirt alone made the hair stand up on Mia's neck. It seemed reasonable that Lars deal with his own carbon footprint and allow Mia to steer clear of Sherpa duty to and from the cleaners. But they had agreed early on in their relationship that each other's passions were not things to be shared, necessarily, just respected. And earlier that month Lars had helped her change their lightbulbs to CFLs. Plus, she reminded herself, he'd been the one to show her the values of going vegetarian. Gratitude for his tutelage coddled Mia into biting her tongue.

He was out. Mia turned on the hallway light to dispel the gloom of winter's early dusk. She hung Lars's shirts in his half of the closet and dropped the sacks and mail on the kitchen table. A light blinked on the answering machine, a Cadillac of a contraption, black with touches of fake dark wood, a technological survivor of the days of Boy George, cassette tapes, and *The Facts of Life*. Mia and Lars were the only people in their age group holding on to antiquity, much less to a landline. Lars, though, liked it for its nostalgic value, Mia for the fact that it gathered messages for both of them in one spot, a tiny proof they were making a home together. They'd endured a fair share of ribbing from friends but the couple would laugh along with the jibes and the machine stayed.

She pushed play and reached for a wine glass.

"Hey, babe, it's me." Lars's voice cut through din in the background. "I'm at Pete and Bryan's. I'll probably be out until late, so don't wait up. And did you get a chance to pick up my shirts? I'm sure you did 'cause you're *awesome*." Mia tried hard to take this as a compliment and not feel on par with Lars's descriptions of the newest game for his Wii. "Oh, one more thing. Dan and Avery? Remember their fight about getting married or splitting up? Guess who bit the bullet and bought a diamond?" He cackled into the phone. "At least *we're* still standing, baby! Still going strong and not selling out! Love you, Mi. See you soon."

Mia poured a generous glass of chilled sauv blanc. The second message began with a beat of silence.

"Hi, honey. It's me. Mom. Your mother." Mia reached over to press pause on the machine. That she chose to simply pause the message instead of delete it outright encouraged Mia to believe she was making significant progress. Mia's mother, Barbara, had been the source of many, many sessions in the care of her therapist, Dr. Liza Finkelstein. After clocking an impressive number of hours with the good doctor, Mia was able to explain with a cool head why Barbara, or Babs as she preferred to be called, was simply not privileged at this point to have a close relationship with her daughter. She had forfeited that right when she'd walked out on Mia and her father the

summer after Mia's high-school graduation. That Mia was headed
to college and would have, in effect, walked out on them both in a
matter of weeks, was of no consequence, as Mia was the child and
Babs was the adult. Mia sighed deeply as she recounted all of these
truths, taking an extra moment to remember the exaggerated pain
that sprang up still, five years after her father's death. It was a car
accident, an icy road, completely unforeseen and unavoidable. Still,
Mia couldn't help but pair her mother's disappearing act with the
death of her father shortly thereafter. The woman brought destruction
with her like some people packed an umbrella in case of rain.

Mia took a long and careful sip of wine and pushed play. "I'm
calling from San Juan, honey. The groups on this cruise are wearing
me out. I've tried reminding them I'm an activities director, not
the Energizer Bunny." Her laugh was dry and quickly interrupted
by a coughing fit. "Sorry about that. I'm fighting a cold. Can you
imagine? A cold in Puerto Rico? And those Al Gore people say we
have a problem with global warming."

Mia glanced at the Inconvenient Truth magnet plastered on the
side of her fridge.

"Aaaanyway, pumpkin, I just wanted to say hello. I hope all is
well in your world. Call me anytime on that number I gave you,
okay? All right, then. Bye now."

Mia had a vague recollection of an international cell number
her mother had given her at one point. If the paper on which it
was written had escaped the recycling bin, it was certainly hiding
somewhere deep within the recesses of her apartment, purposefully
forgotten and inaccessible.

A third beep began another message.

Clearing of a throat. Then, "Yes, this message is for Mia Rathbun. Mia, this is Dr. Manuel Rivas at the Brookview Clinic. We have some, er, results from your tests. I would appreciate a call to the clinic when you receive this message. Ask for me. Thank you." *Click.*

*That's strange,* Mia thought. She couldn't remember a time when an actual physician had called her at home. A nurse or receptionist, yes. But a doctor? She dialed the number for the clinic and was put through to an answering service. The woman on the other end had been given Mia's name and the okay to give her Dr. Rivas's home phone number. Mia's hands were beginning to shake. *His home number?* she thought. What was wrong with her?

The phone at the Rivas home rang once.

Cancer? Did she have cancer? Her grandmother had died of cancer when she was ninety—

Second ring.

Something terminal? Something rare? She'd watched an *Oprah* once about a girl her age who'd—

"Hello, Rivas residence." The speaker sounded like he couldn't be a day over fourteen but was gunning for the rich baritone of a twenty-something.

Mia cleared her throat. "Yes, um, my name is Mia Rathbun. I'm returning a call to Dr. Rivas?"

"Hold on." The baritone had jumped up a half octave just knowing the caller wasn't looking for him. Mia heard rustling and shouting behind the haphazard veil of the boy's hand over the mouthpiece.

"Manuel Rivas." The doctor seemed to be slightly out of breath. Mia could hear the rhythm of some kind of exercise equipment.

"Hello, Dr. Rivas. It's Mia Rathbun. I returned your call to the clinic but they gave me your home number...." She trailed off, feeling like she was an unwitting accomplice to a breach in social etiquette.

"Right, right." His breathing was labored. "Part of our new initiative to humanize doctor-patient interactions." He spoke the last words deliberately, as if recalling the PowerPoint presentation by human resources. "I'm just hopping off the elliptical. Hold on one moment, if you will."

Mia drummed her fingers on the counter. She considered slamming the contents of her wine glass but thought she might need to have her wits about her.

"Stop it! Right now, you hear me?"

Mia sat down. It was getting to be too much. "Excuse me?"

"No, no, not you. I'm sorry. We got a new puppy at this house in a moment of sheer lunacy on the part of my wife. Something to do with Christmas memory making ... Stop it, Ruffles! This is *not* a toy."

The fingers on her free hand massaged her temples. "Dr. Rivas, you left a message regarding my test results?"

A door slammed shut and a high-pitched whine ensued. "That should do it." Dr. Rivas cleared his throat. "I'm sorry, Mia. Now, your results."

Mia closed her eyes.

"We know why you've been bothered with nausea and fatigue."

Mia's voice became very small. "Is it a tumor?"

Dr. Rivas paused. "No, though this will present similarities."

*Oh, dear Lord*, Mia thought.

"Mia, you're pregnant."

The breath stopped moving through her body. Mia's eyes remained open long enough for them to sting. She let out a burst of held air. "But that's impossible." It wasn't a tumor. Not cancer, nothing fatal. Just a seriously misinformed lab tech. She shook her head. "I'm not pregnant."

"I understand these things can be hard to take in at first."

"No," she said. Her head wagged back and forth in denial. "It's the wrong result. There must have been a mix-up in your paperwork. My last name is spelled R-A-T-H-B-U-N. Rathbun, Mia."

"Yes, that's correct," Dr. Rivas said. His certainty was beginning to aggravate his patient.

"I'm on birth control. Like a really, really dependable form. I read the insert. It said if used correctly, there was only a—"

"Two percent chance of failure. That's also correct. But that still means that two out of one hundred women can experience an unintended pregnancy. In addition, sometimes a change of oral contraceptives can cause a weakening in the efficacy of birth control. Research has confirmed this."

"Then your lab must be *incorrect!*" Mia was pacing in her kitchen. This man was on her last nerve.

"Mia, we'd like to meet with you and the baby's father to talk through the next steps."

*Father? Lars? A father?* The thought sent Mia sliding down the wall and onto the linoleum. "I have to go," she said into her knees. "I have to go now. Thank you, Dr. Rivas."

"Mia, it's very important that you receive good prenatal care until you decide what to do."

"Prenatal care," Mia repeated. "Of course." She stared at the handset for a moment. Dr. Rivas's voice floated up to her from some other planet until she found the right button and hung up.

# Full Disclosure

A rumbling in her stomach nudged Mia to stand. The clock on the microwave said eight o'clock. She couldn't be held accountable to exact details, but she thought that meant she'd sat on the kitchen floor for nearly two hours. An unopened package of whole-wheat crackers perched on the edge of the pantry cupboard. Mia stared it down, wondering how it had the nerve to look so normal when the universe had toppled on its head. She ripped open the box and tore through a tube of wrapping. Five crackers in, she decided that was enough dinner for the evening. A dusting of cracker crumbs covered the front of her shirt and she left it there out of spite. Toward what or whom she didn't exactly care.

Halfway between the kitchen and her dresser, Mia felt anger start to rise in red blotches on her face and neck. *We're careful*, she thought as she tossed out pair after pair of socks looking for her pink cashmeres. *We always used protection, we were consenting adults, I took five-count-them*-five *women's studies classes in college.* She dumped the drawer's contents out on the bedspread. One pink sock surfaced. She pulled it on her foot and matched it with a green one with black polka dots.

"I'll have to terminate," she said aloud and stopped. One arm was pulled through her favorite organic cotton sweatshirt. She could glimpse the light bulb overhead through the opening at the neckline. Slowly she pulled the sweatshirt on and sat on the edge of her bed. The room vibrated quietly with the words she'd spoken. She felt her declaration become a heavy mass and roll through her chest to settle, quivering, in her gut. An abortion. Her mind swerved to late-night debates with her mother in high school. They'd glower at each other across the kitchen table, her father disappearing early in the conversation to leave the two females to box it out. The discussions had wearied them both, Babs worrying that she'd failed as a mother to have spawned such a liberal daughter, and Mia despairing that Barbara's archaic thinking about "the sanctity of life" would end up with enough political strength to catapult the country backward into illegal abortions and back-alley dealings in the dark.

On her bed, now a year shy of thirty, Mia shook her head slowly, struck with the certainty that this pregnancy would continue without her intervention. The knowledge unsettled her and she tried to reason her way out of it. *I'm young. It's not the right time. I'm not ready to be a mother....* All true, she knew, but the cumulative noise made by her sound objections was nothing but a whisper compared to the inescapably loud beating of her heart. She was an adult and this was a child, her and Lars's child, growing within her. The heartbeat that was making her head ache was the same percussion their child was hearing within her womb. She felt no self-righteousness, merely the surprising weight of something not much bigger than her pinkie.

"God help me," she said into the room.

The mirror above her dresser drew her eye. In it she saw a girl, paler than the one she would have recognized, swallowed in oversized indigo, circles of dark under each eye, enveloped in fear.

●  ●  ●  ●  ●

Mia had rolled the cocktail napkin that came with her mocha into a petite and symmetrical snake. With her attention now focused on coiling the snake into a circle the size of a quarter, she heard only intermittent phrases of Frankie's story.

"And she couldn't possibly expect me to finish the entire section before we closed, so I told her … I would be happy to accompany her pet mongoose to the circus but only if she bought me cotton candy."

"Um-hm," Mia said. The snake's tail wasn't cooperating.

"And she agreed! So we're all headed to Zanzibar together this Saturday, by zephyr and blimp, of course."

"That sounds great," Mia said. Her bottom lip was tucked under her teeth in concentration.

"Mia."

"Mm?"

"Mia," Frankie said more loudly. "Where are you?"

Mia looked up from her snake. "Where?"

"Yes, where. I think if I ask you *how* you are, you'll respond in some culturally acceptable way that tells me nothing. But if you tell me *where* your head has been traveling while it has busily constructed a woven basket with your refuse, then we might make progress."

"It's a snake. Not a basket."

Frankie raised both eyebrows. Her hair had mellowed into a deep purple since the blue incident. She sipped her macchiato and waited for Mia to give her coordinates.

Mia sighed. Her shoulders slumped and she reflected for the six thousandth time since Dr. Rivas's call that she wished she could cry. Dr. Finkelstein had once said that Mia's inability to emote with tears was evidence of the deliberate emotional distance she put between her and those she loved following the disappointment with her mother. Mia closed her eyes and concentrated on what she hoped would be a teary slam dunk: the accident scene in *Ice Castles*. She started to hum the theme for inspiration.

"Mia, what is it?" Frankie reached over to take her friend's hands. "I've never seen you so loopy."

Mia opened her eyes and stopped with the humming, defeated once more. "Loopy, you say? That's an adjective I wouldn't necessarily employ in this circumstance."

"What circumstance?"

Mia bit the inside of her cheek and turned her full gaze to Frankie's face. "Frank, I'm pregnant."

Frankie coughed up an unfortunate amount of frothed milk, so much so that coffee drinkers at nearby tables began to look concerned, then grossed out.

Mia jumped up to whack her friend on the back. "Are you okay?" she said and handed Frankie a stash of napkins from a dispenser.

Frankie blotted her eyes and blew her nose with an abandon of which Frau Leiderhosen would certainly disapprove. "I'm fine," she said.

Mia envied her the tears that fell slowly down her cheeks. *Maybe I should try choking,* she thought.

Frankie stood and pulled Mia to her feet. She wrapped her bony arms around Mia's body and said into her ear, "Congratulate or commiserate?"

Mia stood, crushed by Frankie's grip, until she noticed the curious stares of onlookers. First the milk coming out of Frankie's nose, now their extended display of affection … People were starting to forget about their own interests.

Mia broke the hug and sat down, taking care not to crush her snake coil. She picked it up again for strength. "Certainly not congratulate. Not yet anyway. I feel, um, conflicted."

Frankie nodded quickly. "Of *course* you do. Isn't that natural?"

"Heck if I know." Mia's shoulders didn't rise above the back of her chair. "Everything seems entirely unnatural these days."

Frankie furrowed her brow in worry. "What did Lars say?"

"Nothing."

"Nothing? That *pig*—"

"No, I mean, I haven't exactly told him yet."

"What?" Frankie was shrieking. "How long have you known?"

"About a week."

"Mia, for the love!"

By this time the people at the two nearest tables had completely abandoned any pretense that they were still reading their newspapers.

"Frankie," Mia said, voice so low only her friend and maybe one of the tables could hear, "can we talk about this as we walk?"

"Of course," Frankie said, all business. She'd gathered the trash on their table in one armful, disposed of it with a flourish, and had donned her vintage pleather disco coat before Mia had finished tucking the napkin snake into her pocket.

"You're speedy," Mia said, eyebrows raised.

Frankie shrugged. "Don't tell Leiderhosen. My speediness does not extend to the mildly interesting but completely outdated Dewey decimal system."

They pushed out into the late February air. The sky spat pathetic, hard snowflakes. It, along with the rest of the city, was tired of going through the motions of winter. Chicago charmed its visitors all the way through New Year's, luring shoppers to Michigan Avenue to sip cocoa at Ghirardelli, indulge themselves at Chanel, ride flush-cheeked around Water Tower Place in a horse-drawn carriage. After the holidays, though, the gray of the city unmasked and naked without the persistent mirth, Chicagoans exhaled one long groan at the dismal weather until its reluctant demise in spring.

"When are you going to tell him?" Frankie asked, eyes squinting upward.

Mia shrugged within her coat. "He's been horribly stressed this week, something about a botched deadline for Bryan. It hasn't felt like the right time yet."

Frankie was quiet. The sidewalks of Logan Square were unusually free of pedestrians, the neighborhood enjoying a brief moment of quiet before the late afternoon rush of humanity back to their homes.

They stepped back from a curb to wait for the light to turn. Frankie linked her arm through Mia's.

"How are you doing with all this?"

Mia kept her eyes trained on the light but could feel Frankie watching her profile. She shivered suddenly when a breeze rattled the brittle branches of the oak tree above them. "I don't think I can answer that yet," she said. "I suppose most of me is waiting to wake up from it. And hoping I can do that before having to spill it to Lars."

The light turned and Frankie pulled Mia gently from her reverie. "I'm no authority on love or pregnancy or anything grown-up like that. But," Frankie paused to gather her courage, "it would seem to me that you shouldn't be alone anymore. You've done this all by yourself for a week and your body was in on the secret long before that. Lars is half of the reason you're even in this situation. He should know what's going on. So he can help."

Mia sighed deeply, feeling familiar weariness seep through her again as it did in waves throughout her days. "I'll tell him. Tonight," she added. Her feeling had been that she should wait for the time when she was feeling less horrendous and he was in better spirits. For her part, at least, Mia didn't think she should assume the fog would be lifting anytime soon.

They'd arrived at the corner of Armitage and Damen, the place of their parting.

Mia could hear Frankie's sniffles as they hugged. Her friend's frail carriage heaved slightly within her parka. "I'm so sorry. And warmest congratulations," she said into Mia's ear. "Whatever the case may be."

Mia held onto her friend, digging her toes into her boots, into the ground below her, feeling herself heavy and firmly planted on the earth, lest she give into her longing to fade away.

● ● ● ● ●

She sat on the couch and waited. The rooms of her apartment were the cleanest they'd been since the day she moved in. No dirt remained to be purged, no soap scum to be scrubbed. Mia took a long and shaky breath. Her eyes drifted to the candle burning on the coffee table. Though she lit the candle only to calm her, not to inspire some romantic notion of the conversation she was waiting to have, its scent of pomegranate battled quietly with the lemon and vinegar odor left from Mia's natural cleaning solution. The sandalwood pillar she'd tried first had sent her hurtling toward the bathroom, so after clearing the stench with windows propped wide open to the cold air outside, she'd tried the pomegranate with better results. Mia watched the flame until she became concerned about her retinas and forced herself to look away.

Lars had called to say he'd be home late. It was nearly nine o'clock when Mia sank onto the couch and she'd been tempted to postpone her news for yet another day. Only the hope that her shoulders would be lighter going to bed that evening kept her rooted to the place she'd staked out, watching the front door.

She uncrossed her legs, suddenly aware that she was bouncing her foot up and down to the rhythm of the Joni Mitchell tune playing on the stereo. *Be honest, be patient, be myself.* She repeated the words Dr. Finkelstein had given her for difficult emotional situations. Dr. F. was currently in New Hampshire showing her Yorkshire terrier, Sparkles, and couldn't answer her calls until early the following week. After the thousands of dollars she'd spent, Mia felt she might be allowed an emergency call during a lull at the dog show, but Dr. Finkelstein was a big advocate of having "me" time. One woman's spa was another's Sparkles.

At quarter to ten Lars's key jangled in the lock. Mia stood, then sat. No need to make this any more awkward than it was sure to be.

"Hey, babe," Lars said. He dropped his bag on the front table and sighed. "What a freaking long day. Maybe I should be a bank teller. Don't they always get off at five?"

Mia watched him toss his wet coat on the floor. He discarded his snow-laced boots near the entry mat and padded to the kitchen. "What'dya eat for dinner?" he asked from inside the fridge.

"Not much. Toast and half a banana. I wasn't very hungry."

"Ouch," he said over the racket of cupboard doors he opened and closed. "That doesn't sound very appetizing. Are you still feeling sick?"

Mia closed her eyes. "Yes. In fact, um, Lars, we need to talk about something."

"Mmm?" Lars peeked into the living room. He was licking a glob of natural peanut butter off a spoon. Mia switched her gaze to the pomegranate candle.

"Go ahead and finish your dinner. Just come in when you're done." She picked up a magazine and tried to look casual and unalarmed. If dogs could do it, maybe boyfriends could also smell fear.

Mia had flipped through the same issue of *Fair Trade Fashion* two and a half times when Lars set down a plate loaded with food. Mia's eyes didn't linger, but she did glimpse two pitas stuffed with greens, globs of tofu, a dollop of hummus, and an orange. He pulled back the tab on a can of guava juice.

"So we need to talk?" Lars gathered the great majority of one pita into his mouth. He looked at Mia as he chewed.

Mia swallowed. She looked into his eyes and not at the stray clump of sprouts dangling out of his mouth. *Short and sweet,* she thought. "I'm pregnant."

He stopped chewing. A dollop of hummus perched on the end of his nose.

Mia felt herself trying not to smile.

Lars watched her and his face relaxed. "Oh, geez, Mia. I thought you were serious. I can't *tell* you how good it is to see you smile. That was almost even mean." He shook his head and took another bite of his dinner.

Mia watched in silence. After a moment Lars looked up. "Oh, no way. You're serious. Are you serious? You're really, uh—"

"I think I'm about two and a half months. It didn't click for a while."

"But that's still okay, right?" Lars's eyes were bulging. He shoved his plate to the center of the coffee table, next to Mia's discarded *Fair Trade.* "That's plenty early enough still, right?"

"For what?"

Lars let out a pinched laugh. "For what? To take *care* of it. To, you know, get an abortion."

Mia flinched.

Lars put both hands up and pushed back on the couch. "Okay, all right." His voice was conciliatory, measured. "Just give me a minute. This is rather, eh, shocking."

Mia sighed. "Tell me about it."

Lars tapped the fingers of his right hand on his knee. The other hand was clenched in a fist. "This is why you've been feeling so horrible, then?"

Mia nodded. She pulled a throw off the back of the couch and draped it around her shoulders. Exhaustion was pulling her toward bed. She let her head drop to the cushion behind her.

"Who else knows?"

Mia shook her head and spoke quietly. "Just my doctor. And Frankie."

Lars ran a hand through his hair. "You told Frankie before you told me?" His eyes sparked with irritation.

"She practically asked. She knew something was wrong." Mia tried not to make that statement any more inflammatory than it was, but Lars was looking for shards of glass on which to cut his hands.

"She noticed but I didn't. Sorry. *Sorry* I'm not intuitive when it comes to subtle changes during the first stages of pregnancy."

"Lars."

"No, that's cool." He stood and swiped his plate from the coffee table with such force that Mia was amazed he didn't leave a heap of tofu on the rug. She listened to him open and shut the fridge, open and shut the pantry, then silence. After labored minutes with no words between them, she rose with the blanket and walked to the kitchen. Lars was leaning against the counter, hands behind him. He looked up at her when she entered.

"I wasn't the most understanding in there." He nodded toward the living room. "Apparently I don't deal well with surprises."

"At least not the reproductive kind," Mia said. She let the door frame support her weight. "Lars," and her voice broke, "I want to go through with it."

He watched her as she spoke.

"I can't believe I'm saying it and I certainly can't believe I'm feeling it," she said. "I've tried to convince myself that an abortion would be the best choice. Especially in the middle of the night when I wake up and can't get back to sleep." Tears, so long sought, finally, blessedly, ran down her cheeks. She blathered on. "But I know I need to do this. I mean, I'm not seventeen or something. I'm twenty-nine. I had full knowledge that sex could lead to unwanted pregnancy. But I still took that chance."

"So you're taking your punishment like a man? Or worse, a martyr?"

"No. Yes. Maybe. I don't know." She blew her nose but the tears kept spilling over. "I'm pregnant with our baby. I love you, Lars. You love me. This is what's supposed to happen, just maybe not in the timing we'd wanted."

Lars nodded slowly. He watched the second hand on the clock above the fridge.

Mia shuddered at the euphoria she felt as the tears let loose. She couldn't wait to tell Dr. Finkelstein! "I just can't tell you what a relief it is to talk about this with you." She moved to him and put her arms around his waist. The blanket fell from her shoulders and puddled around their feet. "Thank you for not condemning me. Thank you for allowing me to feel this way."

"Of course," Lars said. He traced circles with his hand across her back.

Mia yawned into his shirt. "I'm so tired lately. I can barely think straight."

"I can only imagine." Lars said. He stopped with the circles and just held her tightly.

"Let's just take it one day at a time, all right?" Mia let her eyes drift closed. Lars was supporting her whole weight.

"That sounds right," he said. He kissed her on top of the head and walked her to the bedroom.

She fell asleep to the sound of John Coltrane drifting in gentle cadences from the living-room speakers. Lars had kissed her with such tenderness when he tucked her in. *We can do this*, Mia thought, just before dropping into a hard-earned, dark sleep.

When she woke the next morning, he was gone.

# Cravings

"Right, I understand that, Mrs. Freeman." Mia twirled the phone cord around her fingers and resisted the urge to use profanity with a client. "But if you'll try to understand my position here. I cannot force the school district to recognize selling drugs as an after-school activity."

Carl approached her desk, further emphasizing the cosmic rule that things can always get worse.

"… medicinal uses, right … I'm sure Jacob *has* done his research. But we are a government agency, Mrs. Freeman, and—"

Mia let the phone fall back to its cradle. She looked up and smiled her best hope-will-conquer-all grin. "How can I help you, Carl?"

He cleared his throat. "That sounded like a rough convo. Do you want to talk about it? As friends, you know. We could leave the whole I'm-your-boss thing at the door." Mia thought she saw his nose vibrate when he laughed. It was not unlike the whinny of a horse.

"It's a kind offer, Carl, but I think I'll pass."

"Rough day? Maybe I can help. Since my promotion to office team leader, I have really felt an upsurge in my ability to get through to the powers that be." He used a meaty index finger to push his glasses up his nose. Carl watched her for a reaction, shifting from one foot to another, each time causing his overloaded shoulder bag to creak with its weight.

"Thanks, Carl, but I think I'm okay. Just part of the job." The job, Mia thought, that was supposed to be her part in saving the world. She'd majored in social work during college with the firm belief that lasting change would occur only from inside a system that was already broken. She'd swooned at stories of poverty, neglect, and miseducation emanating from the city centers and had cheerily signed on for a life of being overworked and underpaid if it meant she could make a difference. Seven years in and, while she'd have liked to say she'd patched some significant holes, the dam was still on the verge of breaking and her Silly Putty wasn't nearly enough to stop it.

"That's cool, that's cool. Just let me know when I can be of help," Carl said. The bag creaked.

Mia worried about men with shifty eyes.

"Well," she said, gathering the file on Jacob Freeman and returning it to the cabinet beside her desk, "you have a good night, Carl."

"Would you like to join me for dinner?"

The formal execution of the requests always pained Mia. It was never "catch a bite" or "grab something to eat." Instead she felt like she was witnessing a rehearsed prom invitation.

"I don't think so, Carl. Thanks, though, for asking."

"Sure, no problem. I just found this great sports bar down the way. Sully's. Have you heard of it?"

"Yep." Sully's served huge portions of bad bar food with inflated prices. The walls were lined with autographed sports memorabilia, which drew a healthy stream of out-of-town tourists and, apparently, Carl.

"Yeah, it's awesome. So, um, I guess I'll head over there. By myself." Carl stared at Mia as she pulled her coat from a hook by the door.

"See you tomorrow, Carl." She smiled as she buttoned her coat.

"All right." He turned and lumbered toward the front of the office, heavy pack swinging and creaking with his steps.

*Oh, Carl,* Mia thought as she lifted her purse from the floor under her desk. *You really should direct that creepy stare in a different, less fertile direction. Believe me, buddy. I'm doing you a favor.*

Mia flipped the light switch as she passed it on the way out. She'd become the one most likely to close up each evening, initially as an effort to avoid arriving home to an abandoned apartment and now because she'd allowed even her non-Lars social life to dry up like a stream in August. Six weeks had passed since Lars's unceremonious exit and, with the exception of Frankie, Mia's friend list had dwindled to a comfortable nothing.

She put a hand instinctively on her belly as she pulled a vintage pink trench coat around her disappearing waist. She was four months along but her body still didn't flaunt its secret. Her colleagues might have suspected a little overeating after the big breakup but nothing beyond that. Slinging a rubber band around the button of her jeans still gave herself an extra inch. By the end of the day, her body felt heavy and swollen, but her empty apartment, her only witness, could not betray its knowledge of Mia's growing belly. Another good reason not to have friends: No one dropped by unannounced to be greeted by Mia dressed in an increasingly snug T-shirt.

The afternoon light had begun to wane, but sunshine reflected on raindrops, christening every tree branch, every dip in the sidewalk, every windshield. Mia could make out individual, silvery drops quivering on the surface of wrought-iron railings surrounding the brownstones in Logan Square. She trailed a hand along one of them and watched the water shower the sidewalk, her shoes, her coat. Her neighborhood offered the best of Chicago: small restaurants, family-owned businesses, close enough to the center of the city but still affordable for the average social worker. She loved the free-spirited vibe, even felt a jolt of pride when she passed her favorite vegan café, pulsing with impassioned conversation, serious faces over sketchbooks, and an average of one acoustic guitar per table. It had been a coup to find an apartment within walking distance of Urban Hope. When he'd moved in a year or so before, Lars had groused a bit about the new influx of hipsters descending on their formerly bohemian neighborhood, worried their rent would soon be jacked up in response to new demand. So far, though, Logan Square had remained home and was a lovely place to live, work, shop, and eat.

Eat. She smiled to realize again her renewed interest in food. It had been a long haul, but at around thirteen weeks, she'd felt the nausea lift and had treaded, first cautiously and then ravenously, into the world of normal-people food. Not a single whole-wheat cracker had darkened the door of her pantry since.

She heard the strains of Wang Chung coming from her purse and stopped to rummage for her phone.

"Hello?" she said. The number had registered unknown.

"Miggles! How's my perfect little sister?"

"John," Mia said. A smile spread across her face. "It's so good to hear your voice."

"Wait—is that happiness I hear? No guilt trip for not calling more often? No interrogation about my greenhouse gas emissions? No cold shoulder for being Mom's favorite and most brilliant child?"

Mia sighed. "Right, that. Well, today is lovely and springy and not even the lack of attention from my brother, the destruction of the earth, or a dysfunctional relationship with my mother can dampen a girl's spirits."

John whistled. "Boy, oh boy. Who is he?"

Mia snorted. "No boy, dear brother. Unless you're referring to my boss at work who has a problem with excessive perspiration and an unusually thick skin when it comes to rejection. Or perhaps my UPS man, a fine specimen to be sure, but one who waxes his legs and has been known to ask me where I buy my bronzer. Other than those, there is no boy. In fact," she tugged on the door to Gerry's Grocery and lowered her voice once inside, "that must be what you hear in my voice. The complete absence of relationship-related stress." She nodded at Gerry and took a basket with her to the produce aisle.

"What happened to that Scandinavian fellow? Thor? Sven?"

"Lars." Bananas, kiwi, one carrot out of curiosity. "We broke up." She thought about adding the rather important reason for their parting, but decided she'd wait for a gloomier day, maybe even one on which she and John would see each other face-to-face. "How are things in LA? Smoggy?"

"Mmmm, yes. Today's smog index is … dangerous. This is according to the amazingly intelligent phone I just purchased. It knows far more than any one of our teachers back in good old Highlands Cove. Even Mr. Perry. Remember him? Honors chemistry? Painfully smart but unable to make eye contact with other humans?"

Mia had moved down the inner aisles, bypassing the meat but not before sneaking a long whiff of the rotisserie chickens sitting like friendly maître d's in the warmer at the end of the deli counter. She shook it off, reminding herself of all the ethical and nutritional reasons she'd sworn off meat with Lars at the end of college. Instead she focused on the little packets of lentils and quinoa before her. "So LA is good?"

"No comment about Mr. Perry? Wow, you *have* sworn off men."

"Sorry," she said, laughing. "I got distracted. I'm grocery shopping while we talk."

"Oh, fantastic," John groaned. "Let me guess: Your list includes falafel, sprouts, jicama, soy milk, and a cloth bag of fake chocolate chips, just for some crazy fun after the meal."

"Soy milk! Thank you. I would have forgotten."

"How we were raised in the same home is an enigma to me. Even in neurotically healthy LA, you're too much, Mia."

"I think I'll take that as a compliment." She had glimpsed Adam straightening the shelves in the bread-and-cereal aisle and kept moving down the rows. Since her impromptu nap session Mia had done her best to avoid the man. It wasn't that she couldn't figure out what to say; it was that she liked living the conviction that boys did indeed have cooties, and were going to add no benefit to her life. Even casual interactions within platonic relationships had been nixed in her head for the time being, the one exception being her current conversation with her brother.

"… but if she would just stop getting herself plastered all over the tabloids, that would certainly make my job easier. Not that one can give her advice, by the way. Mia, are you there?"

"Pickles," she said. "I need pickles."

"Pickles. I see. Dill or sweet?"

"Oh, definitely dill. The saltier, the better. And cream cheese. Yes! Do you remember those weird little rolls Mrs. Jansen always had on hand for after-school snacks?"

"Mrs. Jansen who wore blue mascara? I'm scared to ask you to explain."

"Dill pickles with cream cheese smeared all over them and then rolled in dried beef? Oh, geez. Do you remember? They were *so* good. I can't believe I haven't thought of them in years."

"So what's a vegetarian to do in this situation? Roll the pickles in cream cheese and black beans?"

Mia made a face. "I'll just do the cheese and pickles I guess." She beelined back toward dairy. "So other than the tabloid problem, work is good?"

"Partially *because* of the tabloid problem, work is good, yes. So listen, when are you coming to visit?"

"Um, soon. Definitely." Now that he mentioned it, Mia had a vague recollection of her brother broaching this subject before. That had been during the epoch of Lars, however, and Lars hated Los Angeles, with its absence of public transportation and excess of collagen. True, he'd never actually been there, but Mia hadn't felt compelled to be his tour guide and somehow she'd never gotten around to budgeting for a trip alone. "How about in a few months? Or six months? How about six months?"

"Six months? I was thinking next weekend or at least before the summer. Why would you wait so long? Mia, you're starting to give me a brotherly complex. I mean, I know I haven't always been the most dedicated sibling but—"

"No, no, that's not it at all." The cream cheese was shelved dangerously close to deli meat, which included shiny, endearing packets of dried beef. She looked both ways before tucking one into her basket. She headed to Gerry's checkout. "I'm just really busy. You know, work and stuff. I think things will calm down in October. November. What about Thanksgiving?"

"Good grief, Mia. It's May." He did little to hide his irritation. "I'm trying here."

"I know, I do. Thanks for the invite, John." She waved at Gerry and balanced the phone on her ear as she unloaded the basket. "We'll definitely set a date. But I think I should call you back. This isn't a very good time."

"Once again, I take a backseat to protecting the fate of innocent animals and meat products." He sighed. "Fine. Call me when you have the chance. I want to hear what's going on, Mia. Do you have some dirty confession or something?" He laughed and she joined him, perhaps a bit too heartily.

"Right. I'll call you back to confess." She closed her eyes and groaned inwardly. "Love you, John. We'll talk soon."

She hung up and stood to face Gerry. "Hi, Gerry. How are you?"

"I'm most certainly very well, Miss Mia. And you are feeling better." He said this as a fact, viewing the strange assortment she'd stacked on the conveyor belt.

"Yes, thank you." During the weeks following the episode at his store, Gerry had kept a close eye on Mia and peppered Frankie with questions as well. Apparently Gerry dabbled in herbal remedies; he had offered Mia samples of his homemade green tea, which he'd also baked into biscuits and served her with honey. They were barely palatable, but Mia had been touched by his concern.

"Hey, Mia." Adam headed to the end of the counter and started placing her things in the bags she'd brought along. "You look fresh and ready for spring." He grinned. She blushed and turned toward Gerry, who had raised one eyebrow as he punched a button for her total.

"Thank you, Adam," she said, trying for her best dental receptionist voice. "What do I owe you, Gerry?"

"Thirty-four seventeen," Gerry said. He looked at his son while Mia fished for her Visa. Adam shrugged but his grin was undeterred.

"These are kind of heavy," Adam said when he handed Mia her bags. "Do you want me to walk you home?"

"No, but thank you for offering," Dental Receptionist Mia replied. "Good to see you both." She cinched the belt of her coat and hefted the bags, immediately regretting her decision to buy three jars of pickles. "See you," she called out cheerily and ducked past Adam as he held the door.

She heard Gerry say as she left, "Funny girl."

Mia looked back when she stopped at the end of the block to adjust the weight of the bags. She knew Adam's eyes followed her until the bright pink of her coat was swallowed by the crowd.

# 6

# Flowers in Bloom

Frankie, newly washed into a stunning auburn, stared unblinking, fork poised above her plate. "Wow."

"Hm?" Mia asked. She looked up briefly from a heap of fusilli but kept close attention on her bowl.

"What a difference a month makes." Frankie stabbed into a mound of fettuccini and began to twirl. "You're a different human." She watched Mia lift a hefty fork load to her mouth. "It's like watching *Jurassic Park*. It's kind of … carnivorous."

Mia thought of the contraband dried beef waiting in her refrigerator and wished she could ask for a sprinkling of prosciutto without using words. One huge change at a time in her best friend was probably enough to expect Frankie to absorb. Mia swallowed a happy mouthful of pasta, pine nuts, feta, broccoli, and sun-dried tomatoes. "The books were right. The cloud lifted after the first trimester and now I can eat."

"I couldn't be more pleased, as your informal and ever-attentive OB/GYN." Frankie had christened herself with this responsibility, first because Mia had avoided seeing one who was trained as such, but even after Mia had found Dr. Mahoney, because Frankie so enjoyed the authority. "You were nearly underweight during your first trimester. Finishing that entire bowl of pasta plus a few slices of whole grain bread is a good start on the way toward a healthy pregnancy."

Mia rolled her eyes and only partly because the focaccia was that good. "Urban myth. One does not need to eat for two, at least not two adult males training for rigorous athletic competition. That's exactly how women end up with an extra thirty pounds to lose after the baby's born."

Frankie nodded. Olive oil and bits of feta had gathered at the corners of Mia's mouth during her healthy weight speech. "Want to try mine?"

"Thanks," Mia said, pushing her bowl toward Frankie as she reached down for a twirl of her noodles. "Mmm," she said appreciatively. "The sauce is perfect. I have never had a bad bowl of pasta at this place."

"Yours is good too, though I don't know that I would have asked for extra broccoli."

Mia shrugged. "Sounded good today. If they'd had butternut squash on hand, I'd have signed up for that, too."

"So have you heard from him?" Frankie watched her friend's face carefully.

Mia shook her head quickly. "No, but the longer this goes on, the more I think that's okay."

Frankie raised her eyebrows. They retained a tinge of yellow from her last dye job. "You're okay with not knowing where the father of your child is and how he could be such a despicable person as to walk away from what he's done?" Her fork clanged against the bottom of the bowl as she dove for another bite.

"He wasn't the only one who 'did.' Plus do I really want a person with that little sense of responsibility having influence on my child?" Mia caught her breath with this thought. She felt one edge of her heart shift slightly.

"Your child." Frankie smiled. "I like it. Are you going to find out if it's a boy or girl? According to my *What to Expect When You're Expecting*, that ultrasound should be right around the corner, around twenty weeks or so."

"No, I think I'll wait." Mia looked at her friend. "I like the auburn, by the way. And you're a really good friend, Frankie."

Frankie fidgeted in her seat. "Let's not get mushy, okay? I'm not very good with mushy."

A figure approached out of the corner of Mia's eye and gained quickly on their table. "Mia? Is that Mia Rathbun?"

Mia looked up into a wide and animated face. "Mrs. Hanworth! What a surprise!" She stood to shake her hand but Mrs. Hanworth pulled her into a hug. The embrace lingered far beyond what Mia would have deemed appropriate. She saw Frankie grin at her discomfort. "What brings you to Chicago?"

"Oh, we're here visiting my cousin's daughter's fiancé. He's a *very* successful surgeon and has *graciously* offered to show me and Merle around town." She gestured to a group of three at a nearby table. Merle gave a wave but didn't look at all persuaded to leave his lasagna. Mrs. Hanworth lowered her voice. "He has a *wonderfully* handsome *bachelor son*, Mia. Just for your information." She pulled her broad shoulders up to rhinestone hoop earrings and wrinkled her nose. "I know your mother would want me to plant the seed!"

Mia turned quickly to her friend. "Frankie, this is my mom's good friend, Marilyn Hanworth. We grew up across the street from her house in Highlands Cove." Frankie smiled sweetly and shook Mrs. Hanworth's hand.

"What lovely hair you have, Frankie. Does red run in your family?"

"Oh, I wouldn't say that," Frankie said breezily. "I love *your* hair, Mrs. Hanworth. How ever do you get it to breathe so, have so much body?"

Mia shot her friend a look, but Frankie's face was straight out of a Nancy Drew book.

"Oh, stop." Mrs. Hanworth patted her beehive and stood up straighter. "Nothing a little Dippity-do and a healthy application of White Rain can't fix up."

Mia was eyeing her pasta and wondered if Mrs. H. would care if she held her bowl while she stood. She glanced back just as the woman was finishing a survey of Mia's more generous physique. *Suck it in*, Mia thought, and tried her best to move her belly back, even a few centimeters. She compensated by jutting her rear out, hoping the bump underneath her shirt would recede into the simple suggestion of a winter's worth of emotional eating and nothing more.

"You look nice, Mia," Mrs. Hanworth said, eyes narrowing to watch Mia's reaction.

Mia smiled and said, "You're too kind."

Mrs. H. tried another route. She turned to Frankie. "She was such a snazzy dresser in high school. Lovely pressed chinos, fitted knit tops that were still tasteful." Her eyes returned to Mia, who was digging her toes into her free-trade leather sandals and wishing they were penny loafers to shut the woman up. She pulled her olive-green cotton sweater away from her middle and squirmed.

Mrs. Hanworth cleared her throat. "But I suppose the styles have changed since then, haven't they? Nothing wrong with being comfortable. Well," she said, her voice lowered. "I'll be sure to tell Babs I saw you. And you tell her," she said, pointing a finger at Mia, "that she owes me a weekend in Vegas, girls only." She pulled Mia into one more hug, twice as inappropriate for the closeness of it, and then bid her farewell.

Mia sighed as she sat down. Her pasta was cold, but she continued at it with the same dedication as before.

"She's a character," Frankie said. "Straight out of Mayberry, only in a coordinating nylon jumpsuit."

Mia snuck a glance over to the Hanworth table. All four were looking at her. She waved and then turned her chair slightly to move out of freak-show range. "That woman has had the same hair for all of my years on this earth and probably before." She cut into another wedge of focaccia. "But she made a mean oatmeal chocolate-chip cookie."

Frankie snorted. "I'm going to have to adjust to this new Mia. The food-loving, broccoli-craving, carb-dwelling Mia."

Mia's smile pinned back cheeks full of pasta. She pointed to Frankie's plate. "Are you going to eat that?"

●  ●  ●  ●  ●

In retrospect Mia could see she should have done more research before choosing a career. One important but neglected question would have been, "How does the average social worker fill the hours of her work day?" She'd made her selection of major during a particularly heady phase of her college experience. Big ideas tugged her from all sides: how to eradicate poverty, the flaws of twenty-first-century feminism, how the prison system failed to effectively rehabilitate. She needed to feel a part of the movement toward societal improvement. Even the words *social work* educed from her a feeling of well-being, a quick uptick of hopefulness that the handbasket containing her world wasn't traveling downward at such high speeds. Mia had enough pragmatism in her to like the extra security offered by a degree that was hire-ready, something a philosophy or history major couldn't provide. So, armed with an inspiring distaste for injustice and the chutzpah to take a whack at the roots of it, Mia found herself quickly and gainfully employed at Urban Hope, a nonprofit housing agency that happily accepted governmental funds as a part of its squeezed budget.

Seven years into her work Mia had yet to meet a root of injustice, much less get the chance to take a whack at it. On days like the one following her lunch with Frankie, the sad majority of her office hours were consumed with paperwork, much of it redundant and all of it far removed from the real needs of the people she served.

A young woman opened the front door, setting off an electronic chime that played the first bars of "Edelweiss" at a speedy electronic tempo. The girl scanned the long, narrow room. She looked to be around fifteen, though sincere effort had been made to increase that number. Her eyes were heavily lined and accompanied a face layered with makeup. She'd pulled her hair into a tight knot at the back of her head. Brush marks commemorated by generous hair gel showed a neat and sculpted road from the forehead back. A billowing navy blue parka swallowed her petite frame.

Carl rose from his desk, which sat nearest the door. "May I help you, miss?" In an effort to appear casual and helpful, he leaned over his desk, propping himself up with one hand, fingers splayed on the desktop.

"Um, maybe." The girl's eyes continued to sweep the room.

Mia pushed back her chair and strode toward the front door. "Hello. I'm Mia. Would you like to come back to my office?" Mia tried to say the word without sneering, knowing Carl would not appreciate the dig on her Office Depot–purchased cubicle setup.

The girl's shoulders relaxed slightly. "All right." She followed Mia to the small space near the back. Carl watched them go, hand still in the three-point stance, face deflated.

Mia gestured to a chair. "I'm afraid we don't have many actual doors around here. This is about as private as we can get. Can I take your coat?"

The girl shook her head as she lowered herself to the chair. "I just have a couple questions."

Mia sat across the desk from the girl and inhaled the lingering scent of cigarette smoke mixed with cheap perfume. She gave silent thanks that smells no longer sent her running for the restroom. "Go ahead and ask anything you'd like. I'll try to help, um, what did you say your name was?"

"I didn't say. It's Flor." The girl spoke unapologetically. The only betrayal of her nerves was the feverish bouncing of her crossed leg.

"Nice to meet you, Flor." Mia smiled. "What questions do you have?" Before Mia had finished speaking, her desk phone rang. "I'm so sorry. Just one moment."

Flor nodded. Mia answered, "Mia Rathbun."

"Oh, my goodness. You sound so professional!" The inimitable chirp of her mother's voice came to Mia from across the ocean.

"Mother," she said, her voice lowered. She turned away slightly from her desk. "Is this an emergency?"

"Of course not, sweetheart. Do you think I would have taken a moment to chitchat before telling you about an emergency?"

"I ask because we discussed how this number was only to be used in the case of an emergency." Mia smiled quickly at Flor, who wasn't watching Mia but was reading with solemn eyes a poem by Maya Angelou that Mia had tacked to her cubicle wall.

"Well, if you'd answer your cell phone or return the messages I leave on your answering machine, I wouldn't have to resort to using the emergency number, now would I?"

"Mother, can I call you back? I'm *working* right now." Mia did a quick mental checklist of any other, more obvious way she could communicate she did not want to be on the phone with the woman.

"I hardly dare trust empty promises, dear, but I don't see that I have much choice." Mia heard the phone move away from Babs's mouth as she said, "Thank you, Ricardo. I *love* the highlights. And tell Lena that facial was *to. Die. For.*" Mia sucked air through her teeth while Babs made kissing noises as a farewell to Ricardo, whoever he was. "Darling?" she said into the phone. Her tone had turned more urgent. "Call me back soon, do you hear me? We need to clear up some important matters."

*Oh, good grief,* Mia thought. *I'm sure we do. Why am I not married yet? When will I come on a cruise with her? Don't I know she gets an employee discount as ship hostess? Why don't John and I plan on coming to Highlands Cove for Christmas this year and could we stay for more than two measly nights?* "Fine. I'll call you when I get off work."

"Promise your mother."

"Mother, please."

"Promise. I was the one to give you life, Miss I'm-Too-Busy."

Mia sighed. "I promise." She hung up without saying good-bye. After a deep breath she turned to face Flor. "Sorry about that."

The girl shrugged. "Don't worry about it. My mom calls me all the time. Hardly ever do I actually want to talk to her."

Mia bit back a smile, remembering the disorienting world of teenagedom. "Thanks. Now, Flor, you have questions for me?"

She nodded and lowered her voice. "I've heard you give out free milk and stuff to people who need it. To, um, mothers for their babies."

Mia shook her head. "We don't, actually, at this office."

Flor chewed her lower lip. The leg bouncing increased in intensity. "Are you sure? Because I've asked around."

"You're almost in the right place. I work more with administrative issues, mostly with government housing and shelters. But we have a sister office upstairs that handles the WIC program. They're the ones with the free milk, diapers, resources for mothers and children. We would never want anyone feeling like she couldn't feed her child because formula's too expensive."

Flor sat forward in her chair a bit. "Do I need to have a driver's license or anything? Because I don't have one yet. I just turned sixteen.

Would I need one if I asked for something like that? Not now, but in a little while." She looked into Mia's face. "In case I was pregnant."

Mia blinked. She'd seen enough craziness at her job over the last few years not to burst into tears, but the jolt of a pregnancy this early in Flor's life still required a moment's pause. The housing division was relatively sheltered when it came to this kind of trouble. And Mia herself had very little experience dealing with problems like Flor's. At sixteen her principal concerns had been acquiring tickets to 'N Sync, deciding which glitter nail polish went best with her eyes, and trying not to sweat in gym class. "No, you would not need a driver's license. They'd want to see some proof of address, but it's a pretty simple process." She cleared her throat. "How far along are you?" Her voice was almost a whisper.

Flor shrugged. "I've missed a couple periods. Still enough time to decide what to do, whether to go through with it or not." She clenched her jaw and kept her eyes on the poem by Angelou.

"I understand," Mia said. *Far more than you're probably giving me credit for.* "If this scenario would turn out to be a real one," she locked eyes with Flor, "and if you should need any help, for anything, I hope you'll come see me." She fished out a card from her desk drawer and flipped it over. "This is my cell phone number." Mia had been told repeatedly, often by Carl the Rule Magistrate, not to give out personal information to clients, but she suspected Flor wouldn't be one to leave a message on the work line. "Call anytime."

"Thanks," Flor said and dropped the card into one of her pockets. When she rose to go, Mia stood with her. "Maybe I'll see you," the girl said by way of good-bye. Mia watched her back until the last note of "Edelweiss" faded from the air.

# 7

## Sweet Spot

Silas sat perched on the top step. He'd brought out a stadium cushion and had propped it against the stone wall at the top of the staircase. The picture of repose, he scanned the day's *Tribune*, which he'd opened to the travel section and used to shield his face from the sun.

"Hi, Silas," Mia said. She smiled when he looked up but his mouth creased into a frown.

"You look dead-dog tired, girl. Work beating all the life out of you?"

Mia sighed. She looked around, wishing for an armchair and cup of mango tea to appear. When it didn't, she plopped down on the step below his. "Silas, can I ask you an indelicate question?"

Silas folded the paper and creased it carefully before laying it on the pavement beside him. As always, he was impeccably dressed and clean shaven. A paisley ascot hugged his neck. With a pipe in hand he might have passed for a classics professor. When the breeze lifted, Mia could smell mint and the slightly sweet memory of aftershave.

"I've never met a question that made me less of a man, indelicate or otherwise. Ask."

"How old are you?"

"Ah," he said, nodding slowly. "You won't believe me, but I don't exactly know."

Mia raised one eyebrow, wary from many entertaining but questionably accurate storytelling sessions she'd enjoyed with her neighbor from the first floor.

"Naw, I'm telling the truth. My mama wasn't so good with dates and numbers." He chuckled. "But I can tell you I celebrate twice a year, just to make sure I'm covered. And at last count I was sixty-seven and one half years old."

Mia let out a low whistle. "That's a lot of years." She turned to him. "What's your secret?"

"You mean to long life?"

"Not just long. Fulfilled. You seem fulfilled, satisfied. How do you do that?"

"Apricot juice cocktails at nine each night and a healthy sex life as long as you can manage it."

Mia's eyes bulged slightly and Silas laughed.

"Just kidding about those apricots." He laughed again, so much so that he needed to extract a handkerchief from his coat to blot his eyes. "My Bonnie would have slapped me on the back for that joke, and not for her approval of it." He wheezed slightly and turned his gaze to Mia. "Honey, you want the good news or the bad news first?"

"Bad."

"I see. A glass-half-empty kind of lady. All right, the bad news is that there is no formula. The secret is a wily one, and just when you think you've got life tucked neatly into your pocket, it rears up and shows you another side, one that makes you weak in the knees for all its toughness."

Mia slumped against the stone railing. "And the good news?"

"The good news is you get to sixty-seven and one half years by walking through your days one moment at a time. Ain't nobody got the right to hurry you up, so you just take a good deep breath and ask the Lord for the strength to get from morning to night."

Mia sighed at the thought of all those mornings and nights ahead of her. "I wish it were closer to apricot juice and a good libido."

Silas rubbed the hint of white whiskers dotting his chin. "Now you need to offer a man some help here. I need more information. What's keeping you from peace of mind? The Book says peace can be like a river in one's soul, and rivers aren't always tame and quiet, you know."

"I would definitely not characterize my life as tame and quiet right now. Think more along the lines of rushing, wild abandon, maybe a rickety canoe that keeps tossing me overboard every few minutes." Mia let her head lean against the railing. She was silent a moment. They watched an elderly woman shuffle down the sidewalk opposite them. She never took her eyes off the pavement but placed one foot carefully in front of the other until she turned the corner. When the woman was out of sight, Mia said, "Silas, I'm going to have a baby."

"Oh, Lord, Lord, Lord," he said, his face broken into a wide grin.

Deep wrinkles creased the sides of his cheeks and eyes, illuminating the decades of joy and sorrow that had crossed his face. "A baby. Well, congratulations, Miss Mia. This is fine, fine news." He nodded to himself, still propped on the back of the stadium chair.

"Thanks," Mia said. "Before you need to ask, the baby is Lars's and he, as you might have noticed, has conveniently disappeared."

"Now that you say it, I haven't seen that boy for quite some time. How's that sitting with you?"

Mia felt a lump in her throat. "Some days are better than others." She swallowed hard. "If you'd asked me yesterday, I would have said I was lucky to dodge a bullet. But today …" Her voice trailed off. Suddenly her pants felt very tight around the middle, even with the rubber-band trick. She stood and looked at Silas. "I should go in. Rest or something. Isn't that what pregnant women are supposed to do?"

He chuckled. "My Bonnie, God rest her soul, was like a tiger when she was pregnant with our little ones. I could not please the woman, no matter how I tried. This was at the very beginning and the very end. But the middle," he shrugged and winked at her. "The middle was the sweetest time. You just about there, that right? Near about four, five months?"

Mia nodded, sad to her bones that Silas knew more about where she was and who she was becoming than the father of her child.

"Sweet spot might be just around the corner," he said. His face softened, his eyes looked long into hers. "The Book says there's a peace that passes understanding. That's what I'll be praying for you." He nodded slowly. "You're gonna be okay, Miss Mia Rathbun. Green, sweet valleys always come, even after a mountain climb you're sure will be the death of you."

"Have a good night, Silas." Mia stepped up to the front door and turned her key in the lock. *What a beautiful mess*, she thought as she forced her feet up the stairs to her apartment. *I'm pregnant, dumped, overworked, emotionally drained, and unloading my fears on an innocent neighbor.* She pushed on the door to her apartment and set about looking for sweatpants.

●  ●  ●  ●  ●

"He is *lying!*" Mia shouted. "You're a fool to take him back!" She shoveled a spoonful of chocolate and peanut butter ice cream into her mouth and continued shouting around it. "It's a good speech, you idiot. Do you honestly think he's changed?" She looked around and found only a hemp drink coaster, which she hurled at Hugh Grant. "Just because you're British, you think you can charm your way right back in. You know what I think of you? I think you're a sad sap of a human who is caught in the grip of an overwhelming ego that allows you to think we are needy, spineless women, that's what." She swallowed the ice cream and could feel drips of it on either side of her mouth. She ran her sleeve across her lips. "And you know nothing about what Julianne is going through, no matter your teary little talk. So you've picked up *What to Expect*. You haven't *been* there, you jerk." She was crying and she felt grand about it.

The start of this debacle had begun minutes after her retrieval of the sweatpants off the bedroom floor. She'd eaten three slices of vegetarian pizza heated up from the day before and had settled on the couch with an unopened pint of Ben & Jerry's. TBS was running a Hugh Grant marathon and *Nine Months* began just as she dipped up her first peanut butter chunk. Now, an hour and a half later, she'd cried through the entire film, particularly loudly in the least emotionally touching parts. There was a scene with Tom Arnold, clearly written for comic relief, which involved Tom and Hugh attacking a man in a dinosaur suit at a toy store. She'd wept bitterly, making noises that she hadn't heard out of herself since a violently hormonal viewing of *Steel Magnolias* in junior high.

Immediately following *Nine Months*, the introductory credits began for *Notting Hill*. Mia tipped her spoon around the edges of the ice cream carton and deliberated whether or not she should walk down to Gerry's for another pint. She was all out of organic popcorn, though a free sample of butter deluxe had come in the mail just before Lars had left and she'd tucked it into the pantry without his notice. Lars nurtured a zealot's distaste for partially hydrogenated oils. *He left at just the right time*, Mia mused bitterly to herself. *Seeing me down all these synthetic concoctions would have forced him into a vicarious toxin cleanse.*

"Julia, you are stunning," Mia told the television, "and I must say, an inspiration to mothers the world over. You have your babies, a devoted husband, a wildly successful career." She ticked off the items on her list with the end of her spoon. "True, I can't identify with two of the three, but *hypothetically*, Julia, we're soul sisters."

*Is this it?* she wondered as Hugh and his friends exchanged witty British banter. *Talking to Julia Roberts as if we're school pals, eating a week's allowance of calories at one sitting. Is this the life of a single mother?*

The phone rang. She ignored it, barely pulling her ears away from the movie when someone began talking on the answering machine. It was Babs. Snippets of her rambling reached the living room, though Mia didn't turn down the volume on the television to hear her better. She knew the gist of her mother's concerns. Call me back, make it soon, why don't you ever call me back? Mia scooted up on the couch far enough to prop the empty Ben & Jerry's carton on the edge of the coffee table. She fluffed a nearby sofa pillow and laid her head on it.

Hugh and Julia were meeting for the first time when the phone rang again. Mia didn't move. "Hellooooo! It's your mother!" Babs trilled from the kitchen. Mia groaned and shifted to the other side of the couch. The woman was stubborn but she'd given every one of those genes to her daughter. Mia squinted to concentrate harder on the screen.

The third message made Mia sit up straight on the couch. "Mia, I know you're there because that charming super in your building said he could hear the television blaring from your apartment."

"Mother!" Mia gasped, upright and frozen on her couch.

"He's such a dear—what's his name? Mr. Fontanelli? Tortelloni?"

"Lamberti!" Mia yelled, then checked herself in case he was in the hall.

"… and he said he'd be happy to get his keys and check to make sure everything's all right, since your own *mother* can't seem to get ahold—"

"Mother," Mia said. The answering machine let out a high-pitched squawk when she picked up the phone. "I'm here."

"Well, of course you are. That's what I was just saying."

Mia brought the cordless into the living room and muted the television. "I cannot believe you called Mr. Lamberti."

"He's such a lovely man. Is he married?"

"Divorced." Mia lay down on the sofa and marveled at Julia's magnificent teeth when she smiled at Hugh.

"I see." Babs was delighted. "I'll have to bring him a little something from the ship next time I visit."

Mia sighed. "I'm not really feeling well. Did you have something specific to discuss?" In the far recesses of her mind, Mia acknowledged that the miffed-teen response she gave her mother was a tired one and that she might consider changing tactics now that she was a grown adult. But old habits became easier and more tenacious, it seemed, the longer one perfected them. She turned her gaze to the ceiling overhead and tried to remember what Dr. Finkelstein had said about moments like this.

"… and why on earth Lars never answers the phone is beyond all means by me, though perhaps he has the sense to be at least a little ashamed of your living situation." Babs paused and Mia knew she was shaking her head. "That boy is very bright but he has strange social skills. There. I said it."

"We all have our flaws, don't we, Mother?" Mia said. She'd drifted into a fetal position and had turned on the closed captioning. It took a great deal of concentration to keep the two story lines of Hugh-Julia and Babs-Mia-Lars separate.

"I'm glad you at least acknowledge that." Babs sounded relieved and ready to settle in to the rightness of her thinking. "I was just saying to my friend, Yvette, here on the ship. Did you ever meet Yvette? Petite, gorgeous little thing from Missoula? Works in hospitality too?"

"Mmm," Mia said, knowing that would suffice.

It did. "Well, Yvette and I were discussing the way young women such as yourself sell themselves short in relationships. She has a twenty-one-year-old daughter who's at school out east somewhere, also living in sin with her boyfriend...."

It was a great mystery to Mia and to the rest of the movie-consuming public why Julia had not married Benjamin Bratt when they'd dated around the time of *Erin Brockovich*. Mia and Frankie had entered this line of discussion a few times, not out of any disloyalty to the loyal and unassuming Danny Moder, Julia's husband and the father of her children, but more to dissect what, exactly, was so unlovable about one of the finer specimens of humanity ever created south of the border. Ben's hair, for example—

"Mia. Mia Grace Rathbun, are you listening to me?"

She cleared her throat. "Not very attentively, I'd have to admit."

"Honestly, I feel like I'm talking to myself."

"You know," Mia yawned into the phone, "we've never been too good on the phone." *Or on planes, in restaurants, in the living room, on road trips* ... "I think we should call it a night before one of us says something we end up feeling miserable about later." She threw her legs over the side of the couch and gathered dirty dishes to take to the kitchen.

"But I haven't even gotten to what we need to discuss."

"We will eventually, Mother. Just not tonight. Let's celebrate, shall we? We've been on the phone for at least four minutes and neither of us is crying. I, for one, find this very heartening."

"There is no need to get sarcastic," Babs said. "You started this when you were in high school and you still haven't gotten over it. I blame that band you listened to all the time.... What was it? ANT? RAP?"

"R.E.M." Mia turned on the kitchen faucet full stream and dunked her dishes into a puddle of dish soap.

"Exactly. That androgynous lead singer, all the whining political songs. That's when this started."

"Don't you want to mention the evil influences of our foreign exchange student, Pieter, from Amsterdam? And what about when I joined Students for a Smog-Free Highlands Cove?"

Babs exhaled loudly. "This is just what I'm saying, Mia. You are completely unable to have a conversation in the present."

"Why would we, when the past is so much more fun?" Mia slammed a dirty pan into the sink and sloshed greasy water all over the countertop.

Babs sighed. "This is going nowhere. You're right. Let's stop for the evening. But I need you to call again tomorrow, Mia. This cannot wait."

"Will do," Mia said. "Good-bye, Mother."

She replaced the phone on its base with a force that nearly snapped off its small and sturdy antenna. The rest of the dishes endured their cleansing to the accompaniment of R.E.M.'s greatest hits, turned up so loud her upstairs neighbor banged on the floorboards until Mia adjusted the volume.

# 8

# Customer Appreciation

Delia pulled Mia's hips toward the sky and then moved to the person on the next mat. Mia pushed out through the pads of her fingers like a good downward-facing-dog girl would, but she still felt tension in her shoulders. She moved quietly to her mat and rested in extended child's pose, a position she had reserved for sissies until her pregnancy, when she became intensely fond of resting in general.

Delia approached her after class. Frankie was busy rolling up her mat but close enough to hear Delia's stage whisper.

"Mia, are you feeling all right?" Her eyes were wide and dark brown. Springy gray curls framed her face and were pulled into a loose ponytail at the nape of her neck.

"I'm fine, thanks, Delia. Just a bit tired."

Frankie joined them at the front of the room. The door closed behind the last student and left the three women alone. Frankie cleared her throat and looked at Mia. "Are you *sure* you're okay?"

Mia watched Frankie for a moment and then turned to Delia. "I'm pregnant."

"Oh!" Delia clapped her hands and pulled Mia into a hug. "I knew it! That little pooch didn't used to be there, though one never wants to assume. Plus, your aura has been cloudy, which can mean either lost love or new life." She spoke as if Mia had changed to color contacts from wire rims, so obvious was the change. Mia thought she might be able to hear Babs's eyes rolling all the way from Puerto Rico.

Delia took Mia's face in her hands. "Congratulations, dear girl."

"Thanks," Mia said, blushing. Delia was the first person outside her immediate circle to hear the news. The sudden openness of her new life made Mia shift uneasily on her bare feet.

Delia turned serious. "Well, I'm very glad you told me because I was concerned about your recent lack of energy during our yoga practices. It's just not like you to appear exhausted, particularly during balance poses."

Mia nodded. "I'm actually feeling better this week. But yes, I've been tired."

Frankie put her arm around Mia's shoulders. "She's doing it all by herself. The baby, I mean. The father is a coward." Frankie glanced at Mia and winced. "Am I not supposed to say that part?"

Mia smirked. "Which part?"

"No worries, girls," Delia said, patting each of them on the arm. "I am nothing if not a discreet yoga instructor. Plus my own mother was a single mom, raised all of us on a shoestring and a prayer. You'll have nothing but support from me." She smiled and the skin around her indigo eyes settled into familiar lines. "There are some things you might want to adjust during our practice, though."

Ten minutes later Mia and Frankie pushed open the glass door leading to the street.

"So you'll need to be careful with binds. And anything with twisting. And all balance poses, especially later."

"Got it," Mia said. She lifted her face to the sun. "And if I have any reservations—"

"—you'll stop immediately before you hurt yourself."

"Right." They turned the corner and cut a diagonal through Humboldt Park. The air was cool but March was already fulfilling its promise with tiny dots of grass pushing through on the lawns edging the sidewalk.

"Because if you don't and I find out later that you've put yourself and your baby at risk," Frankie said in her most deceptively syrupy voice, "I'll report you to your mother. Or to Mr. Lamberti, whichever is most efficient." She roared a sinister laugh and Mia giggled. They walked arm in arm, letting Frankie's cackle rise through the bare branches and up to a colorless sky.

● ● ● ● ●

"Did you think I'd crumble? Did you think I'd lay down and die?" Mia pointed one finger up to the ceiling in victorious disco pose. Late Sunday afternoons meant the noise allowance loosened up a bit in her apartment. Usually she was the one to listen, bemused, at her fellow building-mates' choice of music. Last week she'd heard three songs by Twisted Sister, a Guns N' Roses medley, John Denver, and Amy

Winehouse. This week she was throwing her own into the mix with a soulful, though perhaps not tuneful, sing-along with Gloria Gaynor.

A long-neglected dust-up of the apartment gave her a dual focus. Dancing and cleaning her way through the living room, Mia caught a glimpse of herself in the long mirror propped into one corner. She stopped and stared.

"Good gracious, I'm huge." She spoke her thoughts aloud, though they were completely drowned out by the disco. Black cotton pants downward, Mia still looked like a version of her original self. Her thighs seemed to be widening, and not necessarily symmetrically, she noted. Her hips looked like prime candidates for mom jeans. But at least her lower half still sparked memories of her body before everything had shifted on its axis.

The upper half of her body, swathed in an oversized *Stop Plate Tectonics* sweatshirt Lars had left behind, appeared to belong to someone else. For one, Mia had never, ever, ever had breasts like the ones she now sported. Normally a small-chested girl, Mia had always enjoyed being able to easily harness any bounce factor when she went for a run. She'd never worried when trying on clothes because her chest was certain to fit into small tops and if she needed some *oomph*, there were always push-up bras to the temporary rescue. But this new version of her bosom was shocking. *No other way to say it*, she thought. *Shocking.* She turned to the side, pulling her sweatshirt close to accentuate her profile.

"I'm not sure I don't like them," she said to her reflection. "I wouldn't want to jump around in a mosh pit or anything, especially without good support." But they weren't horrible. Pairing her chest with her belly, however, presented its fair share of worries. Definitely no mosh pit, no auditioning for the Rockettes, no runs along the lake … Her belly had become a substantial and obvious testament to her delicate condition. It wasn't that Mia hadn't been looking in the mirror on a semiregular basis. The proportions of her growth, however, caught her by surprise as she stood in front of the living-room mirror. She'd hoped she still had a week, two weeks before her belly preceded her into a room.

Mia sighed. "I guess the jig is up."

Gloria had finished her battle cry and the Bee Gees were slowing things down with "More Than a Woman." Mia sprayed lemon oil into her dust rag and lowered herself to a sprawl to get the bottom shelf of the coffee table. "More than a woman to me …" she crooned an octave higher than Barry Gibb, which meant only she and some species of canine could hear her yelps.

As she backed up out of her prone position, a pounding on the door reached her ears. She blew a strand of hair out of her eyes, set her cloth and polish on the table, and moved to the door. The visitor resumed pounding.

"Coming!" Mia called out. Mr. Lamberti was likely on her doorstep, coming to ask her to turn down the music. "Am I causing too much of a ruckus, Mr.—"

She stopped.

Adam smiled. "Yes, Miss Rathbun, you are. I've had several complaints and wanted to let you know that the Bee Gees were never meant to be played that loudly without the use of dry ice and a disco ball." He peeked around Mia's frame. "And I don't see either."

She scrunched her shoulders forward in an effort to hide the figure that had just startled her in the mirror. "Adam, what are you doing here?" She looked at the paper bags he carried in his arms and the one at his feet. "Did I order groceries for delivery?"

"Not technically," he drew out the word to show the nuance involved. "Mind if I put these down somewhere?"

"No, of course not." Mia stepped aside, deepening her slouch. "The kitchen table's straight ahead."

Adam bent to pick up the sack at his feet and hoisted it easily with the two he already carried. He stepped into Mia's apartment and inhaled deeply. "Lemon furniture polish. That's a blast from my childhood." He parked his packages on the kitchen table and took a scan of her home. Mia felt relief she'd begun her cleaning spree in the kitchen and was nearly done with the most visible parts of the apartment. "Nice place," he said appreciatively. "I love the colors on the walls."

"Thanks," she said, happy to leave out the detail that Lars had picked every one. She watched him as he surveyed the rooms and tried to convince herself that honey skin and the ability to model for Benetton did *not* make a man attractive. "So, if I didn't *technically* order these groceries, who did? Technically speaking, of course."

His face broke into an easy grin. "If we're striving for complete accuracy?"

"Yes."

"No room for gray areas?"

"That'd be my first choice."

"Then *technically*, I ordered these groceries on your behalf." He began unpacking and looked up, eyes shining. "That probably doesn't tell the whole story, does it?" He placed a jar of salsa and a bag of blue corn chips on the counter.

Mia salivated but dragged her focus back to Adam, which had its own perks. "Not exactly." She watched as he unpacked a lentil salad from the deli, a head of romaine, a package of feta.

"Okay, here's the deal." He straightened to his full height, armed with a tub of cottage cheese and a bottle of mango juice. "I know you're pregnant."

Mia blushed and cleared her throat. She shifted her weight when she realized she was tapping her foot on the linoleum. "You do?"

He nodded. His eyes softened as they searched hers. "I'm sorry to tell you this, but you're a horrible liar. And you have no talent for general deception, either." He shrugged, resigned to the truth.

Mia sat down at one of the kitchen chairs, happy to stop with the shoulder scrunching. "How did I give myself away? Am I that fat already?"

"No," he said slowly, "though I'm not sure the sweatshirts help." He hesitated. "Do I know you well enough to say something like that?"

"Definitely not," Mia said, her tone wry.

"Sorry." He walked to her refrigerator and began clearing room for cartons of organic yogurt and soy milk. "I know you're pregnant because you've been buying crazy stuff. You're a vegetarian, right?"

Mia nodded, knowing what was coming.

"So you've bought dried beef a few times and I think I saw turkey bacon in your cart once."

"It was nitrate free," she offered feebly.

Adam was rearranging the items in her fridge to look more like the dairy section at the store. "Then there was the chocolate, and I don't mean carob, if you get my drift." He raised an eyebrow in her direction but continued his work. "And the biggest single clue: your salt intake. Salsa, pickles, potato chips, cheese … I've seen it all many times before. You're definitely prego."

Mia crossed her legs with a huff and was very grateful she still could manage it. "All right, Grocery Sage. So I'm pregnant. Why are you delivering food to my front door?"

He closed the fridge and stood. A crooked grin accompanied the spark in his eyes. "I like you." He started folding the paper bags. "Sorry these weren't the reusable kind. I know you're into that, but at least they aren't plastic."

Mia shook her head. She'd watched this whole charade, mouth open and mind hopeful, but the time had come to shake it off. She stood. "Adam, thank you very much for your kindness, but I have to at least pay you and your dad for the groceries." She went in search of her checkbook. "How much do I owe you?"

He met her in the hallway by the front door. "Absolutely nothing." He said the words with neither injury nor pride. "You shop at our store every week. Count it as customer appreciation."

He smiled down at her.

Mia thought to brush away a strand of hair that was falling into his eyes but instead she moved a step away from him. "Well, please tell your dad this customer is very grateful for your kindness."

"I will." He opened the door and paused with his hand on the knob. "And the sweatshirt makes no difference either way. You're a pretty pregnant person." He crossed over the threshold and headed for the elevator. "Believe me, not every pickle eater can say that about herself," he said over his shoulder.

Mia could hear the grin in his voice. She forced herself to close the door before he disappeared from view.

# 9

## Guest Appearance

"How much information did you feed him?" Mia said into her office phone. She kept her head down and her voice low, lest Carl should walk by and check on her. Carl's job description did not include hall monitor, but he liked to take ownership of their office's productivity, and talking on the phone to Frankie during business hours would not be looked upon favorably, crush or no crush.

"What information? What did he say?" Frankie was not trying very hard to sound repentant.

"All the details about what I'd been eating, my cravings for salty food? He knew my personal food pyramid better than I know it myself."

Frankie giggled. "I love it! I merely confirmed his suspicions. He asked me if you were expecting a baby. Just like that, very little small talk to warm me up, I might add. Maybe he thought his time was limited, that you'd skulk out of produce at any moment."

"Skulk? I skulk?" Mia moaned, a bit too loudly and had to check her volume. "I do not want to be skulking with halfway to go." She peeked over her cubicle wall and saw Carl stand to stretch. It was ten minutes to five and time for the office to begin the shutdown procedure. For once Mia had decided to kick off when her colleagues did. She tidied her desk while Frankie gave her an update on Ms. Leiderhosen.

"… as if a twelve-year-old girl will really be interested in Plato, right? I mean, I'm sure there are exceptions, but this girl was wearing Hollister from head to toe and kept using 'like' as a transitional word. I finally caught her eye as Leiderhosen was dragging her toward Renaissance poetry and …"

"Edelweiss" sounded at the front of the office. Mia hoped it was Flor, the girl who'd asked about free formula. Weeks had passed with no other word from her, but Mia couldn't shake the feeling she'd meet up with the girl again. She kept the phone and Frankie's chatter up to her ear and peeked around the side of her cubicle. The phone cord stretched just to where she could see Carl's back but not the person who'd entered.

"It's a sincere pleasure to meet you." Carl's words floated back to Mia. When he reached his hand to shake, the new arrival moved into Mia's view.

She dropped the phone with a clang on her desktop and stared.

"This is not happening," she said aloud. Frankie's confused chirps came from the receiver lying prone next to her. Mia picked up the phone. "Frank, I'll need to call you back."

"What was that crazy noise just now? Mia, is everything all right?"

"Most definitely not." She watched Carl escort the guest back to Mia's space and whispered into the phone, "Babs is here."

• • ● • •

Mia stomped along three paces ahead of her mother.

"I don't see how you left me much choice," Babs called from behind. Her leopard-print heels clicked on the sidewalk. "You wouldn't return my calls."

Mia pulled her trench closer around her body. She stopped with a huff to wait for a light to change. Babs caught up, panting.

"It's not as if I *like* being reduced to this kind of surprise visit," Babs continued. She pulled a tissue from her bag and mopped her forehead. "*Most* daughters call their dear old mothers every now and again to catch up, you know."

Mia snapped her head to the side. "I've been busy. And you haven't exactly earned the right to dictate the terms of this relationship. Those rights were forfeited long about the time you left me and Dad to sail the high seas." Dr. Finkelstein's speed dial was burning a hole in Mia's phone. *Be honest, be patient, be myself. Be honest—*

Babs sighed on pitch. "Oh, good gravy, Mia. Must we go over this again? How long will you punish me? For the rest of our lives?"

The light changed and Mia commenced her near-sprint with Babs clicking behind. When they reached the park, Mia slowed. She lowered herself to a bench and waited for Babs to catch up. When her mother reached the bench, Mia turned.

"Before we get one step further in your *surprise visit*, I have something to tell you."

"I'm glad to hear it because I have a few things to tell you too." Babs patted her hair and smiled at a man striding by. "What a well-tailored suit," she said, not as softly as she should have. "Not enough men wear suits to work anymore." The man smiled as he passed, incrementally less discreet in his appraisal of Mia's mother.

"Mother, focus," Mia said. She had the urge to take Babs's face between her hands to lock eyes with her.

Babs turned to face her daughter. "I'm focusing." Her expression softened. "I'm just so happy to finally get the chance to see you. You look wonderful." She smiled, revealing a cruise-appropriate level of charm.

"I'm pregnant."

Babs kept smiling. After a moment she blinked and said through her teeth, "Pardon?"

Mia said the words slowly. "I'm almost five months along. The due date is September 30."

Babs blinked in quick succession, her false eyelashes fluttering in the manner of a stunned Snow White. "When will you and Lars get married?" The smile wasn't completely gone but it had taken a hit.

Mia shook her head. "He left."

"What?" Babs's voice rose in panic. "I don't understand." Her chest heaved as she breathed. "He can't leave. He—he *did* this to you."

Mia sighed. "No, Mother, *we* did this. He chose not to stick around, so I'll have to go through it alone."

At this disclosure Babs burst into tears. She was not a quiet crier. With each inhale she made a sound like a deflating accordion. Park users on both sides of the sidewalk began to stare.

"Mother," Mia said. She scooted nearer to Babs. "Mother, please."

"I've failed!" Babs moaned. "I've failed as a parent! Oh, my good Lord, help me." Her breathing became shallow.

"Take a deep breath." Mia put an arm around her mother's shoulders. "You're starting to hyperventilate." *I'm the one who's pregnant. But please let me comfort you through this difficult time.* It was all she could do not to shriek in exasperation.

"You can't be pregnant out of wedlock. I'm a board member for American Family Alliance!" Babs said. She let her head drop closer to her lap. "I've sent them money every month since the first Bush administration!"

Mia let her arm drop and searched the sky for assistance. "I'm so sorry to have inconvenienced your politics," she said. "We unwed mothers are such a blight to the party platform." She stood. "I'm going home." She started out at a clip. After a few moments she heard Babs's high heels pecking the pavement again in irregular rhythm.

"Did you consider adoption?" she called, making a couple turn and stare wide-eyed at Mia as she passed.

"No," Mia yelled over her shoulder. She motored ahead, hands thrust in her pockets, allowing the front of her coat to flap in the breeze now that there was no need to hide her shape.

"But there are so many deserving couples who simply can't have children." Babs's tone was dangerously close to a whine. "People with lots of money and beautiful houses in the suburbs," she added desperately. "I'm sure they'll overlook your piercings!"

"I can't do this, I can't do this," Mia muttered to her ballet flats, watching the puddles roll over the edges of her shoes but barreling right on anyway. When they reached Mia's block, Silas waved to her from the newsstand on the opposite corner. Mia returned the wave but kept steamrolling ahead. Silas raised his eyebrows at the bleach-blonde woman in heels struggling to keep up with Mia.

At the door of her building, Mia whirled around. "I suppose you should come in. Where are your bags?"

Babs had begun to limp slightly. She leaned against the wall for support. "These are the most adorable shoes but I did not realize I'd be running a marathon in them." She removed one and massaged her arch. "I'd at least have put in a Dr. Scholl's for extra support."

"Mother. Where are your bags?" Mia had a fleeting impulse to take a deep breath and relax but she ignored it in the interests of remaining furious.

"Oh, they're already in your apartment." Her eyes widened innocently. "What? Sam let me in."

"Sam? You mean Mr. Lamberti?" Mia rolled her eyes and unlocked the door. She slammed the Up button for the elevator but didn't wait for it to descend. Four flights later she met Babs waiting outside her door.

"Climbing four flights of stairs would seem inadvisable for someone in your condition," Babs said, leaning against the wall with the leopard heels dangling in one hand.

Mia opened the door to her apartment without a word. She moved through the living room, turning on light switches as she walked. Babs followed her with a running commentary on her choice of décor.

"How quaint. I had no idea you were so interested in Asian influences, dear. The reds are very ... *startling*.... Really they're the only color that saves this room from being dismal what with all the gray and black. Lars must have picked these colors, am I right?"

Mia didn't answer as she was screaming into the pillow on her bed.

"This kitchen is cleaner than I remember from last time. Did you finally hire someone to help? You were never a neat freak. It's always best to acknowledge our weaknesses and move on. I worry about that water spot on the ceiling. Perhaps I should mention something to Sam tomorrow.... Mia? Mia, shall I call something in for dinner?"

Mia emerged from the bedroom, rumpled and changed into the sweatpant ensemble she'd come to favor.

"I see we won't be going out," her mother finished.

Mia pointed toward the drawer by the phone. "Takeout menus are in there. I'll be eating grilled cheese and tomato soup." She padded to the pantry.

"That's not very much for a woman in—"

"My condition. It will suffice, thank you. I've been doing fine thus far." Mia slammed shut the refrigerator door and rummaged in a nearby drawer for a cheese slicer. She got through two strips of cheddar before laying the slicer on the cutting board and turning to her mother.

"Listen." She stopped and sighed. "I need to know why you're here. And how long you're staying."

"Why I'm here?" Babs affected her best wounded look. "I am here, Mia, to visit my only daughter."

Mia shook her head. "But what made you come so suddenly? No advance warning, no fax of your itinerary, no months of calling to warn, I mean, prepare me."

Babs found an ancient canister of organic coffee in the cupboard above the sink. She wrinkled her nose but began filling the small pot on the counter. "I'd heard some strange reports from mutual acquaintances."

"Very diplomatic. Who were your informants?"

"Marilyn Hanworth and your brother."

"You would crumble in an interrogation room."

"True enough." Babs hummed to herself as she opened the canister and measured out a scoop. "At any rate they called within a week of each other and were sure you were off your rocker."

Mia raised her eyebrows. "Off my rocker."

"Well, perhaps not quite to that point." Babs took a long sniff of the coffee and scowled. "When was *this* purchased?"

"During college." Mia flicked on a burner and lobbed a pat of butter into a skillet, unwilling to disclose the packet of freshly ground beans Lars had left in the freezer. She wasn't in the mood to bestow favors. "So now that you know I'm not off my rocker, just knocked up, what are your plans?"

Babs was perusing a menu from Lars's favorite Thai place. "Indefinite."

"I'm sorry?"

Babs looked up and smiled a winner. "I told the ship I have family business to attend to. They love me, I have oodles of vacation time saved up, and I have seniority. So I'm here for as long as need be."

Mia flipped her sandwich but not before it began to burn on the edges. "Right. So maybe a long weekend?"

"I'll think about it," she said breezily and picked up the phone. She punched in a series of numbers and waited. "Yes, King and I Restaurant? Wonderful. This is Barbara Rathbun calling from West Churchill Street. How are you—I'm afraid I didn't catch your name."

Mia plated her sandwich, saved the soup for another time when her appetite merited its consumption, and left the room just as Babs was beginning the story of the typhoon she'd endured in Thailand just that summer. Her laughter followed Mia through a closed bedroom door.

# 10

# All in the Family

"Keep pushing, you're almost there."

Mia wiped her forehead with one of the small white towels stacked beside her. She kept pushing, watching the calorie count on the machine flip numbers every twenty seconds or so.

"Really burning now," the automaton said. Mia pushed down on the pedals of the ancient elliptical machine housed in the workout room of her apartment building. The man-woman who encouraged her in her sweating voiced no difference in inflection. Thus, "Congratulations, you've marked one mile," sounded just as enthusiastic as "Taking a break? Don't rest too long." Mia had looked on every surface of the machine in an effort to silence the voice but to no avail. She'd given up and vowed to remember her iPod the next time she worked out.

Two minutes to her final goal, Mia's cell phone rang. She checked the screen and pushed to answer.

"Hi, John," she said, panting into the phone.

"Mia? Is that you?"

"Yeah," she said watching the seconds tick off the digital clock on the machine.

"Your goal is approaching," man-woman intoned.

"Who was that? And why are you breathing heavily? Um, do you need me to call back at a better time?"

"No. Almost done. I'm exercising." She used her free hand to mop the sweat streaming down her face.

"What did you just say?" Incredulity spilled out of the earpiece of Mia's phone. "Certainly you did not just say that you were exercising to the point of breathing hard? My sister?"

"Excellent job." The automaton sounded unimpressed. "You have reached your goal. Calories burned: two hundred thirty. Time elapsed: twenty minutes."

"Not bad," John said. "But where is the sister I love? The one whose lack of aerobic activity tends to shock people who confuse slender with healthy? Where's the girl who once lectured me on the punishing effects of women getting gym memberships in order to look a certain way?"

"She's gone. You can kiss her and your Christmas presents for the next ten years good-bye." Mia paced the empty room.

"What did I do?" John sounded mournful.

"She's here."

"You're making that up."

Mia took a long swig of water from the cooler in the corner. "I most certainly am not. And you caused this debacle."

"Not true! Have you been reading the tabloids, Mia? Don't get sucked into false information. It might get you rich, but it has its pitfalls."

"You told her I sounded weird. I believe the words were *off her rocker*." Mia glanced at her reflection in the mirror. Even in a frumpy T-shirt and shorts, she couldn't hide her pregnancy. The belly, the big boobs, the roundness of her face, the straight lines down her sides where curves had once been—the chunk factor was going nowhere but up.

"First, there is not one human in our generation who uses the phrase 'off her rocker,' so I'm confident you can determine the source of that comment. Secondly, I merely intimated that you sounded a bit strange. I wondered if she'd talked with you."

"Well, she has now. She's upstairs napping. In my apartment."

"Hence the sudden desire to purge the toxins through a good workout."

"Exactly. I'm thinking of picking up weightlifting. Or kickboxing. I think I'd really benefit from kickboxing."

John lowered his voice. "Is it that bad?"

Mia sat down to stretch her legs. "You have no idea."

"Actually I have some very vivid ideas, all of which propelled me to seek my fortune in a land foreign to Barbara Rathbun. Mimi, I'm so sorry."

Mia sighed. "It will be fine. Here's the deal, John. I'm pregnant." The silence lasted so long Mia thought he'd dropped the call. "John? Are you there?" She heard a faint sniffling noise. "Oh, good grief. Are you crying?"

"No, of course not," he said and cleared his throat loudly. "I'm just trying to wrap my head around the thought of my little sister having a baby." He stopped abruptly and cleared his throat again.

Mia smiled. "You don't have to worry. I'm okay. Taking all the right vitamins, going to the doctor, eating lots of cottage cheese and pickles at the moment, though that will probably change by the end of the week."

"But you sound so well-adjusted."

"The thing about having a child growing within you is that you have very little time left to be maladjusted. I'm doing the best I can."

"That poser. Where is he now? I know people, Mia. He can be brought to pay for what he's done."

Mia rolled her eyes. She lay back on a towel and crossed her legs for a hip stretch. "What, now we're in the Wild West and you have a posse? Or are you thinking more mob boss makes good on some debt he owes you?"

"I'm just saying …"

She laughed. "That's very sweet, but I don't think killing Lars will do a lot of good at this point. He's out of the picture anyway. I haven't heard from him since the day he left." She closed her eyes, feeling a dangerous sting well up from her chest.

"He's still scum. At the very least he should pay child support."

"I don't know that I want him to be involved at all," Mia said, pushing herself to a sitting position. "It's not like we're teenagers, John. I'm twenty-nine years old and I made an adult mistake. I can handle the consequences on my own."

John let out a low whistle. "I'm making an appointment with my life coach this very afternoon. We're going to have to open a whole new line of discussion dealing with my sister who has morphed from a capitalist-lecturing, tofu-inhaling social worker to an elliptical trainer whose rock-solid emotional state is enabling her to have a baby all on her own."

"I'm still a social worker. And I'll probably like tofu again when that particular texture doesn't trigger my gag reflex."

"Now you know how the average meat-eater feels."

"And I still think capitalism suppresses the freedom of the masses."

"But I thought we were making progress."

"Any emotional progress I was making has been thwarted by you snitching me out to Mother. Speaking of," she said, gathering her keys and wallet, "I'm due back upstairs before the queen awakens from her slumber."

"I'm so sorry, Mimi." The sincerity of John's apology covered a multitude of wrongs. "Call me anytime, particularly if you're wielding a sharp object and are considering how to use it."

"Got it." She pushed the elevator button to ascend to her apartment. "Go out there and publicize, great publicist."

He sighed. "So much worthless information. You're the one with the real story."

"Real it is," she said. They hung up and she boarded the flight back up.

●　●　●　●　●

"Urban Hope, Mia Rathbun speaking." She wedged the phone between her shoulder and cheek, continuing to file papers as she talked.

"We don't really deal with sewage at this office. Let me get you the number for Public Works." She soon hung up and turned to the next pile on her desk. The first trimester had wreaked havoc on her productivity. Mia was only that week returning to her typical rhythm at work. She'd been fortunate that Babs's need for a morning massage had eclipsed her curiosity to see Mia in action at the office. They'd made plans to meet for dinner, but that was a good seven hours away and Mia intended to soak up the solitude of each one.

"Hi. I'm back."

Mia looked up from her work to see Flor standing next to her desk. She wore the same heavy parka, though the weather had turned much milder since her first visit.

"Flor, hello. It's great to see you. Please, sit." Mia gestured to the empty chair. She leaned across the desk and folded her hands. "How are you?"

The girl shrugged, her small shoulders barely forcing the coat to move. "All right. I'm pregnant. For real." Her face, fuller than the first time they'd met, betrayed nothing of what her pregnancy meant to her in that moment. She blinked once but let her eyes remain trained on Mia's face.

"Congratulations," Mia said, faltering after the word left her mouth. It was a knee-jerk reaction, those well-wishes, fully ingrained after many years of baby showers, christenings, hospital visits to the maternity ward. Only recently had she realized the relativity of joy and suffering, even with—especially with—the birth of a child.

"Thanks," Flor said. She picked up the paper clip magnet on Mia's desk and started arranging the clips in order of size. "My mom's freaking out. She thinks I should have gotten an abortion, but I told her she can't tell me what to do. It's my baby." The words rushed out of her but she kept her eyes on the methodical organization of the magnet.

"Will you keep the baby or put it up for adoption?" Mia studied Flor's face and severe ponytail, struck again by how young she looked, even with a full palette of makeup.

"Keep it," she said quickly. "No baby of mine is going to live with some stranger."

Mia bit the inside of her cheek. "I can understand exactly how you feel—"

Flor's laugh dripped with cynicism. "I doubt that." She looked up and tilted her head apologetically. "No offense."

Mia nodded. "I understand because I'm pregnant."

Flor's eyes widened.

"And I'm alone too." Mia took a deep breath.

"Are you keeping it?" Flor leaned forward slightly in her chair.

Mia nodded. "I am. But," she added carefully, "I'm much older than you, Flor. I've finished high school, college, I have a good job that can support the two of us."

Flor made a face and looked around the office. "This place is sort of depressing." Her eyes traveled around the room, taking in the beige walls, fake wood veneers on the cubicle partitions, a brittle fern with fronds that dangled sadly off the edge of a file cabinet. "Do you like working here?"

"Not always," Mia answered truthfully. "But for now it's a stable job and I'll need that stability really soon." She cleared her throat and tried to rein the focus back in to Flor. "So you're planning on keeping the baby. What does the father say?"

Flor rolled her eyes with an ease that spoke to many eye-rollings in the past. "The *father* says nothing, other than he wants a paternity test. He says it isn't his." She clenched her jaw. "Believe me, the baby is his." She sat up slightly in her chair. "That's all I want to say about him."

The "Edelweiss" door chime kicked in at the front of the room.

"Are you seeing a doctor for prenatal care?"

"Not yet," Flor said. She'd replaced the paper clip magnet but had moved to arranging Mia's collection of Post-it notepads in rainbow order. "I don't have insurance."

"That's all right," Mia said. She put out an open hand for one of the Post-its. Flor relinquished a fluorescent green. "This is the number and address for a free clinic a few blocks from here. Do you know where the Land Haven Community Center is?"

Flor nodded.

"Great. The clinic is held there and is open every Tuesday, Thursday, and Saturday. Call this number and they'll get you an appointment. Dr. Henshaw is the OB and she's very good."

Flor took the paper and folded it carefully. She tucked it into her pocket. "Thanks," she muttered.

"What about school?" Mia asked.

Flor said nothing in response. She was looking intently at something over Mia's shoulder. Mia turned.

"Hi, honey," Babs whispered. "I don't mean to disturb you, but that Carl person told me I could just come back here." Babs reached around Mia and offered a handful of long pink fingernails to Flor. "Hello, dear. I'm Barbara. I'm Mia's mother. Her *madre*." Babs enunciated each word carefully and loudly.

"Hi," Flor said, her eyes appraising the blonde in a magenta blouse that glittered with rhinestones. Mia watched the wheels click as Flor's eyes moved back to her, taking in Mia's own ensemble: plain black shirt with an empire waist, next-to-no makeup, hair pulled back on the sides in a brown barrette. Flor raised one eyebrow. "You guys don't look alike."

Mia sighed. "Believe me, you're not the first to notice." She turned to Babs. "Mother, would you mind heading back to the front of the office and waiting there? I'll be up soon."

Flor stood. Her side profile gave a tiny glimpse of her expanding belly. "I'm leaving anyway. Thanks for the number," she said to Mia. "Nice to meet you." She nodded at Babs and left.

Babs lowered herself gingerly into the chair where Flor had sat. "What's wrong with that girl?" she whispered to Mia. "Does she need government assistance? Poor thing. She was as pale as a ghost, which looked so unnatural considering her *ethnicity*."

Mia sat with her head in her hands and tried to visualize a safe place where mothers dared not tread. After a long moment of encouraging her head not to explode, she opened her eyes to her mother's face. "Her name is Flor. She's sixteen and she's pregnant."

Babs gasped. "Oh, that's just a tragedy. So, so young with so much life ahead of her. And now she's saddled with a child." She *tsk*ed until she realized the irony of her comment. "But of course," she added, "it's a great blessing that she has an agency like yours to help her. Because she'll *need* help. Unlike you, dear. You'll be *fine*, I'm sure, what with your support network and your degree…." She trailed off and became absorbed in straightening her rings and necklaces.

"What is your plan for the rest of the day, Mother?" Mia made a show of stacking two piles of manila folders together with a loud thud. "What will you do now, when you leave the office?"

"I think we should do whatever it is that you want, dear. After all, this is your city. And you're the one who's pregnant. What sounds good to you?"

Mia shook her head. "Sorry. I won't be off until five." *Like most of the working world,* she added to herself. *Not all of us define a day's work by how soon we get to the lido deck for cocktails.*

"I thought you might say that, so I asked Carl if you might skedaddle a few hours early. What with, you know, the baby."

Mia's head snapped up from the housing inspection she was scanning. "You told Carl I was pregnant?" she hissed.

Babs smiled. "He's thrilled for you."

Mia peeked around the edge of her cubicle wall. Carl looked up from his desk and gave an awkward wave. Mia returned to her desk and groaned quietly. She would need to smooth the waters when Babs wasn't along for the ride. *At least,* she thought, *I can start wearing maternity clothes. And I won't have to dodge any more after-work sports bar propositions. Carl should be grateful for the out.*

"I know!" Babs said, her voice filled with the excitement her cruising compatriots had come to admire so. "Let's find a pretty sidewalk café for lunch and then spend the afternoon tooling around the Art Institute. It's been a very long time since I've seen a decent art museum. The Caribbean is just a *disaster* when it comes to real collections." She lowered her voice. "It's high time I see a respectable European rear end immortalized with paint and brush." She rose and slung her handbag over her shoulder, flashing rainbowed drops of rhinestones around the office. Mia watched her turn on her catwalk as she moved toward the front door and wondered for the millionth time if she should call the hospital where she was born to ensure she'd gone home with the right mother.

# 11

# Side Effects

Mia placed three kinds of hard cheeses into her cart. They joined two small but inordinately expensive boxes of crackers, a bar of Lindt chocolate (70 percent cacao, as requested), two bottles of wine, and a loaf of sourdough. Her initial instructions were to purchase whole grain but the sourdough was the only loaf left made by a local bakery and she knew origins would trump genre. She ran a hand lightly across her face, smoothing her pierced brow out of nervous habit.

In the produce section she wrinkled her nose at the romaine and decided instead on Bibb. Three organic carrots, two ripe tomatoes, a yellow pepper ... produce was a familiar domain. She could make a mean salad. But it was with no small amount of trepidation that she pushed onward toward the back of the store where the butcher waited with a smile. It was one thing to sneak in a package of dried beef here and there but an entirely different enchilada if she'd need to converse with someone over rows of raw meat.

Mia smiled in return, trying her best to look like someone who enjoyed eating the flesh of slaughtered animals. She walked toward the end of the counter and the heated cart that housed Gerry's specialty rotisserie chickens. A few paces from the cart she felt her heart begin to race.

She cleared her throat and called to the meat man. "Excuse me. There are no chickens." She pointed to the cart, which, indeed, sat happily illuminating an empty rack.

"I'm sorry, miss. We ran out about a half hour ago. If you'd like to come back tomorrow, we'll be right back in business." The man had such a nice, friendly face, particularly, Mia thought, considering he spent so much time with blood on his hands. "We have some beautiful cuts of wild Alaska salmon, if you'd like. Or Cornish game hens if you're only in the mood for poultry."

"I don't think you understand," Mia said, her voice rising in pitch and volume. "I *have* to have one of Gerry's chickens. She wants a chicken from Gerry's." Mia's voice became pinched. "She only eats salmon on the Alaska cruise!" The proclamation came out as a whine and Mia felt tears sting her eyes.

The butcher had gone from friendly slayer of animals to terrified male in the presence of female distress. He glanced up the aisles nearest to them and was moving toward the phone when Mia felt a warm hand on her arm.

"Mia, is everything all right?" Adam's eyes searched her face.

"You don't have any chickens," she wailed, gesturing with complete helplessness toward the butcher, who looked infinitely relieved to have been rescued by his boss. "I need a chicken and you don't have any left. How was I to know there was a time limit to something like this? Aren't you *always* supposed to have enough chickens? This isn't Communist Russia, you know!" She exhaled in a broken sob.

"Why don't you come with me?" Adam's words were quiet but sure. He guided her gently by the elbow past the meat counter to a small office in the back. Two bright lamps lit the room and the walls. Adam showed Mia to a couch that sat opposite a cluttered desk.

"Can I get you some tea? Coffee? *Yerba mate*? We have a surplus. It's on sale in aisle eight." Adam's smile seemed to emanate as much from his eyes as from his lips.

"No, I'm fine," Mia said through a shaky breath. She sat back in the couch cushions and wished they were deep enough to absorb her completely. She closed her eyes and tried to calm her erratic pulse.

Adam sat down next to Mia. He faced the desk, resting his elbows on his knees. "Sorry about the mess. This is Dad's domain. It's a pretty accurate picture of how his mind works. Complete disorganization to the outsider but perfectly sensible to him." He turned to Mia. She sat with her head tilted back, eyes closed but tears falling under her eyelashes and down her cheeks. He reached for a tissue and pressed it into her hand. He waited.

She sniffed and then sighed. "I'm crying." She blew her nose, head shaking in disgust or disbelief, she didn't know which. "I'm crying at the grocery store about a chicken."

Adam nodded. "I'm kind of flattered. Not many people feel so strongly about our rotisserie. Maybe I should up our production." He reached over to brush a tear from Mia's cheek. This act of tenderness sent her into a renewed and louder form of weeping. He brought the entire box of tissues to her lap.

"I have to say, your on-again, off-again relationship with meat is fraught with mixed signals."

She shuddered a sob. "I know, I know," she moaned. "I'm shopping for my mother."

Adam brightened. "Your mother? That's great! I had no idea you had family in town."

Mia shook her head emphatically. "She is not 'in town.' I mean, she is, technically. But she won't be for long, thank God. It's only been a week and I just don't know if I can take any more." These last words sounded like they had escaped from a helium-filled balloon. Mia grabbed another handful of tissues and continued. "We've never had the best relationship and now here she is wanting things like Pecorino Romano and chocolate and chicken and I could have just sent her to the store, but I needed some time to breathe and I'm too tired and my body looks like an alien is taking over and I go to the bathroom more than is normal for anyone who isn't diabetic." She slumped in the couch and pulled her knees up to the beginnings of a fetal position.

"What's your number?"

Mia furrowed her brow at him. "My phone number?"

He nodded and tapped the digits into his cell phone. After a moment he said, "Yes, Mrs. Rathbun? Hello, my name is Adam Malouf and I'm co-owner of Gerry's Grocery on North Damen.... I've spoken with your daughter and just wanted to convey personally my apologies for not having the item you requested. We're out of rotisserie chicken this evening, but I'll be happy to substitute any other selection from our meat department, free of charge…. Might I recommend our fillet with Maytag blue cheese crumbles? … Fantastic. I'll wrap two up for you and send them with Mia…. Thank you, Mrs. Rathbun…. All right. Thank you, Barbara…. Yes, pleasure talking with you as well." He clicked shut the phone and dropped it into his pocket.

Mia had stopped crying and was sniffling quietly into her fifteenth Kleenex. "That was very kind of you."

He shrugged. "I'm afraid I know more than I care to about dealing with crazy family dynamics. You don't need to say another word." He winked and Mia had to fight the urge to throw herself into his arms in gratitude.

"How are you feeling?" he asked quietly.

She was brought with a shock back to her present, very unromantic circumstance. "I'm doing pretty well, I suppose. This may sound strange, but I try not to think about it too much."

Adam raised one eyebrow. "Isn't it kind of hard to forget?" He nodded toward her belly. "You're starting to get a hump."

Mia tilted her head to one side. "I hope you mean a 'bump.' A hump is typically attributed to a camel. A *bump* is the acceptable term for cute, beginning pregnancy. Think Angelina, not desert creature."

By the end of her admonition, Adam's cheeks had deepened to blotches of scarlet. "Sorry," he said. "I don't really know much about this kind of thing."

Mia sighed. "Tell me about it." She blotted her eyes with a fresh tissue and looked to Adam for appraisal. "I think I'm ready to face the meat department again. How do I look? Do I have raccoon-mascara eyes?"

One side of his mouth pulled into a shy smile. "I think you look great. A little puffy, but nothing that would scare away customers or anything."

Mia sighed. "Adam, in general, you should avoid using the adjective 'puffy' when describing a woman's appearance for her."

He cringed. "Sorry. I seem to have a hard time lying to you, even when it might not be a bad idea." He cleared his throat and looked at her face anew, wrinkling his brow in concentration. "Take two. Mia, I think you look great. In fact," he looked intently into her eyes, "your eyes are gray right now. They were blue but now they're gray."

Mia looked down at her wad of Kleenexes. "They change when I'm angry. Or when I've been hysterical. Or when I'm swimming."

Adam laughed. "I just feel like I'm going to sink like dead weight when I'm swimming. Nifty changing-eye-color phenomenon seems a lot more interesting." He offered her his hand for help up. She took it and concentrated on smoothing her dromedary rise from the couch. "I'll wrap up your fillets while you finish your shopping." He held the office door open for her.

"Meet you at the front." Mia smiled weakly as she moved toward the frozen foods section and a pint of Eli's premium chocolate ice cream, acceptable only with chunks of semisweet Godiva. "Thank you, Adam," she said, her voice catching in her throat.

"My pleasure," he said. She watched him take long strides as he walked away.

## 12

# Estimated Time of Departure

"I can't believe you let her come." Frankie's eyes were wide with anxiety. "I don't know your mother very well, but I can't see her getting into yoga."

Mia shook her head, eyes trained on Babs, who was tiptoeing across the studio with her borrowed mat and a towel. "She insisted," Mia said, her voice flat with resignation and exhaustion after a long day at work. "Said she'd always wanted to try the yoga class on the ship but it conflicted with Rock 'n' Roll Reunion water aerobics."

The ensemble Babs had chosen to wear caused a ripple of raised eyebrows and double takes, even among the more austere class members. Her tank top was well fitted to a trim and surgically enhanced upper body. The word *SASSY* twirled in gold sequins across the chest and sprayed outward in a burst of gold embroidery. Mia felt deep gratitude for having successfully dissuaded her mother from the matching Lycra shorts (this time *SASSY* adorning her rear) and encouraged her instead to borrow a pair of black cotton capris.

"Excuse me … sorry," Babs whispered loudly to each person she passed on her way back to Mia and Frankie. The class had not yet begun but, taking her cue from the Enya CD Delia had playing, Babs had lowered her voice to a nearly appropriate volume.

"I'm so excited!" she whispered to the girls as she unrolled her mat. "My friend Jeannie *loves* yoga. She says there's nothing better to calm the body and the mind." Babs looked over her shoulder and leaned in conspiratorially. "As long as you don't get sucked into the hippie mystic rot." She raised her eyebrows in warning. "It can be very New Age."

Frankie listened with her mouth opened slightly, not daring to look at Mia. "I hope you like it, Mrs. Rathbun. It's not for everyone, but—"

"Oh, Frankie dear, I'm going to love it. I just know it. And you are such a sweet girl." She shook her head slowly, face serious and pondering. "Mia is very blessed to have such a lovely friend, even if you do such confusing things to your pretty hair." She patted Frankie's hand and smiled.

To Mia's consternation Frankie smiled right back.

Mia cleared her throat. "Mother, class is about to start. We should be quiet now while everyone centers their thoughts."

Babs crossed her legs in half lotus, taking her cue from Frankie's perfect posture. "Center my thoughts. Gotcha." She closed her eyes and rested her hands on folded knees.

Frankie glanced at Mia, who made a point to roll her eyes far back into her head. Frankie shot her a disapproving glance. "Be nice," she mouthed to her friend before closing her own eyes and waiting for class to begin.

*Another falls to the charms of Babs*, Mia mused, eyes closed and cynicism dripping from her toes. Her mind clicked through snapshots of friend after friend who had become enamored with Babs over the years, refusing to believe Mia that beneath the woman's engaging public image lay a self-congratulatory, intolerant woman who cared more for the state of her acrylics than that of her only daughter.

After a few moments Delia's voice cut smoothly through the silence. "Welcome," she said in a cocoa-butter voice. "Today is a beautiful spring day and I'm happy you're sharing part of it with me." She turned to Babs, hands open. "We have a visitor with us."

Babs turned to wave excitedly at the other class members. "Hi, everyone! I'm Barbara, Mia's mother." The class offered a subdued greeting and Mia tried to remain peaceful. "It's my first attempt, so don't give me a hard time if I'm not as bendy as the rest of you." Babs's laughter was joined by most of the class, though there were several serious yoga practitioners who clearly did not appreciate this frivolous disruption.

"We're glad to have you join us, Barbara," Delia said. Her eyes showed a patience and kindness Mia did not feel. "As we move through our poses, please take care to listen to your body."

Mia cringed, sure Babs was brewing a smart remark about listening to her body after menopause, one of her more treasured conversation topics. But Delia brought everyone to a standing position at the top of their mats and the class began.

For the first half hour Babs was remarkably well behaved. Mia watched out of the corner of her eye as she attempted her first full lunge, twisted lunge, side angle stretch. Her mother did begin to sweat through her sequins and looked genuinely baffled when Tom, a heavyset man at the back, lost his battle with pent-up flatulence. Mia shot Babs a warning look in the mirror. Babs bit her cheek and Mia could see Frankie's shoulders shake slightly in laughter, but the moment passed without an outburst, which Mia saw as a sign of great encouragement.

It was the balance pose that provoked the downward spiral.

"From our mountain pose," Delia intoned, "take your time to lift one foot from your mat, knee at a right angle to the floor, and come into stork."

Babs obeyed and pulled one leg up, bent at the knee, foot flexed, body wobbling.

Delia took note and addressed the class. "Remember, balance poses take practice, so if this is where you need to stay for today, listen to your body and know your limits."

Babs pursed her lips and muttered something under her breath about the noises her body was making presently. She kept her leg up, face screwed in concentration.

"When you're ready," Delia said, "move your arms out to the sides of your body, keeping your arms straight and the energy flowing from one side of your body to the other."

Babs snorted.

"And now," Delia continued, "push your raised foot behind you, keeping your knee always lifted, tilting your upper body toward the front of the room and straightening your leg toward the door at the back."

Mia obeyed Delia's instructions but struggled with her balance, mostly because of the wild thrashings occurring to her right.

"Mother," she hissed, "just stay in stork."

"Forget it," Babs hissed back. "I can do this."

She bore an uncanny resemblance to an inebriated Wonder Woman, arms outstretched, body yearning to be parallel with the floor, leg flopping back and forth behind her torso. The sequins merely added strength to the comparison.

"Three more deep breaths here," Delia said. She glanced at Babs, and Mia thought she saw the usually inscrutable face blanch, but Delia recovered quickly and moved her eyes around the room once more. "All right," she said. "Slowly come out of the pose and rest a moment, allowing your body a few breaths-worth of recovery."

Babs lowered herself with a quiet groan to her mat and lay on her back. She closed her eyes and breathed like a sprinter just finishing a wicked two-hundred-meter dash.

Mia tiptoed over to Babs and hovered over her heaving frame. "Are you all right?"

"Mmm," she said, never opening her eyes. "Resting."

Frankie looked on with concern. Mia shrugged and returned to her mat.

Delia cleared her throat. "And now the other side."

"Oh, you have *got* to be kidding," Babs said, full voice and making no attempt to mask her contempt.

Delia laughed softly. "Again, I want to remind everyone that yoga practice is very individualized. What feels good one day, one hour, on one side may not for the opposite. We must listen to our bodies and respond to what they say to us."

Mia saw Babs clench her jaw and rise slowly to her feet. "Sometimes what our bodies say can't be trusted," she whispered to her daughter. "If I depended only on what this old thing said to me," she made a sweeping motion to her body, "I'd never have had the courage to go through with my implants."

Mia stared at her mother in disbelief, watching her shift to the other foot and begin the loud and obnoxious process of forcing her body into warrior three. It took a lot of coaxing, grunting, and no small bit of theatrics to get there, but Babs made it and looked triumphantly in the mirror. Frankie smiled encouragingly. Mia held onto the pose two extra breaths, out of spite, despite Delia's warning glance, and in an act of defiance to her ankles, which would make her pay for her stubbornness for several days.

● ● ● ● ●

On their way back to the apartment after yoga class, Mia and Babs made a stop at Green, Mia's favorite beverage joint. The mingling scents of tea leaves, citrus, and freshly cut grass descended on the women as they entered the shop and approached the front counter.

"Their grass-based drinks are all amazing," Mia said. She turned to her mother, who was perusing the chalkboard menus with unveiled horror.

"How about something less *earthy*?" she asked. Her eyes drifted to the bottom corner of the menu. "What's in the smoothies?"

The girl behind the counter looked up from a dog-eared copy of *A Room of One's Own* that she closed and tucked beside the register. "Organic honey, diffusion of wheatgrass and lemongrass, organic strawberries, organic Costa Rican mango, and organic banana. Dairy free, gluten free."

Babs wrinkled her nose. "I guess I'll try that." She sighed and spoke under her breath as the girl left to concoct the drink. "Mia, have I taught you nothing about fruit drinks? Remember the *real* smoothies we drank all across the Caribbean the last time you cruised with me?"

"I do remember, Mother," Mia said, eyes trained on the menu. "And now that I'm older and wiser, I shudder to think of the pesticides we were pumping into our unsuspecting bodies."

Babs snorted. "Haven't killed me yet." She scanned the room. "I hope they have sugar packets."

After paying for Babs's smoothie and Mia's celery-apple-carrot juice, the two left the shop and wandered through Millennium Park. The sun seemed to have gathered its wits about it after a long and tiresome winter; it blanketed treetops and budding tulips with full-strength rays. Lake Michigan shone in the distance, having traded whitecaps for the glitter of sun-painted diamonds on the tops of its chilly waves. Mia had to sidestep a happy bevy of pigeons who danced in one of the few remaining sidewalk puddles.

Babs lifted her face to the sky. "Lovely day to be at sea."

Mia perked up. "So," she offered, trying to keep her tone casual, "have you decided when you'll head back to the ship?"

Babs took a long draw of her smoothie. She'd dumped roughly a cup of sugar into it before leaving the shop, ignoring the disgust registering on the Virginia Woolf reader when she'd emptied the wicker basket of sugar packets. "I think I'll stay on land awhile. At least until my grandbaby is born."

Mia's heart skipped a beat and she felt an instant surge of adrenaline. "But that's not until the end of September. It's May."

"I know. Won't it be fun?" Babs scrunched her nose at Mia and gave her a side hug. "Think of all the time we'll get to spend together."

"Mother, I think we should talk about this," Mia said. The brightness of the sun, so welcome moments ago, was tapping an insistent finger on her skull with the beginnings of a headache. "My apartment really isn't that big—"

"It was plenty big for you and Lars," Babs said. She slurped up a pull of her drink. The noise made a strange percussion against the slap of her footsteps. "But don't worry. That sweet Sam Lamberti has already reserved an apartment for me in your building. On the first floor, furnished and everything. The renter is some academic type who needed to leave the country for a research project in Bora Bora or somewhere. He was hoping to rent it out and I'm happy to sublet. Of course I offered to pay extra for the inconvenience I cause by not signing a year-long lease, but," she shrugged and smiled the grin that must have encouraged Lamberti's generosity, "Sam simply wouldn't hear of it."

Mia trudged along beside her mother, not even trying to look happy about this turn of news. She made note of the date and vowed forever after to refer to that particular day as Black Saturday, the day her mother had pulled her unwittingly into the Pregnancy Pit of Despair.

"I suppose I can't say anything to dissuade you," Mia said. She saw Silas approaching them slowly, his gait slow and dignified. He'd shed his suit coat in honor of the warmer weather and wore a dress shirt with bow tie and vest.

"I'm happy to stay and take care of you," Babs said, patting Mia on the arm.

"Why, this must be the lovely Mrs. Rathbun." Silas smiled and took Babs's hand for a gentle kiss. "Mr. Lamberti has sung your praises, ma'am."

Babs was too coy to blush but was clearly pleased with the attention. "And who might you be, dear man? Clearly a person who knows how to treat a lady."

"Mother, this is Silas Wilson. His apartment is on the first floor of our building."

Silas winked and leaned in to speak quietly. "Mrs. Rathbun, your daughter is trying to say with all delicacy that I'm an old man who takes up her time with stories and free advice. Such a nice girl you've raised. Flawless manners."

Babs patted his hand. "I can't imagine you're a burden, Mr. Wilson. Plus my daughter has made it her calling to improve the lives of the less fortunate."

Mia felt the color in her cheeks rise. "Actually Silas is very fortunate." Her speech accelerated quickly. "In fact just the other day I was telling him how I envied him his long and fulfilled life."

"Not without its hardships, I might add," Silas said, nodding slowly. "Life's not always what we want it to be, am I right, Mrs. Rathbun?"

"Certainly not." She smiled consolingly. "Your people know a lot about suffering."

Mia's reserve of good will was officially empty. "All right, let's go. Silas, great to see you. I'm sorry."

Silas's eyes twinkled. "No need for apologies, Mia honey. Your mama's just telling things like she sees them. We could all stand for a little more of that." He turned to Babs. "Lovely to meet you, Mrs. Rathbun. Thank you for your concern. I assure you, the good Lord takes care of me just as He does the sparrows." He winked at Mia. "But I'll pass along your kind regards to my people."

Babs patted him on his shoulder. "Wonderful to meet you, Mr. Wilson. I'm sure I'll see you around, now that we'll be neighbors." She shrugged her shoulders happily.

Mia pulled her away from Silas before she could stumble upon any more interracial musings. When they were safely out of Silas's hearing, she tightened her grip on her mother's arm.

"Mia, that's too hard, dear. I don't need you to escort me, for Pete's sake." Babs tried removing Mia's clenched fingers from her forearm.

"Do you *have* an internal censor?" Mia said, looking over her shoulder.

"What are you talking about?" Babs sounded annoyed.

"'Your people?' *Your people?* Mother, this is not Highlands Cove. It's *Chicago*. We have different ethnicities, races, socio-economics…. And no one likes to be grouped according to his or her *people* by a privileged white woman fresh off a cruise ship." Mia was panting. She slowed her pace to catch her breath.

"Well, excuse me, Miss Hoity-Toity PC Queen," Babs said. She huffed along, oversized purse swinging from her shoulder. "I was merely pointing out my sympathy for the black race."

Mia groaned.

"And I don't think Mr. Wilson was offended one iota. I think he liked me." She waited for Mia to open the door to her apartment building.

"My point, Mother," Mia said, pushing the door open with her shoulder, "is that it might be a good idea to think before you speak around here." She rummaged for the tiny key that opened her mailbox in the foyer. Before the little door opened to reveal the day's deliveries, she heard Babs coo.

"Sam, dear, how are you?"

Mr. Lamberti shuffled out from his apartment opposite Silas's and nodded quickly to Mia. "Hi, Mia. Hello, Mrs. Rathbun." He sighed and ran one paw through the wispy gray strands he'd combed over a shiny bald dome.

"Sam, how many times must I insist you call me Barbara?" She lengthened the word until it sounded like the final strains in a Karen Carpenter tune.

Mr. Lamberti shifted on his feet and sniffed self-consciously. "All right," he said, avoiding Babs's gaze but smiling shyly at Mia. "Barbara, then."

Mia sifted through the letters in her box. Electric bill, cell phone bill, subscription offer to *Parents* magazine, which jarred her. Her prime suspect was definitely Frankie, as the girl had engaged in a subtle but tenacious battle to start planning for a nursery and registering for baby gifts.

Babs looked over her shoulder and glimpsed a fund-raising mailer from PETA.

"Oh, for goodness's sake, Mia," she said. "Certainly you aren't one of those militant vegetarians." She turned to Mr. Lamberti. "I'll bet you're a man who can appreciate a good steak. Am I right, Sam?"

Mia didn't hear his response. She was staring at a plain white

envelope she'd found at the bottom of the stack. The handwriting
was Lars's, distinctive and angular, like he'd broken many pens and
pencils from pushing too hard on the point. Mia's heart began to
beat more quickly and she felt her hands gripping the paper to the
point of discomfort.

"I'm going up to shower," she told her mother, who nodded
cheerfully before returning to the discussion of where to get the best
New York strip for the best price.

Mia took the elevator, willing her heart to slow down as she rose,
story by story.

# Hail Mary

Mia forced herself to unwrap slowly from her zip-up sweatshirt. Bending down to untie her shoes, she needed to adjust for the belly that pressed down on her legs. She'd begun to feel the flutterings of a kicker within her womb, though she was never quite sure if she imagined movement or if she really was experiencing the first steps toward communication with her child. It seemed fitting that the baby would start a maternal relationship with kicks and jabs. She often felt the desire to perform such catharsis with her own mother.

She walked slowly down the hall to the bathroom, clutching the letter in her hand. Lowering herself to the plush rug in front of the sink, she carefully slit the envelope from one back corner to the other. He'd written on yellow legal paper, the way he began every piece of writing he did for hire.

*Dear Mia,*

*I'm not exactly sure how to begin a letter like this. Perhaps an apology is the best way, the only way to start.*

*I'm sorry.*

*The emptiness of those words must resound even more loudly where you are, but I offer them anyway as a necessary point of departure.*

Mia heard a creak from the front hall and the sound of her mother taking off her coat. She reached over to shut the bathroom door and turned on the shower.

*I write to you from Seattle, which is sufficiently far away to feel I've removed myself from you and our "situation," but not far enough to feel very good about it.*

Mia felt a wash of anger that their child had been reduced to a word within smug quotation marks, but she couldn't stop herself from reading on.

*I understand if you think I'm a coward and unworthy of contacting you after the way I reacted to your news. You're right. I showed nothing of bravery. Even now I'm hiding behind my cowardice by writing instead of calling.*

*Or how about a visit,* Mia thought wryly. *A visit would be appropriate.*

*But I'm hoping you'll recognize this small step I'm taking and allow me to begin a conversation with you once more. I'm feeling very overwhelmed, Mia, and very scared. This is not what I'd planned for our lives, certainly not now, and I'm having difficulty figuring out how I should respond.*

Mia brushed off a tear that landed on the paper and smudged the ink.

*I'll call soon. Or you can call me, if you'd prefer. I just want to talk. Maybe we can figure this mess out, the two of us. We always were pretty good together.*

*Love, Lars*

She sat with her legs splayed in front of her, the purple stripes on her yoga top muddied with tears. The spray from the shower drifted over the toilet, the sink, the floor, and her hair, but Mia didn't get up to pull the curtain. He was ruining it, she thought. One letter, one look at his penmanship, his awkward sharing of his thoughts, reminders of the intimacy they'd earned after so many years. The defenses she'd carefully constructed over the months he'd been gone were crumbling at their foundations, even as she scurried around trying to keep them upright. *He's a jerk,* she said with authority to herself. *So what if he's a familiar one?*

She stayed there weeping until her eyes began to feel uncomfortably puffy and Babs knocked at the door.

"Mia?" she called. "Are you all right?"

Mia blew her nose into a wad of toilet paper.

"Honey? Can you hear me?" Worry had crept into Babs's tone. "You've been in there a very long time. I thought you were concerned about water conservation."

Mia reached up to turn the doorknob. She looked up at Babs through a fresh onslaught of tears. "Lars was the one worried about water conservation. I'm worried about the energy crisis." Her final words erupted into a wail and Babs dropped to her knees to gather her daughter into an embrace.

"Oh, honey, what's wrong? Are you feeling blue? Is it your figure? Sweetheart, you don't need to worry one bit. All those curves will go back to the right places after the baby's born."

Mia cried into her mother's shirt.

"Now you'll need to be patient with yourself," Babs continued. "It takes nine months to grow a baby and it will take at least nine months to go back down to your regular size. Even then you might have to think about surgery."

Mia shook her head and showed Babs the letter. "Lars wrote. He wants to start talking again."

Babs stared at the paper. Her eyebrows knitted together and she lifted her gaze to Mia. "Is that a good thing or a despicable thing?" She spoke carefully and watched her daughter's face for a reaction.

Mia's mouth lifted into a shaky smile. "That's the question, isn't it?" She shook her head, grateful for her mother's uncharacteristic restraint. "I don't know yet."

Babs nodded slowly. "Honey, I don't know a lot about a lot of things, but I do know matters of the heart are more like a minefield and less like a Hallmark card, no matter what the songs say." She rose from her knees, creaking and moaning with every pop. "I'm old, Mia. I'm getting old."

Mia laughed and reached for another bunch of tissues as her mother turned off the shower.

"Listen," Babs said. She pulled Mia to her feet and cupped her swollen face between her hands. "I'm not one for mush, but this has to be said." She furrowed her brow in concentration as she looked into her daughter's eyes. "You are a beautiful, talented, smart woman with a big, big heart. You got the best of both of your parents and none of our flaws, which is nothing short of a miracle, considering we both had our share." Babs swallowed hard as Mia's eyes welled once more with tears. "You're going to give yourself time to figure out how to respond to this letter. I'll help you if I can, but I'm not sure I'm your best resource when it comes to man advice. Better ask Frankie. Or that nice girl from your high school graduating class—what was her name? Tiffany? Brittany?"

"Lindsay. Lindsay Dunlop."

"Right. She married very well, I hear, and could have some pointers."

Mia sighed and blotted her eyes with Kleenex.

"But before I forget, your obstetrician's office called while you were in the shower. Or on the bathroom floor getting misted."

"What did they say?"

"They called to confirm your ultrasound appointment for

Wednesday at three." Babs's eyes lit up like candles. "May I come? Please? Please, Mia?"

"Come to my appointment?" Mia clutched her head, which had begun to pound with a new flush of hormones in the aftermath of emotion. "I suppose so. If you really want to and have no other plans."

"I'd thought about taking that lovely river cruise, the one about architecture? And I have a mani-pedi appointment at noon, but I can do both of those any day." Babs clapped her hands together. "Oh, thank you. I'm so, so excited. This is the fun part. And don't worry. I'll be quiet as a mouse. You won't even know I'm there unless you *summon* me." She smiled at Mia and pulled an arm around her waist as she ushered her to the living room. "Now you sit down and I'll get you a few squares of dark chocolate. Nature's best mood lifters."

Mia watched Babs swish from the room and allowed a tiny crack to form in her protective wall.

•  •  ●  •  ◦

The next morning was a Sunday and Mia made a special effort to snuggle deeper inside her covers to take advantage of a late morning's sleep. Her eyes were still slightly swollen from the weeping-shower experience the day before, so when she woke at nine unable to drift back to sleep, the heaviness in her eyelids disoriented her into thinking it was much earlier than it was. She pulled on a bathrobe and shuffled in slippers to the kitchen.

"Good morning," Babs said as she beat Mia to the cupboard to retrieve a tea mug.

"You're awfully chipper," Mia said in a man-voice, any unexpected affection for her mother from the day before evaporating in the merciless clarity of morning. "Why are you all dressed up?"

"These old rags?" Babs waved a bored hand across her red pencil skirt, silk blouse, and four-inch heels. "Just something I dug up from the bottom of my bag."

Mia raised one weary eyebrow in her mother's direction.

"And ironed," Babs added. She handed her daughter a steaming cup of tea.

Mia sloshed a bit of cream into the cup and swirled the liquid into a lazy tornado. "Where are you headed?"

"I thought I'd go to church." Babs's back was turned to Mia as she rinsed her breakfast dishes in the sink. "Our services on the ship are usually very disappointing. We have to accommodate all preferences, but usually the Methodists win out. Very opinionated, those Methodists. I've sung many ancient hymns on the deep waters of the Caribbean."

Mia sipped her tea while leaning one hip against the counter. "I didn't know you were still a churchgoer."

Babs shrugged slightly. "I've never been as consistent as my parents would have liked. But there's nothing like the birth of one's first grandbaby to get one to the altar, as it were. This baby will need to be baptized, you know." She wavered at the look on her daughter's face. "Just a little sprinkle?"

Mia shook her head. "I haven't decided on any of that. But as for this morning, there are a million churches in Chicago. I'm sure you'll find one that suits you." She sat down at the kitchen table and opened the newspaper.

"We can go wherever you want," Babs said. She swirled water and soap inside a glass before dumping it out. "I thought we could leave in a half hour or so and start wandering. Surely there's a good ten thirty or eleven o'clock service close by."

Mia smirked over her cup. "Thanks for the invitation, Mother, but I'm no longer required to go to church with you. Adulthood exempts me from the guilt."

Babs looked injured. "Well, I can't force you." She was quiet for a moment. "But it would be some nice mother-daughter time. And I'll take you to lunch afterward."

Mia could feel the weight of this decades-long argument settle with a familiar thud in her chest. "I don't think—"

"I know, I know," Babs said quickly. "The church has been used as an instrument of torture, it spreads propaganda that has nothing to do with the peace-loving, granola Jesus of the Bible, it suppresses the rights of the women and the cause of the poor, and so on and so forth." She wiped her hands on a kitchen towel and looked up at Mia. "I've heard you."

"Great," Mia shrugged. "So we don't have to have this conversation again. You are free to attend church as consistently or inconsistently as you'd like and I'm free to do the same." She turned back to the paper.

"But the church *does* do lots of good things like weddings and funerals. And soup kitchens! You love soup kitchens! Besides, you might just need their help one day, miss, and this is a perfect time to look for a place to start building relationships. I met your father at church, you'll remember." She wagged her finger at her daughter.

"And look how well that turned out," Mia said. She rose to dump the dregs of her tea into the sink.

"Well," Babs said, not a bit flustered by the mention of her failed marriage, "you can't blame the church for that. We'd stopped going by that time anyway." She stopped Mia on her way out of the kitchen. "Mimi, please. It won't hurt you. And I won't bother you about it for the rest of my visit."

Mia wavered. She rubbed her eyes with one hand.

Babs saw the weakening of resolve and jumped in to the silence. "After all, you're in good company, being knocked up with no husband. Think of the Virgin Mary!" She smiled in triumph.

Mia shook her head. "It is amazing I am so well-adjusted," she muttered as she walked to the bathroom.

"Great! I'll just pop downstairs and ask Sam about neighborhood churches."

Mia leaned her head against the tile as she waited for the water to warm. *The Virgin Mary, eh?* she thought. *Not exactly an airtight comparison.* She slipped into the shower and tried to prepare herself for a very long Sabbath.

# 14

# House of Worship

The usher sat them in the front row, so Mia couldn't turn her head to confirm. But a brief sweep of the room when they'd entered had strongly suggested what she'd wondered during the cab ride to the South Side: She and her mother were the only white people in the building.

Ebenezer Church sat aloft a lonely hill in a surprisingly quiet neighborhood. Very few people were out enjoying the spring weather when the cab dropped them off at the entrance. The service had begun before they'd arrived. Silas patted Mia's hand as they ascended the set of stairs at the front of the building.

"Don't you worry, Mia honey," he'd said. "All the people at this church are going to love you and your mama just like you'd been coming every Sunday since you were a child."

Mia had smiled at Silas and willed herself to keep putting one foot in front of the other. The relief of Babs's promise not to pester her about church for the rest of her visit propelled Mia upstairs and into Silas's home church. Babs winked at her as they entered.

"Aren't you glad you came?"

Mia felt the verdict was far from in on that. She'd come down to the lobby of her apartment building and found her mother and Silas laughing together. Babs had jovially explained that Silas had discovered her quest for a church and had invited the ladies to his.

The congregation was in full voice when they entered the sanctuary.

"Oh, I just *love* black music," Babs said to Mia as they made their way down the center aisle.

Silas exchanged warm greetings with parishioners on either side, all the while swaying with the rhythm of the music. After greeting Silas with a kiss or hug, the congregants would turn to Babs and Mia to envelop them in warmth as well.

Babs was in her element. She spoke into the ear of one woman and complimented her on her wide-brimmed purple hat. Another woman farther down the aisle received unsolicited affirmation on how stylish her zebra print heels were, especially in Barbados, where Babs had just visited. When they finally reached an open pew in front of the podium, Mia watched in horror as her mother began to do the two-step, singing along loudly and clapping with great enthusiasm on the wrong beat. Silas seemed to be enjoying sharing his church with friends and would look at Mia every now and again, and pat her arm gently, a kind smile lighting his face and giving extra depth to the lines that traveled there.

After twenty minutes of singing, Silas lowered himself to the pew. Mia leaned over to ask if he was all right.

"Oh, honey, I'm just as good as ever. But these folks can outsing me any day of the week." He nodded his head in time to the music, one smooth, brown hand resting on the red pew fabric beside him, the other hand tapping the beat on his knee.

After another twenty minutes the music softened in gradual decrescendo from a rambunctious waterfall to a hushed and mournful river. Babs swayed with her eyes closed, her tanned legs showing prettily beneath the hem of her skirt. The baby offered a spirited kick in Mia's belly, perhaps disappointed that the auditory fun was coming to a close.

The baby needn't have worried, Mia later thought, as music at Ebenezer took various forms. When the congregants had let the singing die down and had rustled and creaked into the pews, they merely exchanged one melody for another. Pastor Reginald Jenkins prayed from the pulpit and Mia was washed in a second wave of music as the people of the church voiced their agreement in prayer.

"Heavenly Father," Pastor Jenkins prayed, "we praise You."

"We do," Silas said, his voice one of many responding to that of the pastor.

"Jesus, Son of God," Jenkins continued, "we glorify You."

"Yes, Lord," a woman behind Mia said in a joyful voice. She clapped her hands once for emphasis.

"And Holy Spirit," Jenkins said, his voice alive with supplication, "we give You our hearts."

"Take 'em, Lord!" Silas said, stomping the floor once with his foot.

"Almighty God, three in one, we say this morning that we need You. We hunger for You. We want You to meet us here."

The woman behind Mia was humming along with the pastor's words. Mia glanced at her mother and saw she was watching the pastor with eyes wide open.

"Before we get too far into this, though, Lord, we should tell You we are sorry. Sorry for the sins we've committed against You. King David wrote that our iniquities ..." Pastor Jenkins paused and drew out the final *s* in the word. "Our iniquities separate us from You."

The congregation pulsed with sorrow at his words. Mia shifted in her seat.

"We ask you to cleanse us white as snow, O God. Do as You've promised, bridge the gap between Your holiness and our imperfection, and make us clean."

"Yes, Lord!" A man near the back boomed his petition. Several people clapped in agreement.

Mia's mind drifted to the church she and her family had attended in Highlands Cove. Parkview Presbyterian participated in a much more subdued worship format, as far as she could remember. The pastor had read his prayers from a paper on the pulpit. He'd taken his time, looking through scholarly reading glasses perched on the very end of his nose, enunciating each word with deliberate care. Mia knew this to be true as she, like her mother, had the habit of watching people pray when everyone else bowed their heads and closed their eyes. That morning at Ebenezer, Mia wondered how things had changed at the church of her childhood. She'd like to see, for example, if the Sunday school curriculum still boasted an impressive selection of felt-board Bible stories. The various incarnations of a pale and emaciated Jesus on the cross had given her nightmares, regardless of her teacher's assurance that this was the same kind and gentle carpenter featured in other scenes healing sick people and patting the heads of children in bathrobes.

Mia sat with her eyes closed, half-listening to Silas and Pastor Jenkins continue their prayerful volley. Her thoughts lingered on the church of her childhood, where she could still feel the squishy carpet indent as she walked into the sanctuary with John and her parents. She'd studied Christianity in some of her college courses, once through a feminist lens, another time through the eyes of colonized tribal groups in nineteenth-century Latin America. Merging these academic experiences with her own spiritual upbringing had seemed impossible, laughable even, especially since the Rathbuns had discontinued their church attendance by the end of Mia's junior-high years. A short time later her parents divorced and not long after that, Mia's father was dead. She recalled a few Parkview representatives at her dad's funeral and she thought someone from the church had brought a casserole or two in the weeks following his death. But by that time, any worthwhile connection to the church had eroded and Mia had never had reason to return.

A chorus of amens drew Mia out of her reverie. Pastor Jenkins leaned forward with both hands on the pulpit and took stock of his congregation. A man in his late fifties, he was beginning to gray around the temples and the cocoa-colored skin of his face crinkled with joy of full years already behind him.

"Brother Silas, I see you've brought some visitors with you today."

Silas rose slowly to his feet, straightening his jacket and collar as he stood.

"Good morning," Silas said. The congregation called out in a parallel greeting. "I have the honor today of worshipping with two lovely ladies who live in my dear Trump Palace." The congregation laughed in appreciation. "From the fourth floor I present the lovely Mia Rathbun."

Silas gestured for her to stand and she did so begrudgingly. She smiled at the people watching her with kind faces. They called out in greeting and she waved, the color full on her cheeks.

"Miss Mia is expecting a baby this fall, so you ladies might take note and try fattening her up a bit."

The women in the group nodded their approval and blanketed Mia with quiet well-wishes.

"And from the first floor, our newest neighbor, Ms. Barbara Rathbun, Mia's mother."

"Hello," Babs said, waving gaily. "It's a pleasure to be here."

Mia sat down quickly, hoping to encourage Babs to do the same.

"This is my very first time in an African-American church," Babs said.

Mia felt her heart pounding through her shirt.

"And I must say, I think I've been going to the wrong worship service my whole life!"

The congregants chuckled and one shouted, "Amen!" Mia let the breath she'd been holding captive escape her lungs. *It could have been so much worse*, she thought. At least she didn't try to lead the group in a chorus of "Swing Low, Sweet Chariot."

Pastor Jenkins made a few announcements from the pulpit. The ladies' ministry was holding a bake sale to raise funds for a neighborhood school. A family from the congregation had lost their home to a fire and needed donations of furniture and clothing. The offering plates were passed without ceremony and Mia noticed most put something in the plate. Babs threw in a twenty and kept her attention on the pastor as he began his sermon.

"Let's open together in God's Word to Paul's letter to the Galatians. Chapter six, verse two." Pastor Jenkins waited a moment while the hushed ruffle of pages filtered through the congregation. "Paul writes, 'Bear ye one another's burdens, and so fulfil the law of Christ.'" He read the verse again, slowly and with each consonant more pronounced than the first reading. Pastor Jenkins looked up from the worn black Bible he cradled in one hand. "Anybody bearing a burden this morning?"

Several worshippers raised their hands, speaking their agreement and shaking their heads at the weight of what they carried.

Babs raised her hand in the air and leaned over to nudge her daughter. She patted Mia's belly and whispered, "Raise your hand, sweetie. This is a time to be *open* with our needs."

The excitement in her voice made Mia want to jump out one of the windows that lined the aisles. She shook her head firmly and hissed, "I'm here. Don't push it."

"Paul did not make a polite *suggestion* that we carry each other's burdens." Pastor Jenkins's voice trembled with the beginnings of a melody. "He didn't say we should only try reaching our brothers and sisters on our cell phones when we're stuck in traffic or when we have nothing better to do."

Silas chuckled with several others in the group.

"He didn't say to bear each other's burdens because we're nice people and we want people to know it."

"Oh, Lord." The woman behind Mia *tsk*ed to herself.

"No, Paul said we must bear the burdens of our brothers and sisters because it is the *law of Christ*. Not a polite suggestion, but a *law*. I'm not sure about the people in this room, but I've never thought a law was a rule I could take or leave as the mood hit me."

Babs liked this analogy and shouted, "Amen!" Hers was the only voice raised in the small moment and Mia felt her cheeks color again. *What would Dr. Finkelstein say if she could see me now?* she thought. Mia, a self-proclaimed agnostic, languishing in a church service next to the mother who could take credit for funding the orthodontic bills for two of Liza Finkelstein's children. It had not escaped Mia that using part of her father's inheritance to pay a therapist to exorcise the emotional demons created by Babs was ugly irony. But as Dr. Finkelstein liked to remind her patients, we do not choose our families, but we can choose what to do with the havoc they wreak.

Pastor Jenkins had begun a lively discourse on what it meant for Ebenezer Church to be bearing the burdens of those in its community.

"We need to stop expecting people who don't know Jesus to act like they do!" He pounded once on the pulpit with a closed fist.

Babs made some sort of circling motion with her hands and then drew them into a prayerful pose in front of her chest, eyes closed and head nodding. Mia wondered if perhaps Babs was mixing her recent experience at yoga with the trip to Ebenezer. Regardless, Mia knew she had neither the emotional fortitude nor the bladder strength to make it through what was sure to be an animated section of the sermon for her mother. She inched her way out of the pew and toward the back in search of a restroom.

Grateful for the solitude, Mia lingered over the sink, washing her hands and checking out each pore on her face. She rummaged in her bag for lip gloss and a hairbrush. Mid-search, her cell phone vibrated against the outside of her bag. She checked the caller ID and froze with the phone vibrating wildly in her hand. After a deep breath she answered.

"Hello." She couldn't bring herself to speak with a familiarity he no longer deserved.

"Mia?" Lars's voice sounded close enough to be in the same room. He was silent for a moment and then, "How are you?"

Acid pushed into the back of her throat. "Oh, you know. Pregnant, abandoned by the father of my child, getting huge. Couldn't be much better." The bite of her sarcasm surprised Mia a bit but she hadn't exactly rehearsed for the moment.

Lars cleared his throat. "Um, did you get my letter?"

"I did." Her heart was racing so she sat on a folding chair by the window.

"So is it okay that I called?"

Mia sighed. "Lars, I'm not sure what you want from me."

"I don't want anything," Lars said quickly. "I mean, I'm not exactly in the position to be asking favors here."

"Good point." Mia leaned her head back, letting it rest on the smooth pink tile of the wall behind her.

They were silent, long enough for Mia's breathing to calm and her emotions to start spiraling slowly back to the new normal.

"How are you feeling?" Lars ventured.

"Fairly well. The first few months weren't so hot. I couldn't eat much more than crackers and the occasional banana. But now," she sighed. "Now I'm in the second trimester and feeling better." She felt a sudden and overwhelming need for him to be there with her, see her, touch her belly, and talk to the baby she wasn't sure she could face alone. *Be honest, be patient, be myself.* She heard Dr. Finkelstein's slightly nasal voice intoning the mantra in her psyche. *Be honest … and tell him I can't stand what he did but I also can't stand being alone?* Mia felt, rather than heard how hollow and pathetic that sounded. She sat up in her chair, willing her spine to harden.

"Where are you right now?" Lars asked.

"Oh." Mia's thoughts flew back to her present location. "I'm in the ladies' room of Ebenezer Church on the South Side. I'm here with my mother and Silas."

She heard a rustling noise as Lars adjusted the phone to his ear. "Did you just say you're at a church with your mother?"

"Right. And Silas. Remember Silas from the first floor?"

"Of course I do." Confusion dripped out of Lars's voice. "But you're at his church with *your* *mother*? Isn't she on a ship somewhere?"

"Actually she lives on the first floor of our building. My building." The need to self-correct wearied her. "It's amazing who sticks by a person when she really needs it." She thought of Pastor Jenkins and the sermon that thundered on upstairs. *Bearing another's burden isn't as poetic as it sounds,* she thought, the weight of her belly pushing down on her legs until she shifted in the chair.

"Listen, Mia," Lars said. "I really want to try making things better. But placing blame will get us nowhere. We're in this together."

"Really? Because the word *together* usually implies more than one person and so far I've been pretty much on my own in this."

"I know and I'm sorry. Didn't you read the letter? I'm sorry, Mia, and I'm trying to make it right. Can you help me out here?"

"Mm," Mia said as her only reply.

"Can you at least talk without getting so defensive and angry?"

She waited a moment. The baby walloped one side of her womb as a prompt. *Alone.* The word took its time floating in a lazy arc through her mind. "I'll try," she said.

"Great. That's great," Lars said. He sounded relieved. "I'll let you get back to, um, church…. I didn't know you were religious."

"I'm not," Mia said hastily and then felt guilty for saying it. "Sometimes it's just easier not to argue with my mother."

"I remember that," Lars said, a bitter note dropping into his voice. "I'll call soon. Good-bye, Mia."

*Now there's growth,* she thought as she walked slowly back to the sanctuary, her feet whispering their way across the carpeted lobby. *At least this time he said good-bye.*

# 15

# Sounds of Silence

The office of Dr. Mahoney experienced a decorative renaissance during Mia's first trimester. New carpet, new paint, and a series of black-and-white photographs glorifying the pregnant belly made over what had been a spatial tribute to beige and sea foam green. Still-fresh paint fumes pummeled patients entering the waiting room. This caused no small bit of consternation as Dr. Mahoney's patient population was particularly sensitive to strong odors, even those of the latex, nontoxic variety. To remedy the situation, the receptionist offered, free of charge, the use of disposable surgical masks for those patients desiring an olfactory filter while they waited.

A line of pregnant women sat in the new brightly upholstered chairs. Those early on in their gestational stages sat with exemplary prenatal posture and paged through the array of pregnancy and child care magazines. The women who tended toward waddling rather than walking looked significantly less impressed with the periodicals and breathed impatience with the very idea of pregnancy. A woman sitting next to Mia had given up on her maternity wardrobe entirely and wore a top that did not, unfortunately, reach to the bottom of her enormous belly. Mia averted her eyes and vowed never to reach the point of not caring that she showed her groceries, as it were, to a waiting room full of strangers.

Mia caught the eye of a woman sitting opposite her and Babs. She followed the woman's bemused expression and lighted on her mother.

"How can you *stand* not using one of these?" Babs said through her surgical mask. She inhaled into the stiff blue material. "Those odors have to be carcinogenic. Or brain-cell killers."

Mia listened without comment.

Babs pointed once more at the basket of masks. "They're free!" she said, triumphant.

Mia glanced around the room. Several of the women with little to show thus far in their pregnancies clutched the masks, but any woman beyond those first volatile months seemed oblivious to the paint smell. For Mia's part she was grateful for the cause of the fumes and took comfort in the bright new colors of the office: lime green, lipstick red, turquoise, deep purple. She thought the change was inspiring, much more lively than the early nineties motif of pastels and floral art formerly on display.

Babs marked her spot on the article she was reading in *Star Weekly*. She moved her mask to one side and whispered, "I hope you showered this morning."

Mia looked askance at her mother. "Pardon?"

Babs raised her eyebrows in preemptive reproach. "The poor man has his nose in foo-foos all day. I would hope yours would represent our family well."

Mia stared at her mother, who donned the surgical mask once more and returned to her magazine.

"From the looks of his color palette, this doctor must be some firecracker." Babs spoke with the reverence she held for every physician she'd ever known. Mia had watched firsthand as Babs targeted the doctors and their spouses who traveled on cruises she worked. The vacationers were usually very patient with Babs and her pandering to the medical elite, though Mia knew of at least one instance in which an anesthesiologist had asked to be reassigned to a different excursion group when he found out Babs had aligned her workweek with his picks for recreation.

"So? What's he like?" Babs leaned forward in anticipation, for the moment forgetting about the mask. Doctors had this effect on her.

"Dr. Mahoney?" Mia asked, doing her best to keep a straight face. "Oh, he's a firecracker all right. And I'm sure you two will get along like old pals."

Babs sighed happily. In just one afternoon she would get to see the ultrasound of her first grandbaby *and* meet a physician. Mia saw the contentedness settle in Babs's eyes and face.

When the nurse led them back to an open examination room, Babs took her time perusing the framed diplomas lining one wall. "Ooh, Northwestern University for undergrad. I think that's where Emeril went. Or maybe that was a different Northwestern."

Mia left her purse on a chair and climbed the one step up to the exam table. She forced herself to have tall posture, even on what felt like a paper-lined pedestal.

"Dr. Mahoney went to medical school at the Mayo Clinic! Can you believe that, Mia? Remember Great Aunt Ruthie McGilvra? She had her gall bladder removed at the Mayo Clinic. It's a *wonderful* facility. That Arab sheik person died there just last week."

A quick rap sounded and the door flew open. "Hello, Mia. And who's this?" Dr. Mahoney moved quickly to Babs and thrust out his hand. "Dan Mahoney."

"Hello, Dr. Mahoney." Babs was practically purring. "Barbara Rathbun. It's *such* an honor to meet the man who's taken such good medical care of my daughter."

Mia rolled her eyes behind Dr. Mahoney's back. She'd had only a handful of appointments with this man and knew less about him than she knew about the Supreme Court justices, even if he had seen her foo-foo.

"Pleasure," he said and pushed his clipboard roughly onto the counter by the sink. He lathered his hands into an impressive mountain of foam and checked Mia's chart as he rinsed. "So Mia, twenty-one weeks. Any issues?" He tossed a paper towel into the trash receptacle and spun on a wheeled stool to the end of the exam table.

Mia found it disconcerting to have a conversation with a man whose eyes were at her knee-level, but she kept her legs knit tightly together and tried to act natural. "I don't think so. I'm feeling much less nauseous now. And I'm not as tired."

"If I may," Babs interrupted. Mia shot her a look, which went expertly ignored. "Dr. Mahoney, Mia has been working *very* long hours at her job. She comes home exhausted and I can't *imagine* that's good for a growing baby."

Mia looked at Babs in disbelief. Long hours? She was home by six every night and Babs had never mentioned this before.

Dr. Mahoney didn't look at Babs but stopped his scribbling and raised his gaze quickly to Mia. "What do you do for a living again?"

"I'm a social worker."

"So no manual exertion but emotional exhaustion?"

Mia pictured Carl and his aversion to conflict, her office cubicle that had seen nary a human for three days, the welcome visit from Flor the previous week when they'd set her up with the WIC office and discussed their shared distaste for maternity clothes. "No, I don't feel emotionally exhausted."

Dr. Mahoney went back to his clipboard. "Keep an eye on it, Mrs. Rathbun, but I think she's doing fine."

Babs put a hand on one Spanx-ed hip and tried again. "She does yoga."

"Great for the joints," Dr. Mahoney said, flipping back a few pages in Mia's chart. "Might even help with breathing during delivery, though I don't know of any empirical studies to support that. Just be careful with twisting, balancing, anything that doesn't feel right."

Babs's face pinked. Mia could hear the commencement of foot tapping. Perhaps Mayo Clinic wasn't the bastion of medical excellence Aunt Ruthie and the sheik suggested.

"Blood pressure looks good, pulse is fine. Feeling the baby move?"

"Yes." Mia smiled. "Not so much today but I've felt lots of jabs and kicks in the night."

"Great. Let's take a look." Dr. Mahoney retrieved a tape measure from a pocket in his lab coat and asked Mia to lie down and expose her belly. "Measuring just fine, twenty-one centimeters. When was your last pap smear?"

"I had one right before I got pregnant," Mia said, thanking the Lord above for His tender mercies that required only one pap a year. Enduring that kind of cervical exploration with her mother watching from behind the doctor's ear would have put Mia into orbit, or at least premature labor.

"We'll listen for a heartbeat and then get you over to the ultrasound room." Dr. Mahoney turned on the portable Doppler machine he held in one hand and squirted a light blue gel over Mia's belly.

Babs cooed. "Oh, this is so exciting! Hearing my first grandchild's heartbeat!" She moved to the side of the table and watched Dr. Mahoney move the microphone over Mia's middle.

He cleared his throat. "Mrs. Rathbun, do you live here or are you visiting Mia?"

Babs straightened. "Both, really. I'm visiting but have decided to live here until Mia has the baby. Perhaps that might seem *drastic* to some, but I say *nothing* is inconvenient when it comes to my children."

"That's nice," Dr. Mahoney said distractedly.

The hope on Babs's face fell, so quickly had her conversational prowess been curtailed.

Mia watched the doctor's face and felt her heart begin to pound. "What's wrong?" she said. Her mouth had gone dry and she swallowed hard to conjure up some moisture.

Dr. Mahoney did not respond but continued to move the probe

around her belly. After a few more attempts, he switched off the machine. "My Doppler must be off. Let's walk over to ultrasound to get a better look."

"What does that mean?" Babs's voice ratcheted up a few notes on the scale. "Can't you find the heartbeat? Oh, dear God, is there something wrong with the baby?" Babs's lower lip began to tremble and she clutched her daughter's hand.

"Let's not get ahead of ourselves," Dr. Mahoney said, not trying very hard to mask his annoyance with Babs's commentary. "The ultrasound will give us a much more accurate picture of what's going on." He threw open the door and barreled down the hall ahead of the women.

Later, when she tried to remember details of the next moments, Mia was unable to draw any defined edges on the images that pushed through her blurry memories. Babs had held fiercely to her hand as they walked to the other side of the clinic. She remembered being oddly preoccupied with her hands, which had become very cold, so much so that they felt apart from the rest of her body. Perhaps the baby was cold, she thought, wondering if that might explain the quietness in her belly. The technician who normally performed ultrasounds for the clinic left when Dr. Mahoney offered a few quiet words of explanation. The room was dark, photos of the tech's family littering a fabric-covered bulletin board hanging above her desk. Mia watched the ceiling tiles as the doctor readied himself for the sonogram. Babs hovered by Mia's head and occasionally sniffled into a wad of Kleenexes she'd taken from the exam room.

The hush among them broke with Dr. Mahoney's voice. "All right, Mia. I need you lift your blouse to expose your abdomen."

The coolness of the gel made a hard shiver ripple through her body.

"Sorry," Dr. Mahoney muttered. He seemed frustrated with the computer. Babs sniffed when he cursed under his breath.

"Sorry," he said again. "Having a little trouble getting to the right screen."

He placed the probe in the goop on Mia's belly. She waited for long, long moments for him to say something, anything, as he watched the computer screen.

"Jesus, help us," Babs prayed. She painted invisible lines with her shaking forefinger on the back of Mia's hand.

"Not very cooperative," Dr. Mahoney said.

Mia closed her eyes.

Babs said, "Perhaps we should go get the woman who usually does this sort of thing." Mia could hear in the way she spoke that her mother had given up all doctor worship on the man as he was determined to fail her time and again.

"No, I mean your baby is uncooperative." He swung the monitor around with his free hand so they could see. "I guess the kid just didn't want to be found that easily." He paused and they watched the baby's heartbeat flicker regularly in a dark spot in the middle of the chest. Dr. Mahoney shrugged. "As I said, no reason to overreact." He didn't look at Babs when he spoke, but his schoolteacher's scolding was clear in its target. "I can let Lorraine come back in to do all the measurements. She tends not to cuss at computers as much as I do."

Babs snorted through happy tears.

"But from where I sit, it looks like everything is as it should be. Ten fingers, ten toes, and it looks like your baby has one digit in particular that is of interest." He pointed with the cursor and Mia allowed herself the first smile during the last twenty minutes. After the wild acrobatics to avoid the Doppler, the baby lay curled up and cozy, sucking its thumb on the right hand.

"Mia sucked her thumb until she was thirteen," Babs said, wiping the corners of her eyes. "She wouldn't go to summer camp, she was so embarrassed."

Mia said nothing, even though Babs had her confused with John, who had, indeed, sucked his thumb for years but certainly not into junior high. Mia herself had been partial to her blanket, Miss Tims, named after the woman who lived with a trio of porch-prowling cats at the corner of their block.

"My part is done for now." Dr. Mahoney patted Mia awkwardly on the arm. "Tell the ladies up front you need to be back in four weeks for the glucose check. It's routine," he added quickly. A quick nod to Babs and he tromped out the door.

"Well." Babs blew her nose before continuing in hushed tones. "He has the bedside manner of a jackhammer, but he kind of grows on you, don't you think?"

Mia felt her heart begin a begrudging slowdown. She allowed her hand to remain in Babs's grasp for the rest of the appointment.

# 16

# A Little Help from My Friends

"Ooooh, look at this!"

Mia turned to see Frankie holding up a ghastly pink and purple baby outfit. The crocheted top matched a beret clipped jauntily to one side. Purple corduroy bell bottoms trimmed in large green flowers swung below the hanger.

"Frankie, that's not gender neutral. We can't buy a bunch of girl clothes if we don't know the sex of the baby."

"Fine, fine," Frankie said, shoving the outfit back on the rack. "I just want you to see what's out there for baby clothes this season. You'll need to be ready as soon as that doctor holds up your screaming child, vagina or penis included."

"I prefer 'foo-foo' and 'Mr. Wiggle.'" Mia held up a soft green sleeper with tiny fruits and vegetables printed on the fabric. "This is cute, right? It's organic cotton."

Frankie wrinkled her nose. "Don't infect your child with your issues. If you get that, Auntie Frankie will need to find one with cupcakes and Cheetos and made out of duct tape, just to balance you out."

Mia paused in her riffling to rub the back of her neck with one hand. Frankie had been trying to coerce her into a trip to Baby World since the baby was the size of a lima bean, but until that afternoon, Mia had resisted. She just didn't feel ready to ally herself with the consumption side of having a baby. At her appointments with Dr. Mahoney, she'd flipped through a few pregnancy magazines and had been nothing less than horrified with the unfamiliarity of the baby product empire. The vocabulary was strange: layette (stuff the baby would need, like the veggie sleeper and cloths to spit up on), tummy time (time the baby spent on his or her stomach to encourage neck muscle strength), perineum (some part of her anatomy that was sure to experience trials and tribulations during the ordeal of labor), meconium (baby's first tar-like bowel movement). These concepts troubled Mia to the point of ignoring them completely until she absolutely had to confront them. In fact she'd likely still be denying Frankie the pleasures of Baby World were it not for the ultrasound experience several weeks before. Something about seeing that little one, eyes closed in ignorant sleep, thumb planted firmly in the mouth, heart beating with stubborn regularity—the image had flipped a switch in Mia's head and made her begin to see her belly as the very real home of a child. She placed her hand where she felt a flutter from inside and turned to Frankie.

"This place is huge. Can we be done for today and come back some other time?"

"But of course, dear Mia." Frankie's eyes sparked with the promise of a return trip. "Registers are up front." She swung Mia's cart toward the store entrance and took off at a clip. Amid crib sets, baby swings, and high chairs, they passed an entire section devoted to lactation. Mia walked slowly, gathering in the rows of formula, bottles, plastic nipples, and C-shaped pillows meant to ease the discomfort of holding a baby to one's breasts. She had to will herself from clutching protectively at her own bosom when they passed a display of breast pumps. The women in the promotional photos smiled peacefully, their work clothes opened at the chest, pantyhose and navy heels still appropriately donned, while the pumps latched on with two enormous suction cups.

"Good Lord," Mia said aloud and Frankie followed her gaze. "Am I going to have to do that?"

Frankie nodded soberly. "Breast is best. Tailored specifically to the nutritional and developmental needs of your child, your supply regulated by his or her demand, linked to higher IQ scores and fewer incidences of food allergies later in life."

Mia tore her eyes away from the pumping Stepford wife and planted her gaze on her friend. "Frankie, you have to stop reading *What to Expect*. It's starting to creep me out."

Frankie looked incredulous. "Are you kidding? That is the single most compelling book I've read in the last year. And I'm a librarian!" She turned toward the front and resumed her walk toward the register.

The woman who rang up Mia's purchases would have been better matched as a penitentiary warden than as the parting gesture of customer service at a baby supply store. Her hair was pulled back so severely and with such tension at the hairline, Mia found it difficult to concentrate on all the prompts of the credit card machine.

"It's waiting for your signature," the woman said, flicking the back of the machine with an impressively meaty finger.

"Right." Mia obeyed quickly to avoid any corporal repercussions. "Good grief. I barely picked up anything and the total is ninety-eight dollars?" She finished her signature and tapped the screen to approve the purchase.

The woman punched a violent series of numbers on her keypad and said, "It's only starting. By the time you're my age, they suck you dry for all you're worth and leave you for dead. Receipt with you or in the bag?" She held the paper above the counter and waited for Mia's response, her mouth drawn into a line that might have been menacing were they in an alley after dark.

"In the bag, please." Mia's voice became small. She could see Frankie biting her nails in her peripheral vision.

"Enjoy this part, when all you have to do is keep it alive." She handed Mia's bag over the counter and creaked her lip muscles slightly upward. "Have a nice day and thanks for shopping Baby World."

"Thank you," Mia said, holding the bag to her chest and walking shoulder to shoulder with Frankie as they left the store.

"*Somebody* needs to reacquaint herself with the joys of children," Frankie said with considerable more bravado than she'd shown in the store. "That woman is in the wrong line of work."

Mia drank in a deep breath of cooled air and squinted into the sky. Dark, billowy clouds had covered the sun and were preparing to unleash a thunderstorm on the city. The girls quickened their pace to the nearest bus stop and ducked inside the protective shelter as the first voluptuous drops of rain began to fall.

"Frankie, how am I going to pay for a baby?" Mia asked. She lowered herself to the wood bench and waited for Frankie to do the same.

They watched the rain gather momentum, giving a quick and furious bath to the oil-spattered street before them.

"We'll figure it out." Frankie put one gangly arm around Mia's back and pulled her closer. "You just remember you're not alone. I would never allow it."

Mia let her head drop on Frankie's shoulder, which was achingly bony but offered without hesitation.

"If all else fails," Frankie said, "we can always head back to Baby World for some encouragement from the seasoned professionals."

Mia laughed, and Frankie laughed too, under a clap of thunder for emphasis.

●　●　●　●　●

Released from work an hour early, Mia decided to duck into Gerry's for a few items before the after-five rush swamped the store. She didn't like to think of herself as one who lurked but she supposed such a description could be inferred by her behavior once inside. She took care to scan the foot traffic in each aisle before moving quickly to the next item on her list. *It's not Adam's fault I'm emotionally unavailable.* She began the inner pep talk she'd mastered since the boy's kindness to her after the rotisserie chicken incident. *He shouldn't be penalized for being a nice guy.* But there was just too much stickiness that would ensue if she allowed herself to be wrapped into any sort of connection to him. Though he didn't seem fazed by the delicacy of her situation, she was in no condition to be having breakdowns with a man she barely knew, particularly since the man she thought she knew very well had skipped town on her and their baby. Six months into her pregnancy Mia industriously erected a tidy set of defenses in order to survive what she was sure might kill her if she weren't on her most vigilant behavior.

"Hello, Miss Mia," Gerry said when she approached the register, and did what would have educed a karate chop from Mia were he anyone but Gerry. He patted her belly and cooed, "And I do not neglect you, little one. Hello and God's blessings on you." Gerry smiled at Mia and turned to weigh a passel of kiwi. "You are lovely as a pregnant woman, Mia. My son is correct. Not usually is he correct but in this instance I believe he bats one hundred bull's-eye."

Mia blushed and unloaded a baguette from her shopping basket. "Thank you, Gerry. You and your son are very kind."

Gerry said nothing for a moment but Mia thought she saw a flicker of recognition in his eyes. "Your total is seventeen thirty-eight."

She handed over a twenty.

Gerry opened the drawer on his register and spoke to the money he counted. "He has not seen you in a while, am I right?" The attempt was casual but Gerry was not a good liar.

"I've been so busy with work. And my mother's in town...." Mia faltered, knowing she was no more adept at deception than the man bagging her groceries.

"Your change is two dollars and sixty-two cents." Gerry placed the worn bills in her palm and topped them with a small pile of change. He looked at her with kindness that reached straight out of his hazel-peppered eyes and into hers. "Perhaps you'll run into Adam soon. He's a good boy." Gerry smiled and Mia knew he loved his son in a way that allowed Adam to be as confident as he was.

"I agree," Mia said and smiled in return. *Such a good boy,* she added to herself, *that I'm going to do you a favor by avoiding him completely.* "Have a nice night, Gerry." She lifted her shopping bag onto one shoulder and headed into the bustling foot traffic of early dusk.

Fifteen minutes later she stood at her front door and listened. Charlotte Church drifted out to the hallway, which could only mean her mother had trespassed again. Mia sighed as she dug her keys out of her bag. First off, Charlotte Church gave her hives. She had specifically forbidden her mother from playing the girl's music in her presence and had agreed, as a form of reciprocity, to keep her Dido collection to herself. Second and even more disturbing, Mia mused as she pushed open the door with her foot, was the fact that Babs was simply not grasping the concept of boundaries. *She moves to my city, my apartment building, and* still *it's not close enough for her.* Mia fumed as she removed her shoes and coat. *In her crazy relational framework, letting herself into my apartment is not only permissible but expected mother-daughter interaction.* She made a mental note again to call Dr. Finkelstein for an appointment. It had been months since she'd been to Finkelstein Health but Babs's immediate presence was cause for insta-regression.

"Mother!" Mia called. She sounded surly and not a day over seventeen in her tone of voice. "I'm home. In *my* apartment, in *my* building, looking forward to some solitude—"

Mia stopped at the threshold of her living room. She stared and then swallowed hard.

"Honey, I'm so sorry to have to let myself in again. I know how much that *bothers* you, even though I opened my own home to you for the first eighteen years of your life, no questions asked." She lowered her voice to accommodate the foolishness of the situation. "Adam, you should know my daughter is *very touchy* when it comes to personal space."

Adam stifled a grin and nodded gravely. "I understand. I can be a bit of a bear about it myself, Mrs. Rathbun. Must be something about the parent-child bond, the need to be close and yet to distance oneself and strike out on one's own."

Babs gasped and put one hand on her heart. "Why, what a beautiful way of putting that! Adam, you are very wise for such a young man." Babs raised her eyebrows at Mia and bulged her eyes enough to suggest a thyroid issue.

"I studied psychology in college," Adam said, shrugging. "I've forgotten a lot of it, but you'd be surprised how much I use that stuff even at a grocery store." He grinned at Mia. "One never knows when his education might be called upon, especially near the rotisserie."

Mia blushed for the second time that afternoon, both incidences sparked by the man before her. She felt herself getting annoyed at his smugness. "Hello, Adam. What prompted you to break and enter my apartment with my mother?" Mia let the bag on her shoulder slip to the floor and she sat down wearily on her couch.

"This boy," Babs said, shaking her head in disbelief. "He's the one who gave us those delicious fillets a few weeks ago, remember, Mia?" She didn't wait for an acknowledgement from her daughter.

"And *now*, he's been such a dear as to bring by some *lovely* pork tenderloin, already marinated in his father's famous sauce!" Babs beamed at Adam as if he'd just offered her the use of his yacht.

"I'm a vegetarian," Mia said dryly. She recoiled inwardly at the harsh response to Adam's kindness, but he seemed unbothered.

"Right. I also brought a meatless lasagna in case you were averse to the pork." His eyes danced when he watched her face. "But I have heard pregnancy can bring out cravings one might not normally have, even for vegetarians."

Mia stood abruptly. "Thanks for coming by, Adam. It was very thoughtful of you." She looked at Babs, who was throwing eye daggers in Mia's direction. "You two feel free to lock the door on your way out. I'm going to slip to the bathroom for a long, hot soak." She stepped around the two of them and headed down the hall. With the bathroom door shut behind her and the tap turned on, she sat on the edge of the tub with her head in her hands and waited for water hot enough to wash away the tangle of knots in her gut.

# Home Improvement

"You were rude. There's no other way to say it." Babs had pale green paint splattered through her short crop of blonde hair. "He is a sweet boy who brings you meat and you were nothing but nasty to him."

Mia dipped her roller into the pan for a reload of Summer Sage. "I don't see how this is a productive conversation. Adam is a very nice guy but I barely know him. I'm not looking for new friends, certainly not male ones, as they seem to be less than faithful in times of need." She slapped on another set of *W*s, working her roller across the middle of one wall.

"But that's just it," Babs said. She stood with one hip cocked, paint dripping from her brush into the pail she held in one hand. "He *is* being faithful. Much more faithful than others I can bring to mind."

Mia closed her eyes and tried not to count the number of days it had been since Lars had called. "Well, I think Adam sees himself as some sort of savior, or a superhero trying to right the world for unwed mothers. I don't need his pity."

Babs huffed. She stepped up onto the ladder and continued cutting in near the ceiling. "You make it sound like he has *designs* on getting involved with pregnant women. Honestly, Mia. I raised you to have more confidence in human nature than that."

They worked in silence for a few moments. The extra bedroom in Mia's apartment was really a glorified closet. When Lars had lived there, he'd used the space for his office, whiling away impassioned and profanity-filled hours of writing, emerging only for refills on coffee or trips to the restroom. Mia planted both feet in front of the south wall and carefully covered the surface he'd painted a glaring white (it cleared the canvas of his mind, he'd insisted). She watched as the roller erased the blank walls and coated them with a soft green for the baby. Mr. Lamberti had helped remove Lars's IKEA desk from the space and was happy to take it as a donation from Mia. Watching him lug the thing out into the hallway, she'd felt only the slightest tinge of missing her former lover. The desk had fit easily into the elevator and Mia had waved to Mr. Lamberti as the doors closed.

Now, though, as she finished the south wall and began to mask out the trim around the window, Mia's heart sank to a deep cavern inside her. The phone call at Ebenezer had billowed oxygen all over the cinders of her feelings for Lars. She'd thought herself done, beyond, moving onward and upward from their relationship. But the sound of his voice, even when hearing words she didn't like all that much, had pulled out of her all the years she'd spent with him, all the time he'd known her and that she'd been known by him. The knowing felt bigger and sturdier than any sensible dismissal of him. There, in his former haunt, she could easily picture Lars surfacing from a late-night deadline, his thick blond hair standing straight on the top of his head after hours of his hands making passages through it. *It's only a coat of paint,* she reminded herself as the image of Lars at work in this room threatened to stop her project in its tracks, so palpable was the missing of him.

The baby moved as she lowered herself to the floor and Mia put one hand to her womb. As always the movement stopped and Mia smiled. She would have liked to let the baby know that she enjoyed the kicks and was simply saying hello when she placed a warm hand on her own belly. But each time she tried to communicate in this way, the baby stopped as if mystified that it was not alone, that someone or something was applying a heating pad to the spa he or she inhabited. Mia taped the underside of the window sill and ached for Lars to be there to put his hand on her belly, to look at her amazed as they shared the awe that should come with the promise of a child. She was starting to believe that these washes of regret were simply a part of her at that point, that try as she might to rid her mind and body of remembering Lars and watching for his return, she was stuck in a holding pattern. Pining for the disappearance of all heartache wasn't going to speed up its resolution one minute. Treading water might not be the most glamorous way to live, but it did allow one to keep breathing through treacherous tides.

She cleared her throat in an effort to erase her thoughts and start over. "Mother, what color did you paint the nursery before I was born?"

"Nursery?" Babs chortled. "If you mean the dinette area of our trailer with a foldaway kitchen table that made a space big enough for a portable crib, then I did what any caring trailer-park mom would do in the late seventies: I sewed orange- and yellow-flowered crib sheets and bought two matching pacifiers." She laughed at the memory. "We were poorer than church mice at that point. Your father was working double shifts and going to school full-time and I'd gotten sucked into selling knockoff Tupperware."

Mia stopped painting and watched her mother's back as she painted. "I didn't know you and Dad lived in a trailer."

"Didn't you?" Babs didn't sound as surprised as the question implied. "Your father wasn't too keen on bringing up that period of our marriage. He told me once he was ashamed to have brought children into the world with such humble circumstances. We did have some rough neighbors who made the park feel unsafe at times. Drinking, fighting, late-night arguing and such." She shook her head and dipped her brush into the pail. "But it always made me sad your dad felt uncomfortable talking about it because I remember those years as a happy time. We ate more tuna-fish hotdish than I care to recall, but we did just fine. No money for movies or dining out or fancy trips, but there were later years for that kind of thing. There's something sweet about having only each other for company and distraction."

Mia sat beside the window. She sipped on a bottle of water and waited for her mom to continue. Afraid Babs would backtrack to her usual moratorium on meaningful communication, Mia spoke carefully. "It doesn't sound like Dad to be so worried about money and superficial things."

Babs smiled at her daughter and Mia caught her breath at the sudden sadness in her mother's face. "No one knows what's really going on in a marriage other than the two people living inside it." As soon as the words escaped her, Babs's face adjusted again to its normal levity. "But this isn't a time to talk about things like that. Today we're transforming this space into the bedroom for my first grandchild. And she's going to love it."

"Or he." Mia rose slowly to her feet, using the windowsill as a help up. "Today I think it's a boy."

"Why's that?"

"I have a zit on my eyelid, Mother. My eyelid. Only a boy who's dumping copious amounts of testosterone into my blood could cause something so disastrous on the face of a woman."

Babs hooted with such gusto, she snorted on the intake of breath. "It starts from the beginning, don't you know? The stress those boys stir up in our lives and our poor bodies starts from the very stinking beginning."

They laughed together then, and Mia felt the ache in her heart lift nearly to its prepartum weight.

He called that evening.

Mia and Babs were sitting on the floor of the nursery, letting a cool breeze drift in the open window and over their tired limbs and necks. They were laughing the loopy laughter of the overtired, reminiscing about Mia's bad hair and fashion choices in junior high while sharing a deep dish from Lou's—half Green Goddess, half Sausage Deluxe.

"No, no, wait," Babs said, breathless with laughter. "I've got it—Dippity-do bangs with wings on either side of your cheeks. Cheeks, I might add, to which you had liberally applied streaks of Pepto-pink blusher."

Mia was gasping. "Listen, before you get too self-congratulatory, I can bring out some ringers from your dark past." She started to describe a pink and red polka-dot skort ensemble Babs preferred to wear with gold hoop earrings and a matching fabric headband.

"I still wear that!"

Mia groaned.

"I'm serious! Skorts make my legs look long."

Mia was washing down the horror of the image with a gulp of chilled chai when her cell phone rang.

Babs reached behind her and retrieved the phone from under a mound of paint-splashed tarp. She tossed it to Mia.

Mia closed her eyes when she saw the caller ID. "Hi," she said. Despite her efforts otherwise, she could hear a note of eagerness in her voice.

"Hey," Lars said over an undercurrent of traffic noise. "What are you doing right now?"

"Sitting in your office, which morphed today into the beginnings of a baby room." She let her head rest against the closet door and watched Babs start to pick up the debris from their project. Mia stifled a smile, knowing it was far too much to ask for Babs to leave the room and give her privacy for this conversation. Her mother would just as soon jump out onto the fire escape and serenade the moon.

"Cool," he said. Then, clearing his throat, he asked, "Would it be all right if I came for a visit?"

Her heart jumped. "Of course," she said, concentrating on not screaming into the phone. Babs glanced at her daughter but kept at her slow work of rolling up used masking tape. "When were you thinking?"

"Soon. Like this weekend." His voice became muffled, directed toward someone else. "Sorry about that. I'm out with some friends and had to tell them I'd meet up with them when we were done talking."

*He has friends?* she thought. Nearly three months had passed since Lars had left, so she probably shouldn't have felt the betrayal that was seeping into her veins. But he had friends, friends to go out with, friends who would see him later, friends she'd never even met.

She took a deep breath and let it out silently. "So you're coming this weekend?"

"If that works for you," he said. A motorcycle roared by in the background. "I'm supposed to have a meeting with Bryan on Saturday but I thought maybe the trip could serve two purposes." He paused. "That is, if you're up to seeing me."

"I'm up," she said quickly. "I mean, you should prepare yourself. I look a bit different from the last time we saw each other." She meant it to be a joke but Lars didn't laugh.

"Right," he said. "How far along are you now? Five months?"

"Starting my sixth." She rubbed her belly. Babs, who had slipped in and out of the room, perhaps to appear less like an auditory voyeur, handed her a fresh glass of water and looked at Mia's face anxiously.

"Six months? Already? Wow." Lars sounded genuinely surprised. "Well, listen, I should run. But I'll plan on getting there after you're home from work Friday. Maybe we can catch dinner? I've been craving a pad thai from Earth and Water."

"That sounds nice," Mia said. She looked down and realized she'd needled a hole in her paint-splattered jeans to twice its size. "I'll see you Friday," she said and hung up.

"He's coming?" Babs whispered, though there was no danger of being overheard by any government spies. "This weekend?"

"He is indeed," Mia said and took the hands Babs offered her. They pulled her to her feet and she shrugged. "Maybe he's finally getting it. Maybe he's finally ready to face this whole thing with me."

Babs smiled and pulled her daughter into a fierce hug. "I think you're absolutely right. I think he's showing some real initiative." She patted Mia's back as they stood in a moment of silence. Babs pulled away from their embrace and looked Mia in the eye. "He knows he can't sleep here, right?"

Mia screwed up her face. "Why not?"

Babs nodded, eyes mournful. "Because that would be immoral. No ring on the finger, no enjoying the fruits of marriage, if you know what I'm saying." She put up one hand to continue when Mia opened her mouth to protest. "I know, I know. You don't need to say it. It's clear," and she swept a hand toward Mia's belly, "that my daughter has dabbled. You may see it as provincial, but I hope you'll respect my opinion. I am still your mother, you know." She lifted her chin in defiance to the world's failings.

Mia shook her head in disbelief. "Mother, is this really a battle you want to fight *now*? I'm six months pregnant and he is the father of the child."

"Exactamundo, young lady," Babs said, exasperation filtering through. "If you'd listened to me and all those abstinence tapes I bought for you at that Christian conference, we wouldn't even be having this discussion. There would be no nursery to paint." Babs stopped short at her words. "Not that I'm not *thrilled* to be a grandma. I'm just saying that while Lars is visiting, I'll happily offer him my apartment and I'll sleep on your couch." She nodded quickly and bent to pick up the empty pizza box. "At least think about it."

Mia watched her leave and stood with her mouth slightly open in the middle of the room. The depth of her weariness, both physical and emotional, kept her planted where she was.

Babs turned back with her hand on the light switch, "Are you coming, honey?" she said over a yawn.

Mia nodded, too tired to fight all of them or any of them at this hour. Babs padded down the hall and Mia could hear her struggling to fold the pizza box into the trash can, even though Mia had asked her mother on countless occasions to recycle the top lid. Moving slowly toward the door frame of the nursery, she gathered in the evening's last look and flipped off the switch.

# Solidarity

That Thursday, shortly after five, Mia stood on the steps leading to Urban Hope and jiggled the key up and down to make the lock catch. She was the last to leave the office, as Carl had a stamp collectors' club meeting and their two part-time employees had both worked the morning shift. The key Carl had given her, tattooed with the markings of many years of abuse, had a history of foiling Mia's attempts at employing its original function. She howled in exasperation and considered throwing them "accidentally" into one of the grates that flanked each side of the door. Snatching the key out of the hole and drawing back in a threat to toss, she heard a throat clear behind her.

"Bad day?" Flor asked.

Mia turned to see her standing, arms crossed, at the foot of the steps. "This key is worthless," she said, shaking her head. "I've been out here for ten minutes and I can't get it to work."

"Lemme try."

Flor took the key, and Mia stepped aside to give her a shot at the stubborn lock. While she worked, Mia noted Flor's expanding belly, which was finally outside the concealment capabilities of the blue parka.

Flor mumbled something in Spanish, the force of which Mia inferred to mean something Babs wouldn't like. The next moment, Flor raised her hands and did a mini-dance of triumph.

"Got it," she said and handed Mia the keys. "You're lucky I showed up, though, because I had to use all sorts of jacking tricks to get it to work. Nothing too illegal or anything."

Mia nodded quickly and avoided Flor's watchful stare. "Thanks for helping me out."

Flor burst into unfettered, teenaged laughter. "You think I'm serious? Like I could break into anything other than my sister's piggy bank." She hooted and Mia felt the blush creep into her cheeks. "Mia, you're hilarious. I can't believe you have the job you do and you still believe everything everybody says."

Mia smiled at her shoes and turned to walk down the office steps. "No offense, Flor, but I think it's pretty clear that neither of us has a perfect grasp on whom to trust." She gave a gentle pat to Flor's belly.

"All right," Flor said. She nodded in appreciation. "Now I see a bit more sense in you." She smiled and revealed a row of very white teeth, the front two slightly crooked. "I'm walking with you."

They fell into a slow amble down streets just beginning to show the changing palette of sunset. A little girl on a pink bicycle careened past, sparkly streamers on her handlebars whipping the sides of her hands. An older woman whom Mia presumed to be the nanny followed at a distance, every other step hurrying her forward in sensible shoes.

"Wait, Chloe! Wait for Nona!" She gave a weary smile to Mia and Flor as she passed.

"A nanny would be nice," Mia mused aloud. "I could leave my baby with a nanny. Especially if she cooked dinner and had the apartment clean when I got home."

Flor snickered. "You don't need a nanny. You need a wife."

"Flor, a wife does more than domestic duties. She should be a soul mate, a confidante, an equal partner." Mia heard the beginnings of a persuasive argument she'd considered trying out on Lars.

"You're kidding, right? You don't really believe that?"

Mia's posture straightened. "I do. Marriage has evolved since the days of *Leave It To Beaver*. We've come a long way in this country." In her head she could hear Lars's counterarguments increase in volume.

Flor walked in silence for several paces before speaking. "Nope. I can't think of one couple that cuts things down, fifty-fifty. Even my art teacher, Ms. Humphries-Wyatt? She kept her name and all that. She calls her man 'my partner' instead of 'husband.'" Flor raised her voice in a bad fake British accent. "She says stuff like, 'My pahdnah and I went bicycling this weekend in the pahk.'"

"Is she from England?"

Flor shrugged. "I think she's from Missouri. But she has movie posters of Audrey Hepburn all over her office. Anyway, even she and her pahdnah aren't playing like equals. One day she was really hacked off at him, right? And I heard her by the bike rack, yelling at him on her cell. She was taking a smoke break and laying into him, saying how she was sick of doing all the cooking and cleaning and why couldn't *he* pick up their daughter from day care and stay home with her until she got over strep throat?" Flor sighed. "And she even kept her name."

Mia stopped in front of a sidewalk vendor at the entrance to the park. "Can I buy you a drink?" At Flor's confusion she added, "Like a lemonade? Or a Coke?"

Flor looked relieved. "Right. Lemonade, please."

Mia paid for the drinks and they continued on their walk. "Mm," she said. "This tastes good."

Flor nodded and slurped at the end of her straw. "They're better with vodka and cranberry juice."

Mia stared at Flor as she crunched a piece of ice between her teeth.

Flor laughed when she saw Mia's face. "Now didn't we just go over how you can't believe everything you hear?"

Mia scowled into her cup. "I don't know what to believe anymore. And you're not helping."

"What's his name?" Flor plopped herself down on a bench and scattered a bevy of annoyed and squawking pigeons.

Mia sighed as she sat down beside the girl. "I wasn't really referring to him."

"Yes, you were. What's his name?"

"Lars. What about you?"

"Rafa. He's hot." Flor said this as if passing along a tip on how to remove grass stains from white pants. "Which is why it was never going to work."

"What do you mean?" Mia's glass of lemonade had begun to

sweat. She rested it on her belly.

"I was the only girl left in my class who hadn't had sex." She shrugged and took a long pull of her drink. "It wasn't like I was saving myself or anything. I just didn't find anyone that interesting. Rafa, now, he's interesting all right. But he knows it."

Mia asked quietly, "How long were you together?"

"Once." Flor's voice had gone flat. "I found out later he did it on a dare. Wanted to be the first to have me and bet a bunch of his friends that he could get me to sleep with him before I turned sixteen."

Mia let a long breath she'd been holding escape slowly from her lungs. "Flor, I'm so sorry."

"Don't be." She ran her straw around the perimeter of the cup, sucking up with great verve the final drops of her lemonade. "My guidance counselor at school says I'm young, I'll adjust."

Mia smirked. "Doesn't sound like the most empathetic of counselors."

"He's at least a hundred years old. I don't think he likes thinking of kids my age having sex. Makes him nervous." She turned to Mia. "So what's the deal with Lars? Is he hot too?"

Mia pondered the question. "Yes, I suppose he is, though that's probably not what attracted me to him at first."

"Yeah, right," Flor said, dismissing the comment with a snort. "You're not blind, are you?"

"I wonder sometimes," Mia said, worry etching itself into her brow and her thoughts.

"Really? Do you need contacts or something? Because they have brochures about that at my guidance counselor's office, if you want me to pick one up for you."

Mia laughed. "Now who's believing everything they hear?"

Flor shifted her weight in the bench and crossed her arms. Her lips jutted out in a well-executed pout. "Whatever."

"Okay, so Lars. Yes, he's good-looking, but he's also very smart, which I like. And he's passionate."

"All right, now we're getting somewhere," Flor said, nodding seriously. "Passion will do a girl in. *And* get her pregnant, all in the same night."

"Not exactly the kind of passion I was talking about," Mia said. She cleared her throat. "I meant he has the passion to make things better in the world. He's committed to issues, causes."

"Like what?"

"Well, the environment. Human rights. Politics."

Flor rolled her eyes. "Is he *passionate* about you? And the baby?"

Mia's shoulders slumped within her maternity shirt. "I thought he was. Then I thought he wasn't. And now I don't know."

Flor nodded slowly. "Men are an enigma."

Mia looked at the girl. "An enigma?"

"I got extra credit for that word on a vocab test last week. I try to drop it in whenever I can." She grinned at Mia. "Pretty good, right?"

Mia nodded appreciatively. "Very nice. I'm impressed."

"Thank you," the girl said. "I also really like magnanimous, but that's a little harder to work into conversation."

"Hmm," Mia said. "I'll work on some options and let you know the next time we see each other."

"Oh, right. That's why I was stopping by before I had to save you from your front door."

Flor smiled and Mia noticed a deep dimple in one of her cheeks. She wondered if the baby in Flor's womb would mirror the face of its mother or if Rafa's profile would take dominance. She hoped Flor had all the dominant genes, including the dimpled one.

"Are you going to that pregnancy class at the St. Jude's?"

"No, I don't think so." Mia had seen flyers for the prenatal course offerings at the nearest hospital but had chalked them up in her head as information she'd rather glean from books. The idea of being in a room full of happy, expectant couples, their arms and legs all intertwined and supportive while the woman pretended she was in labor, was enough to make Mia run to the frozen section of Gerry's store and clean him out of the entire line of Häagen-Dazs.

"I think we should go." Flor spoke with all the authority that came with her sixteen years. "Don't you freak out when you think about labor?" She shivered. "I've watched, like, fifty episodes of *A Baby Story* on TLC. It's not going to be pretty."

Mia had in fact begun to worry about actually having to give birth. The mechanics of it all left her befuddled. She'd never been one to keep tabs on her anatomy with the use of a hand mirror, as had been suggested by her health teacher in junior high. But she knew enough to be concerned about the physics of getting a child through passages that seemed far too small for the event. The idea defied logic. "I think you need a partner for those classes."

Flor shrugged. "We should probably have a partner for this whole thing, don't you think? Too late for that." Her smile was a touch sad, though the dimple still appeared. "Come on. There's a one-day class coming up for slackers like us. Just one Saturday and we'll be done. Plus we can sit at the back of the class and heckle all the happy yuppie couples who are wearing Gap Maternity."

Mia laughed. The image was oddly comforting. "All right. I'll go."

Flor did another mini-dance, this time from a seated position on a park bench, which only added to the intrigue.

"Thanks for inviting me." Mia scooted to the edge of the seat and creaked to a standing position.

"You're welcome," Flor said when she joined her. Her eyes shone. "It was magnanimous of me, don't you think?"

Mia chuckled as she waved good-bye. "Extremely. Enigmatic, but magnanimous nonetheless."

"Ooooh," Flor called after her. "Enigmatic! I love it as an adjective!"

Mia's smile lasted all the way home.

# Reunion

"I could sing 'Ninety-Nine Bottles of Beer on the Wall.' That always made time go by faster on car trips."

"I'll pass," Mia said. She balanced the phone on her shoulder while she cut a loaf of ciabatta and placed the slices in a waiting basket. "Frankie, I'm not sure if I'm ready for this."

"Of course you are," Frankie said. "You are strong, you are wise, and you are pregnant. This is the dangerous trifecta of female empowerment."

Mia blew a sigh into the mouthpiece.

"You should move the phone when you do that."

"Sorry," Mia said. "I just can't figure out why he isn't here yet. And why he hasn't called."

"Yes, that is *so* unlike him," Frankie said. "Very unusual for him to be thinking of himself first."

"Frankie, please," Mia implored. "We've been through this."

Frankie sighed. "I know. I'm sorry. It's tough for me to remain objective here, Mimi. Men who leave pregnant women to fend for themselves are not at the top of my honor list."

"I thought I was the trifecta of empowerment."

"Out of necessity, my dear. I never said Lars was exempt from his reproductive responsibilities."

Mia didn't hear the rest of Frankie's explanation because of the knock at the door. "Oh. He's here. Someone's knocking. I think he's here." Mia stood with the knife frozen in her right hand. She stared at the door until the knock sounded again.

"You should go." Frankie's voice cut through Mia's paralysis. "You're ready for this, Mimi. He's the one who should be sweating right now. You just be yourself and tell the truth."

"Be myself. Right. Tell the truth." Mia smoothed her hair with her free hand. "I'll call you tomorrow." She snapped the phone shut and walked to the door.

For a moment they stood without speaking, each one drinking in the presence of the other. *He looks good*, Mia thought, remembering Flor's musings about hot absentee fathers. His unruly mop of blond had endured a good haircut, an act Mia hadn't remembered occurring with any frequency when they'd lived together. Brown linen button-down, pressed shorts, leather flip-flops, and two coffees in hand. Seattle personified, and Mia admitted it suited him.

"Hi," he finally said, smiling shyly and letting his eyes drift downward to Mia's belly. After lingering there, he looked up at her face. "You look great. You're all glowy and stuff."

She blushed. "Come in," she said and led the way into his former residence.

He moved through the kitchen and set the two coffees on the countertop. "Wow. It smells really good in here," he said, the words lifted up in surprise. In all of their years together, Mia had cooked a homemade meal perhaps a dozen times and those either because of inclement weather or having to do with a national holiday.

"I hope you're hungry for pasta." She reached over casually, stirring the pan of vegetables sautéing on the rear burner. For good measure she tossed in a carefree pinch of kosher salt, arranging her face in an appropriately bored expression.

"So you cook now." Lars shook his head. "I guess I have been gone for a while."

*Three months, a week, and two days,* Mia thought and bit her lips to keep the words safe in her head. "Thanks for bringing coffee." She nodded toward the cups sitting in wait on the counter.

"Do you still like Costa Rican blend with hazelnut?" He handed her the steaming cup.

"Actually I've given up caffeine for the pregnancy," she said carefully.

"Oh, right. Sorry. I should have thought of that." Lars shifted on his feet.

"But I'm sure it won't hurt the baby if I drink just a bit." She smiled at him. "It was thoughtful of you to remember."

His shoulders relaxed slightly.

*Reconcile, reconcile, reconcile,* Mia thought, taking the cup from Lars and drawing a careful sip. *We'll both have to meet halfway in this, so why not start with a cup of coffee?*

Three months could do a number on one's digestive track, particularly when sharing each calorie with a uterine cohabitant. The idea of her favorite coffee had sounded like such a good idea, but it tasted like warm metal in Mia's mouth. She stopped stirring the whole-wheat linguini and froze, the liquid steaming up her mouth but fighting its natural exit down her throat. When she could take it no longer, she dropped the wooden spoon into the boiling water and lunged for the kitchen sink, where she spat hot coffee down the drain. She rinsed out her mouth at the sink without looking up. When she finally let herself glance at Lars, she saw him sitting at the kitchen table, head in hands.

"Sorry," she said. "I guess I don't like coffee anymore."

He nodded behind his hands. "I should have called first. Apparently three months is long enough for a person to change her eating, drinking, and cooking habits."

"In normal circumstances it's probably not that long. But pregnancy can be a real humdinger." Mia forced a hollow laugh, willing him to at least take his head out of his hands. *Levity, levity, reconcile, reconcile,* she thought and was relieved when Lars's phone rang.

He checked the screen and said, "I need to take this.... Hi," he said into the phone as he left the kitchen and walked toward his former office.

Mia took a series of deep breaths, trying to focus on Delia's calming yoga instructions to let the good air in, bad air out. She would have worked herself into pigeon pose or even crow, had it not posed a danger to the child, a number of kitchen appliances, and the pasta she needed to drain. Steam billowed out of the colander and into her face and she marveled at how nervous she and Lars both seemed. *What used to be our normal?* she wondered. How did they act when they were a couple rather than a family-in-the-making? She didn't feel like it should be so difficult to jump back into their former roles, but the tension between them so far felt deep, almost dangerous, as if one false move could send the whole thing crashing down.

"What's this about crashing?" Lars stood in the doorway to the kitchen.

Mia offered a blank stare.

Lars pointed to the plates in Mia's hands, filled and steaming. "You were just saying something to the vegetables about something crashing down."

*Keep inner dialogue inner,* Mia chastised herself. She shrugged. "Some people talk to their plants. I talk to my food." She set the pastas down with a thud.

"The office looks nice," Lars said when he'd taken the chair opposite her. "Much better, actually, than when I would disappear into its bowels for days."

Their laughter was soft and tentative but it reminded them of all the time they'd shared. Emboldened, Mia said, "I thought green would be pretty but still gender neutral. I'm not finding out the sex before the baby's born. I mean," she stopped herself, "that's open for negotiation. Maybe we could still find out, if you felt strongly about it."

Lars said nothing and Mia shoveled a healthy bite of zucchini into her mouth. *Too much, too soon,* she lamented internally. But he nodded slowly and said, "I think you're right to wait. More suspense. Life has so few surprises. Why rob yourself of this one?"

Mia sipped a glass of iced water and willed herself not to think of Lars's last reaction to one of life's surprises. "Tell me about Seattle."

Lars tore into a slice of bread and immersed it in a saucer of olive oil until a stream ran down the crust and back into the dish. He took his time answering Mia, crunching on the bread and leaving his lips slightly parted so she could watch the progress of each bite. She pulled her eyes away and focused on her side salad, wondering if this was a new habit acquired in the Pacific Northwest or if she'd merely been immune to it before he'd left.

"I love it there," Lars said at last. "The geography is amazing. I can be at the beach and in the mountains within the same day. And the vibe is cool. Very laid-back, and much more earth-conscious than the Midwest." He took a bite of salad. Mia wanted to reach over and hold his jaw shut. How had the smacking not driven her to the brink all those years? Perhaps she was just overly sensitive in her current condition.

She cleared her throat. "And you've found some friends?"

"Friends?" he asked quickly. "Why do you say that?"

"Um, because when you called last week, you were out with them. You told someone you'd catch up with the group after we talked." Mia raised her eyebrows. "Certainly it's not too personal to ask if you have friends."

"Too personal? No, of course not." Lars laughed and waved the thought away with his hand. "I hadn't remembered telling you anything about them, is all. That night I was out with some people from my apartment building. Lots of young professional types, an architect, a nurse, a medical resident. Kate, this girl who lives next door, is a lawyer. She does lots of work with the legislature on behalf of environmental causes." He pushed his empty plate away and smiled at Mia. "Great dinner. I'm impressed."

"It's really very simple."

"That's good," he said, looking long into her face. "Sometimes I think we do ourselves an injustice by making things too difficult."

He reached over to take her hand and she felt warmth spread from his fingers and through her entire body. Mia closed her eyes slowly and willed them open once again. Her breathing became shallow, her chest rising and falling with each breath. "You're right," she said, keeping his gaze. "We make things too complicated."

"Mia?" he asked.

She nodded, unable to speak.

They stood and he approached her. She gave into the kiss, her brain and body firing on all cylinders. The intensity of her desire for him took her off guard. So much time had passed since she'd thought of herself as anything other than a glorified stroller, her knees were shaking at the mere idea of being with Lars again.

"Mmm," he said into her hair, and then he giggled. "I've never made out with a pregnant chick."

She smiled into his neck. "You never should have gotten me knocked up if it bothers you."

"Bother me?" He shifted slightly to the side to get better access to her lips. The belly was creating a detour. "Do I seem bothered?"

Mia closed her eyes and leaned into him the best she could around her expanding midriff. She was so relieved, somewhere in the deep, obscured recesses of her heart, that he still found her attractive. He still wanted to kiss her and hold her. The thought made a lump form in her throat and she felt herself wanting to weep.

"Yoo-hoo!" A call came from the front door. "I'm home!"

Lars snapped back from their embrace. "Who's that?" he whispered, startled, eyes darting toward the entrance to the apartment.

Mia rubbed her temples with fingers that still tingled with adrenaline. "It's my mother."

"Hello, hello, you two!" Babs came for Lars with arms wide open. She wore a new velour jumpsuit in hot pink. Mia had seen her eyeing many versions of it when they passed street vendors offering knockoffs of brand names. Since becoming a regular attendee of Silas's church, Babs had expressed a strong preference for black urban culture. Never mind that Silas and many of Ebenezer's aging parishioners weren't exactly experts on what was current among trendsetters in fashion. Babs embraced her newfound appreciation for what she believed was African-American with gusto, starting with an exploration into velour. "Congratulations, Daddy-to-be!"

Lars cleared his throat while Babs clung to him in an enthusiastic embrace. "Thanks, uh, Barbara. We haven't seen each other for a while...." He trailed off, searching Mia for clues on how to handle the woman.

"Oh, it's been at least two years, don't you think? The last two times I visited Mia, you were absolutely *swamped* with work, as I recall. Something about tribes in Africa that just couldn't get along ... and another time there was a flood somewhere down South?"

"Right. Sudan and Hurricane Katrina." Lars smirked, appearing to remember the way the woman had confounded him and driven him from his own apartment when she took time off from her current-events-ignorant gallivanting across the Caribbean. "Plus," he added with a thoughtful expression Mia knew was trouble, "you never were too fond of me, as I recall, Barbara. Didn't you once refer to me as a—what was it?—tree-loving, bark-eating mooch?" He winked at Babs. "Mia and I got a real kick out of that one."

If Babs was flustered, she didn't show it. Instead she laughed with all the good nature that comes with floating on a ship in perfect weather for ten months of every year. "Oh, Lars, you're such a jokester. I'm sure we've all done or said things we didn't mean. I'll make you a deal: I'll apologize for my saucy comment and you apologize for getting Mia pregnant and then abandoning her." Babs smiled up at Lars, turning it on full wattage.

Lars laughed conspiratorially and mock-punched Babs in the shoulder. Mia watched the two of them and wished she were one for hard liquor. What had she done, merging the genetic pools of the two insane people standing before her?

"Well, as long as you two are reacquainted, we should show Lars to his sleeping arrangements. Right, Mother?" Mia cleared her throat and waited for Babs's announcement.

"True dat," she said and clapped her hands excitedly. "Lars, my apartment is ready for you. I cleaned *all day*, so I hope you appreciate it. New sheets on the bed, fridge is stocked with snacks, though I don't believe in all that organic nonsense you and Mia love to preach. There's a vase of fresh flowers in the living room and clean and fluffy towels in the bathroom." She shrugged her shoulders in joy. "My crib is your crib!"

Lars couldn't tear his eyes from Babs—the velour, the lipstick-ed middle-aged mouth that had just said the words *true dat* and *crib*.

Mia touched his arm and spoke slowly to avoid having to say it twice. "Lars, I thought it would be better for you to sleep at Mother's place while she stayed with me."

"Why?" Lars's eyes remained on Babs, but a note of irritation had crept into his voice.

"You're not married, Mister Man," Babs said. She wagged one hot-pink fingernail in his face. "I know it might seem a little late for modesty, but until there's a ring on Mia's finger, you'll be perfectly fine in 1B."

Mia had to hold back a smile as Lars stood gaping like a linen-clad gorilla. She wasn't exactly thrilled with the sleeping arrangements, especially after the interruption to their romantic reunion, hand and head tingling included. But after all he'd put her through, Mia had to admit the idea of Lars pining and restless in a foreign apartment brought a certain amount of satisfaction. *Not revenge, exactly,* she thought. *Just a teachable moment.*

Babs led the way out of the kitchen and Lars put an arm around Mia to hold her back several paces.

"I thought you two couldn't stand each other," he enunciated into her ear.

"We couldn't," Mia said.

Lars tightened his grip on her shoulder. "Then why are we deferring to her?"

Mia shook her shoulder slightly to loosen his hold. Her heart beat wildly in her chest. She looked into his face as they stepped into the corridor. "She's been here. You haven't. And she's my mother. That's worth something, I'd say."

Lars shook his head in disgust and rolled his suitcase back out into the hall.

# Baby Steps

By the next evening both Mia and Lars were eager for an escape. They'd eaten breakfast with Babs and Silas at a soul-food restaurant Babs insisted they try. With stomachs full of grits and molasses ham, and ears bleeding from the number of words Babs had managed to work into such a small space of time, they returned to the apartment. Lars had been elected laborer with Babs and Mia as joint forewomen, ordering him around with a list of heavy lifting and nursery furniture assembly they'd earmarked for his visit. Lars, though able to debate the themes of class war and the savior complex in Dostoyevsky's early works, hovered just above failure status as a handyman. He tarried over jobs that should have taken a quarter the time, shouting expletives and filling entire rooms with the $CO_2$ expelled from dramatic sighing. After a while Babs was unable to hide her disdain and resorted to sarcasm, a tool Mia had seen her mother employ only in dire circumstances. By the end of the afternoon, Mia had to pull Babs aside and let her know she and Lars were headed out for the evening.

"That sounds like da bomb," Babs said. "You kids have fun." She strode with purpose toward the back bedroom. "I'll be happy to have the place to myself."

Lars and Mia exchanged glances and were out the door within five minutes.

"Seriously, Mia, I don't know how you're doing it," Lars said when they turned a corner at the end of the block. "You are way more patient than I would have given you credit for."

Mia swung a light sweater in one hand as she walked. The sidewalk still radiated heat from a day's worth of summer sun, but she'd brought an extra layer to protect her shoulders from the air-conditioning at Earth and Water. "I know. I wouldn't have thought in a million years that living with my mother in the same apartment complex would be anything but torture. But I don't know." She walked in silence for a moment, deep in thought. "It hasn't been that horrible."

"Doesn't she idolize Ronald Reagan?"

"No, it's Nancy."

"Same thing. And didn't she cry when you told her you were a vegetarian?"

Mia giggled. "Yes. Meat is very important to her."

"And isn't this the woman who thought the recycling movement was a government conspiracy spearheaded by Bill Clinton to distract from the Monica Lewinsky scandal?"

"I know," Mia said, shrugging in surrender. "And none of her crazy ideas have changed. But no one has killed anyone yet, so that has to be a good sign, right?"

Lars held the door to the restaurant for her to pass through. "I'd still lock up my valuables and consider taking a self-defense class."

Mia laughed and he rewarded her with a grin that set her back to the first time they met. *Dangerous combo, hormonal imbalance and loneliness,* she thought as the host showed them to a table by the window.

They shared a quiet meal, lingering over Mia's tofu burger and Lars's pad thai. Lars's open-mouthed chewing abated with the challenge of noodle slurping, which made Mia's tofu burger all the more appetizing. She also savored the slow pace of their conversation, relieved they'd reclaimed some of the naturalness of their relationship. Mia laughed as Lars told her of the editor at a Seattle activist newspaper where he'd landed a few articles. Despite being the self-proclaimed voice of anticapitalism in the Pacific Northwest, the man had a fetish for Krispy Kreme doughnuts, a vice that caused him endless ribbing from his fellow journalists. Lars had once dropped in unannounced and found the editor hiding under his desk, mouth framed in frosting and eyes bugging out with the effects of sugar and simple-carbohydrate overload.

Mia talked a bit about her work and started to discuss her relationship with Flor, but the girl's name reminded Lars of a story he'd written involving a woman who'd created a life-sized sculpture of Che Guevara with her orchid collection. When the check came, Lars offered to pay instead of their usual split down the middle, and Mia showed him her gratitude with a kiss across the table.

"Thank you," she said softly, their faces still touching.

"If a tofu burger can get me that kind of gratitude, maybe we should order a few more to go." Lars leaned in for another kiss.

When they finished, she smiled. "I mean, thank you for coming to visit. I'm glad you're here."

They were a few blocks from her building when Lars stopped abruptly.

"Ice cream. Are you up for ice cream? That store—what's it called?—on the corner, where we used to shop sometimes?"

"Gerry's?" Mia said, her heart beginning to pound.

"Right. Gerry's. Don't they have nondairy double chocolate by Stella Mae's Creamery? You know, that's a Seattle company. I've been gorging on all their stuff since I moved." He pulled her by the hand and started in the direction of Gerry's. "I'm sure they had it at this store. Remember that neurotic old guy who owns the place?"

"Vaguely," Mia said. Her voice had gotten small, but Lars rambled on.

"I always thought he didn't like me, though I'm not sure what I did to offend him. His organic selection is abysmal."

"Abysmal. Right." Mia scanned the storefronts as they passed, hoping for a plausible distraction that would allow her to avoid accompanying Lars to Gerry's. With the exception of a gun shop, everything was closed for the evening. Her caffeine intake may have changed since Lars had left, but she didn't think he'd buy a sudden interest in firearms.

As they neared the store, Mia could see the green and white stripes on the overhang that yawned over the entrance. She squared her shoulders. *What have I to be nervous about?* she asked herself. A look of defiance crossed her face. *It's not like there's anything between me and Adam. And what could be more natural than a man taking the pregnant mother of his child for ice cream?*

Lars held her hand as they moved toward the frozen section, Mia scanning the aisles as they walked. It appeared the only workers in the store were high-school students stocking shelves and a plain-looking girl working on a sudoku puzzle at the one open register. Mia made a mental note to accomplish more of her shopping on Saturday evenings as they seemed to be the time when Gerry's store was cleared of its two owners.

"Rainbow Delight ... Tropicana Dream ... here!" Lars emerged with a pink nose from the recesses of the cooler. "Chocoholic Nirvana. Just what I'm craving."

Mia padded after him quietly. Tiptoeing, in general, was not always the most effective way to avoid unwanted human interaction, but it had kept her in good stead in elementary school when she was up past her bedtime. Lars held out his hand for change from the plain girl, and Mia had walked several steps to the front entrance when she heard her name. She turned slowly to see Adam wiping his hands on a green-striped apron. A smile spread across his face and remained stubbornly fixed when his gaze shifted to Lars.

"Adam. Hi," Mia said. She took a step forward and then stopped. "Have you met Lars?" She offered no label—no "my boyfriend," "father of my child," "man who went AWOL and was in large part responsible for the weeping I did in your office a month ago."

"Hi," Adam said, stepping to where Lars stood and offering his hand. "Adam Malouf."

"Lars Skjørland. Good to meet you, Adam." Lars looked at Adam's dirt-caked apron. "Produce section, I hope?" he said with an easy laugh.

"Yes," Adam said, nodding. "By the end of a Saturday, we usually need a full restock of vegetables and fruits."

Lars nodded. A knowing look crossed his face. "I worked as a produce boy in high school. It was a great way to learn how grocery stores are so much at fault for price gouging, food-born illnesses, and pesticide-drenched 'nutrition.'" Lars made sarcastic quotation marks with his fingers.

Mia cleared her throat. "Lars, Adam and his father, Gerry, own the store."

Lars blinked once and must have decided he'd said nothing but the obvious. "Then you and your dad know the uphill battle of getting good quality food to the people who need it most. Do you participate in Food For America?"

Adam shifted on his feet. The plain girl, who'd been watching the volley with wide eyes, turned her attention back to the sudoku to spare her boss extra discomfort.

"We take part in several local programs to feed the hungry but Food For America is not one of them."

Lars nodded slowly. He narrowed his eyes and said, "A lot to be done, my friend. I hope you realize the gravity of our present situation."

"Well," Adam said, keeping Lars's gaze, "I appreciate your concern. We do our best to help. I'm no expert, but I'd say most real change happens in our families first, with the way we take care of the people closest to us." He turned with eyes sparkling. "Wouldn't you say, Mia?"

She swallowed. "I would," she said simply.

"Right on," Lars said, his face the picture of deep consideration. "I'm glad we talked, Aaron."

"Adam." Mia and Adam spoke at the same time. She blinked away the intensity of his gaze. "Have a good night," she said and backed toward the door.

"Good to meet you, Lars," Adam said. Mia couldn't dissect the undertone of his words without looking at his face and by that time she was out the door.

# Namasté

They stood on the front steps of Mia's apartment building. Though just after ten in the morning, Mia felt a slow trickle of perspiration meander between her shoulder blades and down her back. The forecast called for highs in the mid-nineties with life-sapping humidity. Babs had already left for church with Silas and had moaned about the deplorable lack of ocean breezes to clear the air. Mia stood on the top stair, feeling her feet swelling in her flip-flops. She fiddled with her necklace, taking turns watching Lars's face and glancing down the street for the cab he'd called.

"This was good," he said, brushing a strand of hair from her eyes.

The act of tenderness made Mia's head spin, though it could have been the heat bearing down on her dark hair.

"I'm glad you came," she said.

She felt a bit like she did in junior high when Gina, the most popular girl in class and lead cheerleader, had invited her to a slumber party. She'd wanted to throw her skinny arms around the girl's neck and bathe her in tears of gratitude, but had instead poured the depth of her affection into an overpriced birthday gift. Babs had been incensed at Mia's spending and had made her forfeit her allowance for months to pay for the limited-edition, splatter-paint Jordache jeans.

The memory brought a stinging realization that she wouldn't have been able to fit one calf into those jeans this particular morning, should they have made an appearance on the front stoop. Mia straightened her back and ventured, "We didn't have time to talk about everything."

"Don't worry," Lars said. He pulled her to him and enveloped her in a sticky hug. "We'll get to all that. I just wanted to ease into this again, you know?"

Mia nodded into his armpit and then lifted her head to fresh, muggy air. She wanted to ease in again too, but felt a different kind of urgency as her ligaments expanded.

A cab rolled to a stop in front of the building and Lars pulled away from their embrace. He leaned over and kissed Mia briefly on her nose and forehead.

"I'll call you, all right?" He smiled as he lifted his suitcase down the steps.

Mia merely nodded. She stood and waved as the cab pulled away. Lars flashed a grin and waved back, and within minutes they were miles apart.

● ● ● ● ●

Wednesday after work Mia met Frankie and Babs at yoga class. Delia was particularly focused on opening the hip muscles, so they spent a lot of time in various forms of pigeon pose. Mia could hear Babs grunt each time the stretch deepened. She thought she heard her mumble something about "birds that have no other purpose than public pooping," but by the time she looked at Babs's reflection in the mirror, the woman was the picture of calm. Her hair was swept away from her face, revealing a full palette of exuberant makeup. Though certainly not the only characteristic that caused her mother to stand out among other yoga enthusiasts, Babs's predilection for caked-on foundation, eye shadow, liner, and lips allowed for a startling contrast among the chemical-free crowd.

"And now let us enjoy the rest our bodies deserve." Delia wove among the class members, rubbing her hands together to release the scent of a sandalwood stick she held. "Please allow yourself to drift back on your mat, one vertebra at a time, until you are in corpse pose."

The first time Babs had heard the name for this particular pose, she'd grimaced at Mia. Not a fan of mortality, Babs. Mia distinctly remembered a time in her early adolescence when her mother had refused to attend a funeral with Mia's father, insisting that seeing the deceased "looking like Silly Putty" in a coffin would only erase the fond memories she had of the friend alive. To boot, Babs had not attended the funeral for her own ex-husband, opting instead to send an over-the-top floral arrangement that had received nearly as much attention as Mia and John in the receiving line.

No longer able to lie comfortably on her back, Mia turned her legs to one side and curled into a fetal position on her mat.

"Allow the strength of Mother Earth to pull you toward the ground," Delia said.

Mia could hear Babs begin to hum what she swore was a hymn. "You *are* the earth. Embrace heaviness. Release."

Mia could hear a wobbly version of "How Great Thou Art" drifting quietly from Babs's mat. When it appeared Delia was finished with her exhortations, Babs quit her own and Mia could see her mother's body go still and relax. Mia's mind drifted back and forth between her intention to clear it and a beehive of thoughts about Lars and his visit. She'd hoped to have more time to talk about the baby, but each time she tiptoed into that zone, either he had changed the subject or she had chickened out. Thinking now of her reticence made her disgusted with herself, but only until she remembered with gratitude how nice things had felt between them. No discord, no fighting, no anger. *Lars is right*, she thought. *We'll have time later to talk about the hard things. For now we should just enjoy getting back to our "normal."*

"Begin to awaken the body by wiggling your fingers and toes," Delia said. Mia didn't look, but she knew her teacher sat in full lotus at the front of the room, eyes closed.

"When you are ready, come to a seated position with eyelids softened."

Mia saw Babs cross her legs with an excess of tired drama. Her mother made her eyes into slits but did not close them.

"Bring your hands to heart center and let us end our time together." Delia bowed slightly and said, "*Namasté.*"

The class responded in kind and people began to rise from their mats and roll them up for the walk or ride home.

"Great class," Frankie said. She had her mat slung over one bony shoulder.

"Frankie, I love the orange," Babs said when she'd had a chance to take in Frankie's newest hair color. "To be honest, I didn't think I would, but you picked just the right hue for your skin tone. You must be a winter?"

"Oh, my gosh. I haven't thought of that for years! My mom made me have my colors done in junior high and I thought she was insane."

The three of them started for the door. Mia had to make a conscious effort to walk like a human, not a duck.

"I *was* a winter in fact," Frankie continued. "Which meant I was supposed to wear all these happy, loud colors that did not go with my current obsession with Velvet Underground and Blue Oyster Cult." She giggled.

"Well, I don't know much about velvet oysters, but your mother was right. We usually are." Babs elbowed Mia gently. "Did you have a good workout, Mia?"

Mia nodded. "I suppose. I feel tired today. Some of those hip openers were tough."

"Heavenly days, yes," Babs said. She sighed. "At my age my hips want to start closing for good, if you know what I mean."

Frankie and Babs shared a laugh but Mia didn't want to even approach thinking about her mother's hips, open or closed.

"I've found lots of wonderful ways to get around the whole woo-woo thing," Babs said. They'd reached the street and were making their way through a rush of after-work foot traffic.

"The woo-woo thing?" Frankie asked.

"You know, the 'you are the earth,' 'be present' garbage. All that drivel about reaching for the sun, feeling the warmth of our hearts connecting, blah, blah, blah."

Frankie said nothing but Mia saw her smile at her shoes.

"Yoga, I've decided, is mostly about God. Heart center? God. Fingers stretching for the sky? Fingers stretching for God. And the most *obvious* one is that thing she does at the end. Everyone saying that Hindu prayer."

"You mean *namasté?*"

"Yes. I just get around it by bowing my head and saying 'Jesus, Jesus, Jesus' instead."

"Mother, *namasté* is a greeting. It means hello. Or good-bye."

"Well, which is it? Good-bye or hello?"

"Ooh, this is sounding like a Beatles song," Frankie said.

"I don't know. Maybe both." Mia steered her mother through a herd of tourists and nearly lost her in a two-step with a man wearing ropes of gold jewelry.

Babs continued, undeterred. "I don't buy that definition for a minute," she said. "I've seen way too much of the world to believe that, Mia Rathbun. This is New Age brainwashing at its best. And just when you're feeling all gooey and relaxed. Off your guard."

"So you say Jesus instead?" Frankie asked.

Mia looked at Frankie's face to stop her from any more encouragement, but her friend seemed genuinely interested.

"Yep. Just one more way I get to praisin'."

Mia groaned softly, worrying that sometime soon her mother's poor impersonations of an African-American worship service would get her into trouble.

"I like it," Frankie said with conviction. "You've got spice, Mrs. Rathbun. I like that in a cruise ship hostess." She hopped to the space in between them and slung her arms around Babs and Mia.

"And you have spice as well, Frankie," Babs said. Her mascara had blurred under her eyes with the yoga workout and only the outline of her lipstick remained. "I like that in an orange-haired librarian."

The three walked with arms linked, and Mia couldn't help but smile at the annoyance of those who needed to move in order to let them pass.

⚬ ⚬ ● ● ⚬

Sunday morning Adam was sitting on the front step of her building when Mia arrived home from a leisurely breakfast at Lolo's. She swallowed hard and willed her feet to move at a casual pace, rather than backing up slowly and rewinding her progress down the street. She caught his gaze and he stood quickly, waving awkwardly with one hand and brushing off the rump of his pants with the other.

"Hi, Adam," Mia said breezily as she approached. "How are you?"

"Fine," he said, nodding. His brow furrowed into a seriousness Mia hadn't seen in him. "I have to talk with you."

She chuckled, the nerves in her stomach betraying her by the shake of her voice. "What, no 'How are *you*, Mia?' No time for small talk?"

Adam looked confused, but complied. "Oh. Sorry. How are *you*, Mia?"

She smiled. "Fine, thank you." She swept a glance over his clothes.

"Pressed dress pants, crisp oxford, even a tie, though loosened at the neck. Hmmm … Odd time of day for a wedding … A funeral?"

One side of his mouth crept up into a smile and his shoulders relaxed a bit. "No, though there have been many times when a funeral might have been more exciting. I'm taking my dad to church." He glanced at his watch. "In fact he's going to go nuts if I'm not at the store in exactly seven minutes."

"But," she stammered, "how long did you wait here? How did you know I'd be coming home?" She hesitated to employ the word *stalker*, but there were warning signs.

He shrugged. "I didn't. You had three more minutes before I bolted." He put both hands on his hips and then let them drop to his sides. "I just want you to know I care about you."

Her eyes darted past him for an escape route and he hurried to continue.

"No, no, not like that. Not that that would be such a horrible thing, but you don't seem, well—" He sighed and ran a hand through his hair. "Okay. Try to understand me here." His eyes searched Mia's face with an intensity that made her heart jump into her throat.

"You care about me," she said.

"Right. I think you're a great person and I like you. I'm saying, do you have an excess of friends right now?"

Mia bristled. "Adam, what are getting at?"

He groaned. "I am *so* bad at this kind of thing," he said, almost to himself. He moved toward her and took one of her hands in both of his. "I want to be your friend, Mia. If you have no more room for extra friends, I understand, but if there's space in your life right now, I want to help fill it." He dropped her hand and looked uncharacteristically unsure of himself. "I know it's none of my business, but it would really irk me if you settled for loser relationships just because you're pregnant. Or if you thought you deserved to hang around with—" He stopped abruptly, his expression sheepish. "Please tell me I've made at least one tiny bit of sense."

She squinted at his face. Mia noticed for the first time the crop of thick lashes that framed his hazel eyes. "Not with words, per se, but I think you're trying to say that we should be friends."

"Yes!" he said. Relief spilled out of the word. "It seemed like you were avoiding me after we ran out of chickens the day *yerba mate* was on special and then I saw you in the store but you were weird, no offense—"

She laughed. "All right. I get it. So I'll stop being weird and you'll stop worrying about me not having enough friends while I'm in the family way."

He hugged her tightly and kissed her on the top of her head. "Great. A win-win for both of us. I'll see you later. Gerry's not one for patience." He headed off at a clip but turned back to shout, "I left a bag of groceries with the super. Lamberti? He said he'd put the ice cream in his freezer until you made it home." Adam grinned at her and began jogging toward the store.

She stared after him, shaking her head. He ran like an athlete, which surprised her for some reason. *There is no way that shirt will make it to church without sweat and serious wrinkling*, she thought, and felt flattered by the sacrifice.

## 22

# Belly Flops 101

The lighting in the childbirth education room at St. Jude's barely illumined the space, so much so that Flor and Mia stood motionless for several beats upon entering. When her eyes adjusted to the semidarkness, Mia could see a splattering of couples seated on the carpet. People talked in hushed tones, so Mia lowered her voice as well.

"What do we do now?" she whispered to Flor, who stood beside her in a belly-hugging tank top that had printed on its front *You Wish*.

Flor shrugged. "I guess we sit." She led the way to an empty spot only inches from the front of the room.

Mia lowered herself to the floor, barely preventing a moan from escaping her lips. At twenty-eight weeks she could not figure out how to balance the strange distribution of weight in her body. The previous week, she'd literally fallen into Carl's arms at work. He'd been flustered beyond the point of conversation, no matter her assurances that pregnancy had made her a disaster in motion. She didn't bother explaining how it felt to be toting around a beach ball inhabited by an aspiring Mary Lou Retton and that it could make a girl clumsy. Carl simply smiled and blushed, blushed and smiled. Now faced with the childbirth class, Mia hoped her training wouldn't require any feats of balance, strength, coordination, or flexibility. Twelve weeks to go and she was already throwing herself at unsuspecting victims.

She glanced around the room and almost burst out laughing. About six other couples were scattered on the carpet, and every single one of them was canoodling. Some of the women rested their heads against their partners' shoulders, whispering, giggling, appearing to bask in the soft lighting and the closeness that came with baby making and carrying. Others enjoyed backrubs offered by serious-looking men, one of them in a ball cap that proclaimed *This Dad Does Diapers.*

"I think I'm going to puke," Mia said to Flor, whose eyes followed Mia's gaze to the couple nearest them. The man was facing the woman, each of them with legs crossed and all twenty fingers entwined. Mia heard the man whisper, "I love you too, cupcake," and the two leaned forward into a lengthy kiss.

Flor snickered. "I'd rather be alone than be called cupcake for the rest of my life."

Mia laughed too, but wasn't sure she agreed. Cynicism felt better than loneliness, though, so she decided anew to embrace her independence and the opportunity to share this experience with Flor.

"So why didn't your mom come?" Flor smacked her gum as a percussive end to her question.

"She would have," Mia said, "but I asked her not to. Hospitals make her even more high strung than normal. Plus I didn't think she'd be a particularly good birth coach."

Flor looked at Mia askance. "But you thought the teenager with no experience would be better? At least your mom has had kids." She pulled her hair out of the elastic that held it in a low ponytail and went to work with rapid hands pulling it right back where it'd been. "And it's not like we'll be able to coach each other for real."

"I know," Mia said, shrugging. "I just couldn't do this with her. What about your mom? Where is she?"

Flor snorted. "She thinks I'm nuts for wanting to know what's going to happen. She says I'd be much better off just hooking myself up to an epidural in the parking lot and trying to survive."

The girl fingered one earring and Mia saw again, sharply, how very young she was, despite the deepening maturation of her body with each week.

"I might put it up for adoption," Flor said, not looking at Mia when she spoke. She busied her hands with picking invisible specks of lint off her pressed jeans.

"Really?" Mia tried to keep her voice level, knowing only Flor could make that choice and that her own input had to remain as neutral as possible.

Flor shrugged. "I saw *Juno*. That girl was cool."

Mia nodded slowly and tried not to smile. "It's a big decision. You're smart to consider every option."

The door to the room flew open with a clang when metal hit the cement wall behind it.

"Hello, hello, hello!" A woman who could have been blood sisters with Bette Midler floated into the room, a brightly colored caftan flowing behind her outstretched arms. "So very sorry I'm late. My acupuncture appointment ran over and that is *hardly* a thing one wants to rush." She filled the room with loud, musical laughter.

Mia glanced at the couples and saw mostly shock registering on their faces. Canoodling and hushed reverence for the act of childbirth were not easily paired with the woman with wild blonde curls standing before them. The cross-legged pair huddled closer together and clasped hands in a united front.

"My name is Tillie Lawrence and I've been teaching slacker childbirth education for twelve years here at St. Jude." She looked around the room in mock embarrassment. "Did I just say slacker? I'm so sorry. I meant to say the *abbreviated, efficient* childbirth preparation class." She winked. "I'm sure none of you are slackers."

The entwined couple next to Mia looked offended. The man patted his wife on the back and whispered into her ear. Flor, by comparison, leaned over to Mia and said, "I like this chick."

"Just a bit about me," Tillie said while unloading a few items from a cart at the front of the room. "I'm a nurse by training and still moonlight in the ER when the need arises. Most of my time, however, is now dedicated to being a grandmother of an exceptionally beautiful two-year-old, Betsy, and performing in community theater productions in the area." She swept the room with a glance. "Anyone see me in *Sister Act* last spring? Anyone? Anyone? Beuller?" A laugh tumbled out of her throat. "Better for you. It was *not* my best performance. Even so—" and she broke into a loud alto chorus of "There's No Business Like Show Business."

Flor chuckled, shaking her head when Tillie did a jazz square. Mia didn't know whether to stay where she was and hope Tillie's twelve years of experience would kick in any minute, or if she should escape to the information desk and report the woman.

"To begin, I like to show a video of the birth process, just so we're all on the same page. You know," Tillie said, tilting her head to the side in thought, "giving birth is a lot like doing a belly flop off the high dive. It's intimidating, certainly not something you'd want to do every day, and it will very likely leave some physical and emotional scarring. But"—she held up one finger in dramatic pause—"you will never, ever regret it, if only to be able to say you've done it and done it with panache."

Tillie busied herself with the DVD player, not bothering to lower her voice when she cursed at its unwillingness to cooperate. Mia looked to her side and saw what appeared to be trouble brewing in Pretzel Couple's paradise. The woman relinquished her grip on her husband's hand and nodded toward the door. Her husband seemed to be placating her long enough for the video to start.

"Is this going to be like those creepy videos we had to watch in biology class?" Flor asked quietly. "There was one that showed a bloody, gooped-up baby with the umbilical cord hanging from its stomach." Flor shuddered. "They should have at least washed him off first."

The creepy health-class videos turned out to pale in comparison with Tillie's introduction to childbirth. Mia watched, transfixed, as woman after woman in labor flashed onto the screen, many emitting sounds more commonly heard in the animal kingdom. The narrator of the video, in an inexplicably calm British accent, assured his audience that childbirth was a natural and beautiful part of the human experience and nothing to be feared. Mia felt strong opposition to this advice, particularly during a portion of the video that focused, literally, on the exit of a child from the birth canal.

"Oh, dear God," Flor said. Mia saw the blood had drained from the girl's face.

All cultures had birthing rituals, the narrator droned on, and we Westerners would do well to pay attention to women like those in the Amazon, who merely dropped into a squatting position on the rainforest floor and unceremoniously pushed out their babies with nature's help of gravitational pull.

"I am *not* having a baby in the same position I use to poop," Flor said, her voice getting louder with each comment. Mia thought to ask her to keep it down, but she couldn't tear her eyes away from the television screen.

By the end of the film, Mia swore she'd heard some pockets of sniffling within the room. Pretzel Couple was newly entwined, both faces exhibiting a fresh wave of horror.

"Well," Tillie sang out, punching several buttons on the remote before the screen went fuzzy first and then black. "Any questions?"

Someone snickered at the back of the room.

"Great," Tillie said and clapped her hands once. "Let's talk about what we can do to make it through the whole ordeal. We'll start with breathing techniques."

Flor and Mia obeyed each of Tillie's instructions, working their way through overviews of Lamaze, the Bradley Method, home, and water births. At one point, when the couples paired off to practice the method of their choice, Tillie floated over to them, humming "Some Enchanted Evening."

"I see you two are flying solo?" she said, crouching down to be eye level. Her eyes sparked with warmth.

Mia nodded. "We came together but we're—"

"Single unwed mothers," Flor finished. She smiled at Tillie. "You're making this class way more interesting than I thought it would be."

Tillie patted Flor on the knee. "That's very kind of you to say. There are always two camps in my classes: those who are happy to know the whole truth and nothing but the truth, like yourself, and those who would rather think childbirth is like it is on TV, where the woman is barely breaking a sweat and still has lipstick on when the baby is placed on her chest." She nodded quickly toward the Pretzels. "Better to know the full story, I say." She stood and sang quietly, "Dun. Dun. Dun. Another one bites the dust." She'd walked two steps before saying over her shoulder, "I was a single mom too. You'll do just fine."

Two hours later, after a deluge of information dumped on them in the form of Xeroxed handouts, some of them the light purple color of a mimeograph machine, Flor and Mia left the classroom, shuffling slowly behind the other couples.

"Have a wonderful birth experience," Tillie called after them. "Remember to breathe deeply, to ask for drugs unless you're hell-bent on not doing so, and to think of your birth plan as a suggestion, not the Ten Commandments." Mia looked back at Tillie, who smiled knowingly. "Things don't always go as planned."

*Tell me about it,* Mia thought to herself as Tillie serenaded them one last time, her voice rising and falling in wild vibrato to the strains "Don't Cry for Me, Argentina."

Mia said good-bye to Flor at the bus stop near the hospital. "Thanks for doing this with me. I don't think I would have come on my own."

Flor put her hands on Mia's shoulders and took on a serious face. "We social outcasts have to stick together." She raised both hands for Mia to slap ten. The bus groaned to a slow stop in front of them.

"I'll see you," Mia said as Flor climbed up the steps to the bus driver. Mia waved as they drove off, but Flor sat on the opposite side and didn't see her friend through the dust-caked window.

# 23

# Modern Convenience

It was one in the morning and Mia should have been dreaming, but sleep was winning at the game of hide-and-seek they'd been playing all night. Her belly was big enough to prevent most reclined positions from being comfortable. She needed a pillow stuck between her knees at all times, lest her lower back ache and hips stiffen to an octogenarian's pace the following day. She'd done a prenatal version of tossing and turning for two full hours, twisting her torso around to one side, grabbing the sheets with both hands to help flip herself over to the other. After multiple rounds of this charade, Mia wriggled to an upright position against her headboard and sighed into the silence.

"This is ridiculous." Her voice sounded unnaturally loud in the darkened room. She sat for a moment, watching the street lights outside her window cast an eerie orange on the pavement below. The air conditioner grunted its cyclical roar to life. Her bedroom's chill belied the oppressive heat outside. Summer held on with a tenacious grip, though the end of August would arrive the following day. Mia dangled her swollen feet over the side of the bed. The wood floor complained under her tread as she moved to the living room to retrieve her laptop.

Tucking a blanket under her belly and draping the rest over her legs and feet, Mia booted up the computer and waited as the screen welcomed her back. She logged onto her e-mail account and held her breath as it retrieved new mail.

"Two new messages," she said, triumphant. She clicked on the icon that led her to the messages and felt her heart pick up speed when she saw one was from Lars.

Phone conversations since he'd visited had become more wearying than communicative. They'd tried, really they had. She'd call him, he'd call her, and sometimes they'd even reach each other in person instead of colliding with voice mail. Perhaps Mia was reading too much into their calls, but she'd become frustrated with the lack of real connection. While on the phone, they spent an imbalanced amount of time on Lars's work issues, her weekend plans, and other such fluff before one of them would need to cut the conversation short and return to his or her life and obligations. One evening, when Mia had tried without success to get Lars on the phone for two hours, she'd thrown her cell on the couch and resorted to writing an e-mail instead. She'd been surprised to find the words had come easily, unfettered by the fear of saying the wrong thing, unhurried to get to what she needed to say before the conversation ended. To her delight, Lars had written a lengthy and thoughtful reply, weighing in on her concerns and sharing some questions he had about her pregnancy and the baby, none of which he'd ever uttered in person.

Mia opened the new mail and found Lars had sent the message only a half hour before. She forced herself to open the other message first. It was from her brother and the subject heading read "Extreme Times."

Mimi,

I can't believe she is still there. Are you okay? Have you resorted to cutting yourself? Wearing ashes as a subtle hint? Singing dirges as friendly greetings?
I have to tell you, I didn't know you had this in you, this patience of Job. Certainly the whole ordeal is wearing on you: It can't be good for a pregnancy to have such elevated stress levels, even if she is renting the apartment downstairs.
Should I be doing something? Rescuing you in some way? I'd offer to have her come stay with me, but, well, I don't think I've reached your level of nirvana yet.
Is this a by-product of yoga? If so, I need to sign up for down dog ASAP.

Love you,
John

Mia laughed as she wrote a quick reply, assuring her brother that she had not yet felt the need for bodily harm and that Babs was so busy with the Ladies' Auxiliary from Ebenezer, she'd had less and less time to plague Mia. In fact, she dared to write, the visit from her mother had been a positive one. Dr. Finkelstein had even left a voice mail from the South Florida Terrier Invitational that she was proud of Mia's conscientious inner work and that she'd love to hear a victory report when she returned.

She clicked to send John's message and opened the one from Lars.

M—
Thanks for writing this morning. You're always so encouraging to me, and this was a day I was in dire need of a verbal pat on the back. The poor saps with whom I work on a daily basis have great passion for what they do and believe, but they do not know good writing from a hole in the ground. This had to and did come to a head this morning when my editor asked me to rewrite a piece due this afternoon, griping, in effect, over my usage of polysyllabic words and "highfalutin social theory" (his phrase) the average reader would neither appreciate nor understand. After a prolonged discourse during which I stated my position with brilliance and unparalleled patience while he played with the bobblehead of Napoleon Dynamite he keeps on his desk, we decided to agree to disagree, which meant I had to start over and dumb the blasted thing down to a third-grade reading level.
So thanks for your e-mail. You were the only decent human being in my life today.

*Decent* may not have been first on the list of adjectives Mia wanted to hear from Lars, but it was late, she was sleep-deprived, and she took it as a compliment.

The story about your mother being the only white woman getting her nails filled at Leila's was priceless. Do you think she'd mind if I wrote it up as a comedic piece for the paper? I'd change the names if she wanted. It would be such a fantastic glimpse into twenty-first-century race relations in Middle America.
Yes, I definitely want to see the ultrasound video. I'm thinking of coming out to see you again, maybe sometime in September?

When is your due date again? I'm thinking you said October, so I could always wait until then, but maybe it would be good to have another visit before the pressure of the Big Day, particularly since needles make me pass out. I'm sure you're planning on a drug-free birth, but just in case ...

It was true. Lars had some bizarre condition that caused him to pass out cold at the sight of needles. Mia had seen it in action during a blood drive their senior year. She'd stopped to talk with a friend on the periphery of the room where students were donating pints for the local blood bank, and when she turned to Lars, he'd dropped to the floor. Her friend had summoned medical help and after a generous supply of juice and cookies on hand for the real donors, he'd been able to lean on Mia and walk back to his apartment off campus. Mia had once tried to rib him about the incident, but he'd become very defensive and had thrown out lots of eager explanations of "vasovagal syncope" and his "involuntary response syndrome." Thinking of Lars on the floor of the delivery room made her roll her eyes, another reason e-mail was an appropriate medium for the two of them at that point.

I'll call you soon. Not tomorrow because my friend Kate (remember I told you about her? The environmental lawyer who lives in my building?) is making me go on a hike that sounds like it may kill me. She's super intense, very athletic. Apparently she's climbed a few fourteeners, though tomorrow's hike, she's assured me, isn't supposed to be as arduous. Still, I'm packing extra energy bars and Gatorade. I think that when faced with heat exhaustion or consuming glucose-fructose syrup, I'm within good sense to choose the latter.

Off to bed now, where you are already sleeping peacefully. Give
the belly a rub for me.
Lars

Mia shut down her computer slowly, staring at the blinking
mouse arrow until it faded. The room went black in the absence of
the glow from the screen.

*Athletic? Super intense?* Mia turned his words about Kate over in
her head as she waddled back to her bedroom. For the life of her, she
could not imagine Lars strapping on his hiking boots and heading up
a mountain. God had blessed him with a wiry frame that remained
unchanged regardless of activity level or calories consumed. His
interests, however, had never ventured into the athletic realm. When
living in Chicago, Lars's idea of a good workout had been walking to
a restaurant instead of taking a cab.

*Climbing a mountain? By choice?* Mia lowered her body onto the
sheets once more, turning onto her side and tucking a pillow between
her knees. She closed her eyes and tried not to imagine what Kate the
Super Intense looked like in hiking shorts. Images of perfectly toned
abs and arms floated in and out of her mind's eye before she'd push
them out with deliberate speed. She fell asleep, pursued all night by
dreams of mountains, breathless steps, and elusive summits.

# 24

# Labor Pains

"I completely agree, Tom. But try telling that to Madge and Bill from Poughkeepsie." Babs took a dainty bite of her hot fudge sundae. "They've been waiting for their Caribbean cruise for months and they're not going to skip the day excursion into Nassau just because *I* think it's overrated."

The man behind the ice-cream counter shook his head at the tragedy. "Well, we can do so much, right, Ms. Rathbun?" He shrugged and handed her change from a five. "You enjoy your ice cream now and don't worry that beautiful head of yours over what we cannot control."

Mia had to giggle when Babs winked at Tom and patted his hand affectionately. The woman was shameless, but for the first time in her life, Mia was feeling more amused by her mother's antics than irritated. Perhaps it was the inescapable presence of the child within her that was nudging Mia to cut her mother some slack, to look at her as she was wired instead of how Mia wished she would behave. If the old adage was true—that a daughter received a kind of circular justice in the way her own child treated her—then she'd need to start climbing out of the naughty hole in quick order. She pushed out the chair opposite hers when Babs approached.

"Thank you, sweetie," Babs said, sitting carefully on the black wrought iron. "Tom and I were just discussing the perils of tourist traps. Did you know that he and his wife have been on thirty-two cruises? Thirty-two! I'm surprised our paths haven't crossed before." She shook her head and dipped into a bite of fudge muddied with whipped cream.

Mia took a lick of double-dip rainbow sherbet. "Do you miss being on the ship?"

"Oh, sure, I do," Babs said. Huge gold hoops swung in her earlobes as she nodded. "I miss the water, the people, the food." She shrugged. "But it's nice to be on land again for a longer period of time. If I were on the ship, I wouldn't be able to see you and see my grandbaby growing." She reached out and patted Mia's belly. "This is time I won't be able to get back. My job can wait."

"They've been very understanding." Mia had been surprised and impressed with how much latitude Crown Caribe Cruises had given her mother. Apparently the cruise business was more liberal than the rest of the working world in terms of grandparent maternity leave.

"Didn't I tell you? I was fired." Babs pulled a cherry off its stem with her teeth.

"What?" Mia's voice startled Tom behind the counter. She waved apologetically and continued with a softer tone. "You lost your job?"

"I did," Babs said, her eyes glinting in mischief. "Isn't that so romantic? I've never been fired before. And my first time was for the sake of my illegitimate grandchild." Babs's eyes filled with a longing for *Wuthering Heights*. "Someday I'll be able to tell this little one how much I sacrificed to witness the birth."

"Mother," Mia said, blotting the sides of her cone with a napkin to catch the drips. "You should go back. This is not something to lose a job over."

"It most certainly is," Babs said, huffy. "I can't think of a better cause. Besides, they'll take me back."

"They will?" Mia didn't know how much stock to put in Babs's job security awareness.

Babs waved away Mia's concern with five nails painted Rousing Raspberry. "Of course. I've already had one call from Stan in personnel. I'm not easily replaced, I'll have you know." She pointed her plastic spoon at Mia for emphasis.

"I know." A memory of Mia's father sitting on the couch, head in hands and weeping quietly came back to her so forcefully, she caught her breath.

"What is it? A contraction?" Babs jumped up from the table, nearly toppling her dish of ice cream. "Oh, dear Gussie. Tom! Tom! My daughter's going into labor!" She looked at Mia in horror. "But you still have five weeks left!"

Mia shook her head and called to Tom. "I'm fine. Everything's fine."

Tom was clutching his heart with one mottled hand. "Thank goodness. I don't know how to deliver babies." He shuffled to the back room, face still etched with panic.

"Are you sure you're all right?" Babs lowered to her chair with reluctance.

"Mother, you are *way* too reactionary," Mia said. She took a deep breath. "When you said you were irreplaceable, I had a memory of Dad right after you left."

Babs's eyes clouded over and she picked up the dish of melting ice cream. "What did you remember?"

"Coming into the living room and seeing him on the couch, holding his coat over his face and crying into it to muffle the sound. He didn't know I was watching."

Babs picked at the few remaining spoonfuls of cream. She waited so long to speak, Mia thought the conversation was over. When she looked up at Mia, her eyes were large and sorrowful. "I know you weren't there to see it and that you have no reason to believe me on this, but the divorce was very hard on me, too." She closed her mouth and Mia saw the muscles in her jaw flex.

"What happened?" Mia asked. "And please give me a more complete response than 'We grew apart.' That has never satisfied." She spoke softly and concentrated on keeping her emotions in check. This was the closest Mia had come to a civil conversation with her mother about the divorce. She didn't want Babs to abort the mission before they got to new territory.

"What happened?" Babs repeated quietly. She folded a paper napkin into a neat triangle. "We spent nearly twenty years building a marriage that was completely out of balance. Your dad and I both made lots of mistakes, lots of teeny steps toward not knowing each other, not loving each other well. And in one quick motion I kicked the whole, fragile thing to the ground and took off." The words seemed to pain her. She closed her eyes briefly, wincing. "It must sound cliché, but I couldn't take the cage anymore." She stopped abruptly, jarred back into the moment and her present company. "Your father was a good man, Mia. We all have our faults, but he was a good man."

"Mother, please." Mia pleaded with her eyes. "I'm a grown woman. I need more of the truth to make sense of what happened. Please."

Babs swallowed hard. "He was very controlling. Nothing that you would have noticed. Most of what happened occurred between the two of us. We were very careful to shelter you and John from any conflict we had." She shrugged. "Maybe that was a bad idea. When the whole façade shattered, you two were so shocked. The rug was pulled right out and you didn't even know there was a floor underneath."

Mia watched her mother's face. "I do remember some things. Like waking up in the middle of the night and hearing you two argue."

Babs raised an eyebrow. "We tried keeping it down."

"Did you go to counseling?"

Babs snorted. "I tried it. But your dad thought it was a waste of money. And since the money was his to distribute ..." She faltered. "Listen, I wasn't innocent, either. I said things, did things to get his attention that, looking back, were only adding fuel to the fire instead of quenching it." Her face softened. "In many ways we stayed at the emotional maturity we were when we married. We were so young," she said, her head shaking in retrospective disbelief. "I was eighteen. He was not even a year older. We should have grown up together, but we didn't."

Myriad questions peppered Mia's thoughts, but she settled for one. "Did you love him?"

"To the very last," Babs said without hesitation. "I suppose a part of me will for the rest of my life. I was free without him, but a marriage binds you in ways that go further and deeper than the license and the ring. I will always love him." Her voice caught. She began to unravel the folded napkin before her.

Mia watched her mother, feeling like a voyeur in such a moment of raw grief. The two women sat there, holding the sorrow between them, cradling it carefully lest it wash over its cracked and broken surface and bring them to their knees.

● ● ● ● ●

The window air-conditioning unit in Mia's apartment provided a grumpy soundtrack to the silence in the room. Mia, Adam, Frankie, and Babs hovered over the Scrabble board, waiting again for Frankie to take her turn.

"We need a time limit," Mia said. She shifted her weight to her right side, taking a sharp breath when pain in her sciatic nerve hollered from her hip.

Adam's face was eighty percent compassion, twenty percent goof. "Sorry. Anything I can get you? I can run down to the store. We got an extra shipment of Vicks VapoRub. My dad uses it for everything."

Frankie snorted but Babs nodded. "Your father is a wise man, Adam. In addition to clearing up blocked sinuses, Vicks has been known to soothe earaches, prevent tooth decay, and build strong bones. I had a cruiser once who said she used it in her banana bread to clear up a head cold."

"Really?" Adam was intrigued.

"Ignore her," Mia said. "Frankie, seriously. Take your turn or Adam will run and get Vicks and then he and Babs will be lost to the evening."

Adam grinned at his wooden squares and his low laugh made Mia's heart jump. She quickly averted her eyes downward and took inventory of her game pieces.

"All right, all right, testy pregnant one. I'm ready." Frankie set down her pieces with a flourish and spread her hands in victory. "Xanadu. Sixty million points for using an *x* and an extra fifty thousand for being so culturally aware." She grinned at the group and commenced an awkward victory dance involving an excess of elbows.

"What's a xanadu?" Babs asked. She wrinkled her face with the word as if she feared the definition had to do with a tropical fungus or unsightly face rash.

Mia rolled her eyes. "Really bad Olivia Newton-John film, circa 1980. Currently experiencing a rebirth as a kitschy Broadway production in New York."

Adam let out a low whistle. "Impressive, Frankie. Both in terms of points racked and knowledge of the music theater scene. Too bad you can't use proper nouns."

Frankie whined as Adam cleared the board of her pieces and did his own version of a victory dance.

Babs sighed and fell back into her armchair. "I'll never win at this game. And to be honest, I don't care a who-diddy. I hated playing it as a child, I hated playing it as a housewife in Highlands Cove, and I hate playing it with you young people who know what's showing in New York City." She smiled sweetly at Adam. "I only came because Adam asked me so nicely."

Mia took great pleasure in seeing Adam blush. "He *is* a nice boy, isn't he?" She reached over and pinched one of his cheeks.

"Shut up," he said like a surly adolescent, though the spark in his eye betrayed how much he enjoyed her ribbing. "I merely brought your mother a box of Godiva dark and a slice of toffee caramel cheesecake from our deli." He lowered his voice. "You have the same gift waiting in your fridge."

"I heard that!" Frankie said, already up from her chair and skipping for the kitchen. "What? Don't best friends count for anything? Adam, you must assume the best friend will want Godiva dark too."

They could hear her rustling around in the fridge when the telephone rang.

Adam jumped up from the couch. "You sit," he said to Mia. "Pregnant people don't need to answer phones."

"Well, la-ti-da." Babs's blue shadow framed bulging eyes. "Must be nice to have someone dote on you in your *condition*." She looked at Mia knowingly.

"He's a very good *friend* to me, Mother," Mia said. She drew out the consonants to dispel any doubts.

"Mia." Adam had one hand over the mouthpiece. "It's someone from St. Jude's Hospital." He shrugged and whispered, "She said she was calling from labor and delivery."

"Do they make advance calls now?" Babs said in a loud voice. "Like reservations at a hotel?"

Mia took the phone from Adam. "Hello?" she said.

"Mia Rathbun?" The woman at the other end sounded like she had a cold.

"Yes, this is she."

"My name is Claudia. I'm an OB nurse at St. Jude's and I'm calling about a patient, Flor Rodriguez?"

"Flor? Is she all right?" Mia's mind raced. Flor's due date was after hers by at least five weeks, which meant she had two months before she should be anywhere near the delivery room.

"She had her baby," Claudia said and paused to blow her nose. "Sorry. Allergies. Ms. Rodriguez had her baby and will recover fine. The baby has been taken to NICU and will be in the hospital for a while."

"Oh." Mia realized she was gripping the phone so hard her fingernails had blanched. "Can I see her?"

"Yes, that's why I called. Ms. Rodriguez has you down as an emergency contact and we nurses thought we should call. She's been here over a day and hasn't had one visitor. You can stop by tonight before eight o'clock. Just check in at the labor and delivery desk and they'll point you toward her room."

"Thank you," Mia said and clicked to hang up. She turned to face Adam, Frankie, and Babs. "Flor had her baby. It's in neonatal intensive care.... I didn't even ask it if was a boy or girl." Her eyes welled up.

Frankie sat beside her on the couch. Mia leaned into her and let her head rest on Frankie's scrawny shoulder.

"I'll take you to the hospital," Adam said, already punching in a number for a cab on his cell.

"I'll go too," Frankie said. She hugged Mia around the shoulders. "She's going to be okay, right?"

Mia nodded. "I think so. I can't imagine how she feels.... I barely know her and she put me down as her emergency contact. Her mom probably didn't even go with her to the hospital."

Adam rose and helped Mia to her feet. "Ms. Rathbun, do you want to come?"

"Oh. Um, not exactly." Babs's face had a tortured expression. She looked at Mia.

"You stay," Mia said, attempting a wobbly smile. "It's okay. Hospitals creep her out," she said to the friends who walked with her to the apartment door.

"I'll just be here praying then," Babs said, waving at the group until the door closed.

# 25

# Pressed but Not Crushed

Flor's eyes were closed and the room was beginning to darken as waning sunlight filtered through flimsy yellow curtains. Mia, Adam, and Frankie huddled in the doorway, watching her frail frame rise and fall with each breath. The room was spacious and with only a bed and a small sofa to fill it, Flor's tiny body seemed overcome with the extra space, a mile separating her from the window, another mile between her and the bathroom door. Mia turned to her friends and motioned for them to leave, but Flor rustled under the bedcovers and opened her eyes.

"Hey," she said, a shy smile spreading across her face. "Come in, you freaks."

The three of them moved as one entity toward the bed. Frankie held onto Mia's arm. Adam had both hands shoved into his jean pockets.

"You guys look like you're on your way to the principal's office," Flor said. She pushed herself up and gained about an inch before wincing.

"Are you okay?" Mia asked. "Should we call a nurse?"

Flor let her head drop softly onto the pillow and rolled her eyes. "Just wait, sister. You're next."

Frankie patted Mia's arm at a frantic pace and said nothing, content to stare with wide eyes at Flor, the wonder woman of sixteen who'd just birthed a real live baby and lived to be a smart aleck about it.

"I'm Flor," the girl said. "I'd shake hands and all that, but maybe that can wait until I'm not hooked up to an IV."

"I'm so sorry. Flor, these are my friends, Frankie Irving and Adam Malouf."

A round of soft hellos circled the room. Frankie cleared her throat. "Flor, how are you feeling? And you can answer that however you'd please: emotionally, physically, spiritually …"

"Or you could say nothing," Adam said, too loudly. "We're cool with silence."

"Jeez," Flor said. "You people are crazy." She shook her head but Mia could see in her face that she was enjoying the attention. "Well, let me see. I just squeezed something the size of a cantaloupe through an opening that's normally about the width of a grape. Maybe a lime, if the need arises." She cast a glance at Adam, who was taking great care to memorize the serial number on a beeping monitor. "Sorry, dude. Just being honest."

Adam nodded quickly. "You know, I think you ladies might be more comfortable, and Lord knows I would, if I spent some quality time in the waiting room. Flor," he looked into her face and couldn't suppress a grin, "good work."

"Thanks," she said. She raised her hand for a high five and he complied.

"A five," he said, relief spilling out of his voice. "I know what to do with a high five. And in more mundane circumstances, I feel very comfortable with citrus fruits and their respective sizes, but—"

"We'll see you downstairs, Adam," Frankie said. She turned his shoulders to the door and he nearly skipped out.

Flor laughed and looked at Mia. "You should totally go out with him. He's really cute. And he talks funny." She nodded. "It's important that a relationship maintain a sense of humor and unpredictability."

Mia cocked her head to one side. "Excuse me?"

Flor shrugged. "One of the nurses brought me an old *Marie Claire* this afternoon. There's some really great advice in that thing."

"So … where's your mom?" Mia tried to keep her tone casual.

"Probably at work. I'm not sure." Flor picked at the fuzz on the hospital blanket. "She left a message with the desk that she'd come by sometime today but I haven't talked with her yet."

"And the baby?" Mia leaned her elbows on the railing of the bed. She wanted to hold Flor's hand, hug her, do something more tangible for her friend when she asked this difficult question, but she stayed rooted to the floor, careful not to assume what Flor would need from her.

"The baby." Flor sighed. "It's a girl. She's really tiny. Just under five pounds." She fixed her eyes on the ceiling as she talked. "I held her for a while after she was born. She looks like me." Her voice broke and she closed her eyes tightly.

Mia took her hand and Frankie moved to the side table for Kleenex. She already had two rivers of black mascara forging paths down her cheeks.

"What did you decide?" Mia's belly pushed up against the side rail.

Flor took a shaky breath and let it out slowly. She took the tissue Frankie offered. "I'm giving her up."

They cried in silence, Frankie sitting at the foot of the bed, Mia holding Flor's hand. Darkness continued to fall around them but no one moved toward the light.

Flor's voice sounded prematurely ancient. "I want her so bad, it's making me hurt. But I looked through all those files at the adoption agency, you know?" She shook her head, tears streaming down her face. "And I know I can't take care of her like those people can. I don't have a job, I don't even have a diploma for a job. She wouldn't have a dad. She'd barely have a mom." She shook her head. "I want to do it by myself but I want to be real about it too." Her shoulders slumped under the hospital gown.

Mia clung to Flor's hand as she wept.

Frankie blew her nose in a most unladylike way. Mia startled, which made Flor laugh.

"Sorry," Frankie said, shaking her head. "I can make a lot of noise through this schnoz." She blew again to prove her point. "But since I have your attention," she said, pulling another tissue out of the box, "I want you to know." She searched Flor's eyes through the semidarkness. "You are the most courageous woman I have ever met." Frankie bit her lower lip as it trembled.

A new wave of hot tears fell down Flor's cheeks. "Thank you," she said quietly. "I'll try to remember that. Because I don't feel very brave right now."

The baby pulled what might have been an elbow or a foot across the middle of Mia's belly and she instinctively placed her hand on her womb. She kept one hand firmly gripping Flor's, watching the care with which Frankie poured a glass of water for the girl. She could hear the musical voice of Silas's pastor at Ebenezer Church, lifting and falling while he exhorted his congregation to bear each other's burdens. *This burden*, she thought, *hurts with its weight.* She brushed a strand of cocoa-colored hair off Flor's brow. *But it will not crush us.* There, in that darkened and quiet room at the bedside of a young and abandoned mother, they were not crushed.

●　●　●　●　●

Adam dropped Mia off at her apartment and only after she insisted did he let the cab drive away without walking her up to the fourth floor. She assured him she was fine, just tired.

"But your eyes are all red and swollen," he said. It occurred to her that he might have thought this a compliment, he said it so gently. "What if you slip and fall? I'd never forgive myself."

"I'm fine, really," she said. She patted his cheek with one hand. "You're a very nice boy, Adam Malouf. I'm lucky to have a friend like you."

He blushed and waved at the cab driver, who was getting impatient. "Friends don't let pregnant friends with swollen eyes from crying walk to their apartments alone."

"Adam, it's one flight of stairs and an elevator." Mia opened the

car door and tried her best to look nimble as she got out. "Thanks. I'll
call you sometime soon." She smiled and shut the car door, knowing
his eyes followed her up the stairs to the building and as she opened
the outside door to the lobby. Still hearing the car idling in the street,
she turned to wave. The taxi began to crawl forward, irritation all
over the driver's face.

She shook her head as she entered the building. Babs must have
employed her maternally gifted supersonic hearing, for the minute
the door opened to the lobby, she threw the one to her apartment
open as well.

"How is she?" she asked, moving toward Mia with rapid clicks
on the tile. Mia looked down at the silver bedroom slippers topped
with bouncing feather poms.

"Honey, tell me! Hurry! I could barely concentrate on my
cucumber mask, I've been so worried." She patted the large curlers
wound through her hair. "I did this just as a distraction. I don't even
like my hair curly."

Through the theatrics Mia thought she glimpsed genuine concern
in her mother's eyes. "She's doing all right, I guess. The baby is tiny
but the doctors say she'll be fine after a few weeks in the hospital."

"It's a girl? Oh, that's wonderful," Babs said. She pulled a silk black
robe more tightly around herself. Mia glimpsed a cotton nightshirt
underneath but feared nothing dwelt below thigh level. Her mother
had never been one for a full set of pajamas. John, in particular, had
cited this as the principal reason he would forever be a guest at the
Highlands Cove Inn rather than wake up in his childhood home and
be subjected to a view of his mother's morning apparel.

"When will Flor be able to go home? Will the baby have to join her later?" Babs tucked an errant spike of blonde into a curler.

"The baby won't be going home with Flor," Mia said. "She's been put up for adoption." Mia felt tears threaten again, remembering the way Flor had watched the ceiling as she told them her decision.

"Oh, that poor girl," Babs said. She shook her head sadly. "I can't imagine how she feels." The lines around her mouth deepened. Without a full face of makeup, Babs aged ten years. Circles under her eyes gave her a defeated air, the punishments of the world seeming to catch up to her perpetual enthusiasm for conquering it.

"I'm going upstairs," Mia said.

Her mother pulled her into a fierce hug. "I'm not one to squawk about the glories of motherhood," Babs said into Mia's ear. "But there's nothing like it on earth. Even a sixteen-year-old child knows that. I'll be praying for her." She released from the hug and hurried to her apartment, closing the door quietly behind her.

Mia pulled her tired body through the space left between her and her bed. She dropped her purse on the kitchen counter, kicked off her shoes on her way to the bedroom, and disrobed without turning on a single light. She lay on her side, cocooned under the covers of her bed. Her cell phone rested in her hand and she dialed his number without allowing herself the indulgence of analysis.

"Mia?" he said upon answering.

"Hi," she said, tears streaming down her face. She heard one drop onto the sheets.

"Are you okay? What's wrong?" Lars spoke quickly.

"I'm okay," she said. "I'm crying."

"Why? Is it your mom?"

Mia sniffed into her comforter. "No. It's just that—" she stopped, her mind crowded with images of Flor, the cavernous hospital room, the isolation of a single mother, even after the most intimate act of giving birth. "I need you to be here. Now. I need you to come here and be with me and help me and not leave me alone." The words tumbled out and she made no effort to rein them in. Her pillow was wet with salty tears.

"Oh," Lars said. His pause was brief. "Okay."

Mia sniffed. "Okay?"

"Okay. I'll talk with my editor at the paper and ask for an extended leave. Maybe I can be there by the weekend."

Mia blotted her eyes with the corner of the sheet. "Thank you," she whispered.

"I'll call you tomorrow, all right?"

"Yes," she said.

The phone remained cradled and warm in her hand even after she fell asleep.

# Socialite

Mia let the line go dead and held the office phone between her cheek and shoulder while she made a notation in the file. Maybelle Anderson, age seventy-five, had called to request a window air conditioner for her subsidized apartment in Florrisant Estates. She said she'd waited until the beginning of September with the hopes that the government could get a better deal. Mia shuddered to think of how the woman had survived August, one of the hottest on record and a time in which she herself had been brought to swollen knees when outdoors for more than ten minutes at a time. Though never one for roughing it, pregnancy had made an official priss out of Mia. She'd walked each morning for exercise, but only if she got moving before seven-thirty. Anytime after that she could be found cuddling her window AC unit.

"Ms. Anderson," she'd said a moment before, "you should feel free to call us with your concerns when they occur. Don't worry about getting us the sale price, particularly when it comes to your health." *You'll do us a bigger favor by not croaking during a heat wave and getting our negligence splashed all over the papers,* Mia thought as she pulled up a number on her computer for the heating and cooling contractor used by Urban Hope.

"Oh, honey, you're sweet. I didn't want to bother. And besides, summers when I was a girl were much worse than they are now. I remember my grandma heating up a kettle of tea on the front porch in five minutes, and that was before noon." Maybelle laughed into the phone, raspy and barking. Mia heard her take a deep breath and then sigh happily, "Ah, shoot."

"We'll get someone out to your apartment as soon as we can," Mia said.

"I know you will." She lowered her voice. "And you and I both know that may or may not be before *next* summer." Another cackle and then a parting command: "Now don't forget to tell your people about that sale at Sam's Club. It's only good through next week and it will save you a nice little bit. Lord knows we can all stand to save in this economy. Tell the Sam's Club folks that Maybelle Anderson sent you. Maybe they'll knock a few more dollars off!"

Mia smiled as she e-mailed the request to the contractor, making sure to CC a copy to Carl. She clicked "send" just as the big man himself rapped two hairy knuckles at the edge of her cubicle.

"Hi, Carl," she said. "Nice shirt."

"Oh, this?" he said in a way that told her it was a brand-new purchase and that he'd strutted in front of his mirror before work, checking out the goods. It was dark blue with bright orange splashes of jungle animals. The collar was too big for his neck and the lapels splayed out nearly to the edge of the shoulder seams. "It's all right, I guess. I'm going to a little get-together after work. You know, poker party." He shrugged to betray his complete inexperience with poker and parties.

"That's great," Mia said, nodding with all seriousness. "Maybe that will become your lucky shirt."

"Totally," Carl said, absorbing fully the greatness of her idea. "My lucky shirt." He looked past her, lost in thought, plotting, she supposed, the breathtaking and illicit adventures to be had in orange monkeys and pleated Dockers.

She waited a beat and then cleared her throat to remind Carl he was in her cubicle and not at a table in Vegas.

"Oh. Um, here." He produced a small gift bag from behind his back. "Sorry I can't make it to your shower."

"Carl, this is very kind of you," Mia said. She reached out to take the bag. Babs and Frankie, against her feeble protests, had planned a baby shower for that weekend, hosted in Babs's apartment and attended by a handful of friends. That Babs had even invited Carl was a bit sketchy, but the list had looked anemic. Ever the ship hostess, Babs was conditioned to believe bigger was always better, even if it meant rummaging around the periphery to drum up revelers. "You certainly didn't need to get a gift."

"I wanted to," Carl said. He placed both hands on his braided leather belt. Mia was fairly sure they were clammy.

She reached into the bag and pulled out a teddy bear adorned with a fussy yellow and purple ribbon. "Adorable," she said and smiled up at him. "This is very sweet. I'll put it right in the nursery when I get home." She started to fold the tissue paper but Carl stopped her.

"There's something else. Actually the bear isn't really the important part. But my mom said I should add something babyish to the gift I picked out." He gestured to the bag.

Mia retrieved a letter-sized envelope and looked up at Carl.

"It's a savings bond. Guaranteed investment, safe and predictable, good for the government." He nodded quickly. "Win-win for everyone. I also printed off information regarding college tuition savings plans for single parents." He blushed. "If you're interested. And if you're still single."

"I am interested and I am single," Mia said. She stood up and circled Carl in an uncomfortable side embrace, intuiting that the press of her belly would make him curl up in his lucky shirt and seek the comfort of his mother. "Thank you, Carl. This was very thoughtful. I'm touched."

"You're welcome." He pulled back and patted his product-laden hair. "I hope you have a good time at the shower. Tell your mom I said hello." He turned and scurried back to his desk and an oasis of computer solitaire.

Mia tucked the bear and the envelope into her purse and decided not to dwell on what else her mother had planned for the weekend. She could only hope that Frankie's influence tempered her mother's tendencies toward the limbo and strip shuffleboard.

●  ●  ●  ●  ●

"I sent a gift to Mom's address. It's very chi-chi. You and Courteney Cox will be hot mama twins." John sounded very pleased with himself.

"Thanks, brother dear. I hope it's a breast pump. I really need a breast pump." Mia stirred in a cup of couscous and covered the pot to steam.

"Oh, please, no." John made a shivering sound. "I never want to hear another word about your breasts or what you do to them, all right? I can barely imagine my little sister large with child, much less what happens when the child exits. So, no. My shopping was a success due to the very hip and very rich people I serve. Breasts never entered the conversation, thank God."

Mia giggled. "Okay, then I won't worry you with how enormous they've gotten."

"Stop it."

"Like, we're talking *way* bigger than that girl you dated in high school. What was her name? Jill? Julie?"

"Please stop."

"Jenni! Jenni Holland. My boobs are bigger than Jenni Holland's."

"I can't believe I'm still on the phone."

"And we also don't need to talk about the pelvic floor exercises I've been doing—"

"That's it. I'm hanging up now. Good-bye, dear sister."

"Hey! Great news. I think I lost my mucous plug last night!"

"Have a great shower. La la la la, I'm hanging up now and can't hear anything else you say."

Mia laughed. "Love you. Thanks for the gift. I just hope it's a dual-side because I'll need to be efficient when I'm pumping."

*Click.*

Mia hooted into the empty kitchen. "Boys are so not made for baby bearing," she said aloud. The pronouncement made her think of Lars, so she scrolled through her recent calls and clicked on his number.

Voice mail. "Hey, this is Lars. I'd love to talk with you and learn from you, but I'm unavailable in this moment. Which is not to say I'm not *present* in this moment. Heh, heh. So leave a message, all right? I'll call you back and we'll connect."

Mia waited for the beep. "Hi. It's me. Just calling to see how you are and to tell you I'm really excited to see you this weekend. I know Mother said she was going to call you about the shower, which will be Saturday morning at ten. Don't worry—I made them promise no gross games like sniffing out chocolate in diapers or eating Gerber peas and carrots. Just come. It will be fun. A very daddylike thing to do." She cleared her throat. "Okay, well, I'll talk with you later. Call me when you get a chance."

She hung up and wondered immediately if she should have used the word *daddy* in her message. Surely the noun had crossed Lars's mind in the past few months. And the shoe fit, as it were. Still, she wanted so badly for Lars to make his own strides in his own time, not to be the catalyst for his commitment to making things work with her and their baby.

The timer on the microwave started to beep and she removed a pot from the burner, opening the lid and seeing a pile of steamed vegetables waiting to top the couscous, along with a drizzle of olive oil, a dash of fresh pepper, and a sprinkle of salt. Mia wished there were cameras to capture the depth of domesticity she displayed in that moment, sitting down to a healthy, home-cooked dinner that didn't send her unfaithful pregnant thoughts and her palette wandering into the meat department for solace and something substantial. She bit into a stem of broccoli, grateful for Adam's guidance with this concoction a few days prior. He'd seen her in the store and had, through the course of his wandering alongside her cart, pulled everything off the shelves needed to make the couscous recipe. As she crunched into a red pepper, Mia smiled to remember his enthusiasm as he picked through Gerry's produce section. He'd muttered through sixteen heads of cauliflower before settling on the perfect specimen allowed into her cart. She didn't have the heart to tell him the first fifteen had looked remarkably identical to the winner. A girl knew when *not* to argue with a man in his element.

She was pushing the tines of her fork into the remaining freckles of couscous when her mother called from outside her apartment door.

"Hello! Anybody home? It's your mother and I know when you're lying, so think carefully before you answer." Babs called her instructions through the wood and laughed at her own joke.

Mia waddled to the door and unlocked the chain. "Hi," she said and made way for Babs to enter.

"Wassup, girlfriend?" Babs asked as she strode into the kitchen wearing a flouncy bohemian skirt topped with an oversized top she'd cinched at the waist with a gold belt. "Oh, are you eating dinner? Sorry to bother." Babs poked in the pots still sitting on the stove. "Eww. Veggies, veggies, and more veggies. And what's this?"

"Couscous. Kind of a mix between pasta and rice. It's Middle Eastern."

"Well, that explains it," Babs said, replacing the lid to the pot. "I've never been there. Too much violence." Babs stabbed a fork into a carrot stick and bit down loudly. "I've heard the Mediterranean is lovely but I'll take the political neutrality of the Caribbean any day of the week." She made a face and put her fork down on the counter. "I'll never understand how you can survive on rabbit food."

Mia shrugged as she rinsed her plate. "To each her own, Mother. Not everyone likes a big, bloody cow flank for dinner."

Babs guffawed. "You sure used to. When you were in junior high, before all this vegetarian nonsense, you could eat us under the table at Amarillo Steakhouse. Remember that place over on Meridian Drive?"

"Of course," Mia said. She pulled out a clean dish towel and dried her dripping plate. "In college I read all about their horrendous employee treatment, their refusal to allow unionization, the unusually high occurrence of salmonella incidences at their restaurants." She grimaced. "I couldn't feel better about my decision to swear off eating there and everywhere like it."

Babs's heels clicked over to the table, calling breezily over her shoulder, "Suit yourself. But I know you'll be hungry again in an hour. And I hope you don't infect my grandbaby with your food neuroses."

Mia took a deep breath and tried to concentrate on the progress she'd made with her mother in the last few months. For Babs's part she'd only picked at the vegetarian "problem" a handful of times since her arrival, which was a huge index of growth in Mia's opinion. Her mother had largely ignored Mia's piercings and the tattoos on her back and ankles after her initial uproar and grief, a period which lasted most of the first month. When Babs moved into her own place, most of the comments about Mia's membership in PETA, the Sierra

Club, Rainforest4Ever, and the Democratic party had fallen by the wayside. In return Mia had forsworn her tirades against talk radio, she'd stopped cringing outwardly each time Babs showed up in spandex and any number of sweatshop-birthed ensembles, and she'd refrained from lecturing when Babs referred to people groups in antiquated terminology. All in all, they had made great strides in agreeing to disagree. No longer did Mia fear a call from the *Dr. Phil* show, asking her to appear on-air for an intervention set up by her mother.

"Now about this baby shower tomorrow." Babs sighed like an Oscar contender. "I have run into *so* many obstacles trying to make this a classy event. And between you and me," she lowered her voice, "Frankie is not exactly the best resource for *glamour* around these parts."

"Really?" Mia turned her head to stave off a smile. She sat down across from her mother.

"Oh, no, she is not. She was no help in trying to procure a chocolate fountain *or* an ice sculptor."

Mia's eyes grew wide. "You're having an ice sculpture?"

"Of course not," Babs said. "Chicago prices are ridiculous. Now, if our onboard sculptor, Juan, were here? He'd whip out a stork and cradle in no time flat and probably only charge me for the ice." She shook her head sadly. "People in this city have no conscience. We're talking down payment on a house in Highlands Cove, sister girl. I ain't playing."

Mia couldn't contain her laughter, born mostly out of relief that she would not be luring Lars, albeit unwittingly, to a mock-up wedding reception orchestrated by her mother. "So ice is out. And the chocolate fountain?"

"No go." Sadness cloaked Babs's face. "I called everywhere. Either the rental fee was exorbitant, and I mean *exorbitant*, or they were booked into November. I guess chocolate-fountain season doesn't take a break in September." Babs huffed, a pout pulling down her cheeks and the corners of her mouth.

"Thank you for trying," Mia said, putting her hand on Babs's and smiling at her mother. "I really appreciate all you're doing."

Babs sat up straighter and looked away, suddenly self-conscious. "Of course I would throw a baby shower for my only daughter. I only wish I could find more gold lamé. I found lots of purple and silver at the prom clearance at the Party Store, but I can't find enough gold to cover the drapery. They did have these adorable shot glasses to go with my theme—have I told you about the theme?"

Mia shook her head but put out a hand to stop Babs from further disclosure. "I want it to be a surprise," she said. "Lars and I should be surprised, don't you think?"

"Lars?" Babs said. Her eyes widened to doe-size. "Did you talk with him?"

"No, I could only get his voice mail," Mia said. "But you invited him, right?"

Babs paused before answering. "Yes, yes, of course. A baby shower without the father of the little one?" She let out a high-pitched laugh. "Unthinkable. Of course I invited him. Talked with him just last night." She cleared her throat and jumped up from the table.

"I'm really so happy," Mia said. She rubbed a slow circle on her belly. "The baby's almost here, I'm surrounded by people who've supported me, Lars is coming home." She looked up at Babs, eyes shining. "Everything's working out."

Babs made a funny sound in her throat and then threw her arms around her daughter's neck. "You'll be fine," she said, patting Mia's back in rapid rhythm. "You've always been a smart girl. You're going to do just fine."

Mia pulled away and drew a deep breath. "I'll be even better when it's not just me. It will feel so good to be an *us*, you know?"

Babs's mouth pulled into a tight smile and Mia thought her eyes didn't match the upward motion of her mouth. "Us is almost always better than I," she said. She spun toward the door, her skirt undulating in a wave of color. "I'm off. See you tomorrow at ten." She paused at the door and spoke over her shoulder but without meeting Mia's gaze. "You and Lars, I mean. See you and Lars at ten."

Mia watched her shut the door and reflected again on the strange conversational skills of her mother. For a woman whose very job description required her to be social, she was one odd duck. The baby moved in slow motion in Mia's womb, every day outgrowing the limited real estate. She looked down at the beach-ball-sized bump before her and said, "You won't be campaigning for gold lamé drapes, right? Even if that gene makes its way to you, please promise me you'll ignore it." The baby kicked, hard, into Mia's ribcage and she laughed through her gasp.

# 27

# Breach of Etiquette

Frankie offered Mia a plate heaped with deviled eggs, fruit salad, a bagel topped with cream cheese and capers, and the coffee cake Adam had brought. "His late mother's recipe," Frankie whispered, nodding at the cake. "So even if you hate it, make sure to rave."

Mia nodded and took a seat near the window. She inched the chair forward several inches to avoid a collision with a cascade of lamé tumbling from her mother's curtain rods. Mr. Lamberti, looking unusually sullen, saluted her with his paper coffee cup. A timid girl from Frankie's library sat next to him, nibbling on a croissant and looking around nervously for Frankie. Mia smiled at her and waved.

"Thanks for coming, Victoria," she said.

The words startled the girl so badly, she sloshed orange juice onto her plate. Mr. Lamberti looked with eagle eyes at the spillage, monitoring if any had made its way to the floor. Victoria, her face an instant crimson, set to blotting the edge of her plate with a palm tree napkin.

Mia sighed under her breath and turned her attention to Silas, who'd assumed a regal pose on the chair beside her. His plate sat filled to overflowing but untouched on a side table to his right.

"Thanks for coming, Silas," Mia said. She leaned over to kiss a weathered, brown cheek.

"Now, Miss Mia, don't be getting too familiar." He cocked his head in mock warning. "What if your mama sees you all fresh and pretty, making the moves on the older gentleman in the group?"

"Shh," Mia said. She ducked her head slightly and whispered, "Don't tip her off. But wait a minute—since when does she have proprietary rights on you?"

Silas shrugged, both palms up. "I'm just saying. Your mother does have jealous tendencies." He dug a purple plastic fork into fruit salad.

Mia took a sip of mimosa, which her mother had publicized was made with nonalcoholic champagne in the interest of the child-bearing among them. Babs had outdone herself in her choice of décor. In addition to the sparkly window treatments, there was black and purple confetti strewn about the food table, black and purple streamers twisted into wild configurations around every linear surface and an impressively large mylar banner hanging above the couch that read *Welcome to Paradise, North High Revelers*. Her mother had blacked out the words *North High* with a Sharpie, filling the spaces with nearly symmetrical stars. Emerging from the kitchen in a turquoise and orange strapless sundress, Babs approached Mia with a wide smile.

"Hi, honey," she said, leaning down to kiss Mia on the top of her head and draping a plastic lei around her neck. "Welcome to paradise. I'm glad you filled your plate." She took inventory of the food before Mia and nodded in approval. "That bagel would be much better with lox but I know how you are about real protein. Frankie wanted to have a tofu breakfast casserole, but I just couldn't do that kind of thing in good conscience. Not at a party I hosted." She shivered.

Mia cleared her throat. "Hi, Mother. Thanks for the shower." She smiled. "Your place looks lovely."

"Very shiny," Silas added. His eyes wandered the room in careful appraisal. "I'm sure I've never seen a blow-up palm tree quite that majestic."

Babs's gaze followed his to the traveling strand of lights pulsing thick fingers over inflated leaves. She sighed happily. "I know. It's perfect, isn't it?" She sorted through the stack of leis on her arm and came up with a hot pink one for Silas. Placing it carefully around his neck, she leaned down and pecked him on the lips. "Thanks for coming, love button."

"Love button?" Mia asked, her mouth full of the best coffee cake she'd ever tasted. "Did you just call him *love button?*"

"Hush," Babs said. She patted Silas on the shoulder and straightened her already perfect spinal column. "I am your mother but I'm still entitled to my privacy." Winking at the man before her, she added, "She'll get used to the idea, sweetheart. Interracial dating is still rather new to our culture."

Mia stared after her as she swayed, hips in full glory, back to the kitchen.

"She's a lot of woman for a man of my years," Silas said, "but I think I can handle her."

"Wow." Mia felt slightly ill at the thought of her mother using the words *love button* with any man, much less one who felt confidence in his ability to handle her. "I didn't know you two were seeing each other. Um, forgive me for saying so, Silas, but aren't you a little older than she is?"

"Nine years her senior," Silas said quickly. "Just about right, in my view. She says she prefers a man with the frivolity of youth firmly behind him. My own frivolity chooses to make its appearance judiciously." He chuckled, then placed a warm hand over hers. His eyes leaped with feisty contentment. "We never know how God's going to ease the burden, do we? Your mother has a big heart, Mia. And many *talents*." His eyes widened and Mia became very nervous that Babs's stand on abstinence outside of marriage did not extend to men with their youth firmly behind them. "Did you know she can name all the parts of a ship, bow to stern?"

Mia had no chance to answer before Silas continued.

"She can twirl a baton! And the woman is *fierce* with a hot glue gun, I'll tell you." He shook his head in wonderment. "The things she can make with yarn and birdseed …"

Mia felt her heart surge with gratitude to see Adam approaching.

"Hi," he said and sat down in an empty seat beside her. He looked past Mia and grinned. "Hey, Silas. How's it going?"

"Very well, Adam, very well. Good to see you, young man. Your dad coming?"

Adam shook his head. "I'm afraid not. He had an emergency

consistory meeting at his church. Something about a communion wine theft."

Silas shook his head and *tsk*ed his empathy. "Part of the reason we went to grape juice a few years back. Lowers the liability."

Adam turned to Mia. "You look pretty."

She cleared her throat and turned to the tiny wedge of coffee cake left on her plate. "That cake was amazing. Did you make it?"

"Try not to act so shocked." Adam rolled his eyes. "Honestly, what does a guy have to do these days to get some respect in the kitchen?"

"Not much, in my opinion," Mia said. "I'd be happy with cold cereal and a cup of tea. But this cake puts you safely into rock star territory."

"Thanks," Adam mumbled. "My mom used to make it. She would have liked you." The confession made him shift in his chair, seeming to regret the disclosure as soon as he made it. His voice louder, he asked, "Where's Lars? Frankie said he'd be here."

Mia glanced at the clock on her mom's bookshelf and was surprised it was already half past the hour. "I'm sure he's on his way. He's probably just running late." She dipped her hand into her purse to retrieve her cell phone. No new messages pulled up and she dropped it back into her bag. "He didn't call, so he must be close." She pulled her hair into a ponytail and let the whole mass of curls drop again.

"It's warm, isn't it?" Adam rose from his chair. "I'll open a window."

She watched him and tried to shake off the wooden, heavy feeling that was making progress in her chest. *He'll be here*, she assured her rattled nerves. *You are far too jumpy. Just relax and enjoy the party.*

Frankie came to the center of the living room and welcomed the small group of friends. Assured by Mia that they needn't wait to begin, she initiated a game that required players to match up baby photos with famous people, local celebrities, and those in attendance at Mia's shower. They laughed when Silas pretended his photo was one of a curly-headed blond boy.

"What's the problem?" Silas asked, his mouth twitching to stay in a straight line. "As an adult I simply tan easily."

Mia laughed with the others and caught herself glancing at Babs's front door. After checking her phone again for messages and finding none, she stood from her chair and caught Babs's eye. "I'm going to call Lars," she said quietly while the others marveled at Adam's conehead in his hospital baby photo. "Maybe something's wrong."

"Wait," Babs said, her hand on Mia's forearm. "What about the gifts? Don't you want to open those first?" She started worrying her bottom lip with her teeth.

"No," Mia said, drawing out the word and peering into her mother's face. "Why wouldn't I just call him to make sure he's all right?"

"No reason," Babs said, revealing in the avoidance of her eyes some unknown but very good reason.

"Mother, what's going on?" Mia's whisper had turned to a hiss. "What aren't you telling me?"

"He's not coming." The words blurted out of Babs's mouth at full volume. "I told him not to." She flinched.

"What? Why?" Mia's mind raced, her thoughts trying to grab onto the image of Lars, not in the room with her and ready to start their new life, laughing over baby photos and eating coffee cake, but in Seattle, far, far away.

"I called to invite him to the shower." Babs looked panicked. "He didn't know if he could make it, and I told him he really should try harder, which led, somehow to an argument. He insulted you, Mia," she said, eyes pleading. "He said you were doing fine without him and that you didn't know what you wanted."

"But this is not a conversation *you* are supposed to have." Mia spoke through gritted teeth. "This is none of your business, Mother. It has never been any of your business."

"I certainly disagree with that," Babs said, making no effort to lower her voice. "You won't understand this for a few more weeks, but once you're someone's mother, you can't abdicate. There's no turning back, no matter how screwed up each of you becomes."

"Screwed up, huh?" Mia said, eyes flashing. "Yep, I suppose I am a screwup. Learned from the best."

"That's my whole point," Babs said, following Mia as she moved to pick up her purse. "I see all these warning signs, all these red flags that you're headed down a path that will give a whole lot of mediocrity to your life.... You're settling, Mia, and I can't just stand by and watch you do it."

Tears made hot paths down Mia's cheeks. She whirled around to face her mother. "Today was supposed to be—I'm running out of—" She closed her eyes to the stares of those in the room.

"Do you know what the sermon was about this Sunday?" Babs's voice was quiet and measured. "Pastor Jenkins talked about how perfect love casts out fear. Mimi, you're waiting for him because you're *scared*. But real love casts fear out of the picture."

Silas shifted noisily in his seat.

"You don't know what you're talking about," Mia said. She clutched her bag to her chest and froze inside the silent circle of friends surrounding her. Mia glanced at Adam, who sat with his head in his hands, and Frankie, who was swaying lightly side to side, as if trying to comfort a babe in arms. "I'm sorry, everybody. I can't do this anymore." She shook her head, tears falling on the hands she'd clasped around her purse. Feeling a sudden and heavy weight in her belly, she turned to the door and walked out, leaving a room of awkward stillness in her wake.

# 28

# Gloves Off

Saturday, September 22. 11:30 a.m.
**To:** denytheman@earthmark.com
**From:** miamiabobia@chicagonet.com
**Subject:** Sorry
Please call. I heard about the tiff you had with Mother. She was
out of line. We need to talk.
**mia**

Saturday, September 22. 2:30 p.m.
**To:** denytheman@earthmark.com
**From:** miamiabobia@chicagonet.com
**Subject:** Waiting by the phone
I've left two voice messages and have texted you three times
this hour. Please call. I'm starting to feel like a knocked-up
stalker.
**mia**

Saturday, September 22. 3:30 p.m.
**To:** denytheman@earthmark.com
**From:** miamiabobia@chicagonet.com
**Subject:** Starting to scare me
I can't exactly fly to you at 38 weeks of pregnancy. Believe me,
I'd consider it.
CALL ME PLEASE. AS SOON AS YOU CAN.
m

● ● ● ● ●

Mia had drifted into a restless nap when her cell phone vibrated under the couch pillow. Two rings in she was awake but befuddled, wondering how all four of her limbs could be asleep and confused by the light streaming through the windows. Third ring and she jumped, fumbling to answer the phone before it went to voice mail.

"Hello?" she said, breathless. "Lars?"

"Oh, thank God." Frankie's voice broke even in the short expanse of those three words. "I was starting to think you'd moved into a van down by the river. Why haven't you been answering my calls?" Relief gave way quickly to righteous anger.

"Sorry," Mia said. She succumbed to a loud yawn. "I couldn't talk to anyone for awhile. Adam tried calling, you did, my mother did.… No offense, Frank. I'm just worn out emotionally. Not exactly the kind of baby shower one sees photographed in *Martha Stewart Living*."

"Are you referring to the paradise prom theme or the only slightly more noticeable but intriguing mother-daughter spat we all witnessed over our Costco quiche?"

Mia groaned. "I'm fully awake now. And I'm realizing I still haven't talked with Lars. Can I call you back?" She tried running her fingers through the train wreck of curls at her scalp but got no more than a few inches in.

"Sure. But Mia, if I may." Frankie cleared her throat. "You know I love you no matter what, right?"

"Yes, thank you."

"And that I'll love this baby of yours probably to the point of being unhealthy."

"Yes."

"Okay. I just want that to be clear." She paused and then added, "He has never deserved you. Just make sure you're sticking with this out of love instead of out of shared history."

Mia could hear Frankie hold her breath and then exhale in a rush. "No one really understands a relationship until they're in it," Mia said. Her voice betrayed a bone-deep weariness. "But I know you say that stuff because you care about me." A beep sounded in her ear and she pulled the phone away. "He's calling. I have to go."

"Call me later and I'll come over with the gifts."

"Right," Mia said, her heart already racing to the other line. "Lars?"

"Hey," he said. She couldn't be sure without the confirmation of visual cues, but he didn't sound upset. In fact she thought he sounded rather relaxed.

"How are you?" She would tread lightly, she thought, gather more information.

"Great," he said. Was that a woman's voice in the background? "I'm feeling very centered."

"That's good," she said. She could feel her brow furrowing above her eyes and made a conscious effort to smooth her forehead. "Lars, I'm so sorry my mother butted into our business. I should have known our temporary truce was too good to last."

"No worries," he said. "Hey, we should talk about this in person."

"Yes," she said, letting her shoulders relax. "When can you come out here?"

"What do you mean? I *am* here. I'm staying at the Palmer downtown since your mom didn't exactly offer her place." His laugh was easy. "We already ate but do you want to meet at Zuba's for biscotti or something?"

"Sure." *Did he say* we? "I'll be there in a half hour."

"Right on," he said, before hanging up with a congenial farewell.

She was in a cab and only blocks from Zuba's Tea Shack before it occurred to her that their good-bye had felt like one between friends.

● ● ● ● ●

Dusk had wrapped an indigo cloak around the city when Mia left the street outside and stepped into the ochres and greens of Zuba's. An eclectic mix of copper light fixtures cast a warm glow over the counter and the small tables encircling it. She spotted Lars at a table near the back. His eyebrows lifted over a steaming cup of tea and he waved her over. She smiled and tugged her shirt over and under her belly, keeping her fingers at the seam to protect herself. En route to Lars, a woman emerging from the restroom caught her attention. Her first thought was that she hoped the long legs and swinging

mane of shiny hair would sit at a table out of Lars's view. The girl
was not good for a pregnant woman's self-image. She walked at a
languorous pace toward Mia and it took a moment to realize the
woman was smiling at her.

"Mia?" she said when their paths met a few feet from Lars.

"Hello." Mia's tone was cautious. Did she know this woman?
Work? Her neighborhood? A quick mental inventory produced no
connection.

The woman pushed forward a tan, lean arm, which made Mia's
plump and dimpled arms jump out from her sides for what she
hoped was an instant slimmer. "Kate Ashworth. I've heard so many
great things about you."

Lars stood and hugged Mia with great care, as if she and her
water might break on the spot. "Hey," he said, pulling back from
their embrace. He looked down at her belly and his eyes widened.
"You're almost ready to pop, aren't you?"

Mia's hand returned to a protective stance at the hem of her shirt.
She glanced at the woman beside her. "I'm sorry, but are you two
here together?" The supreme effort it was requiring Mia to connect
the pieces of this puzzle, after the day she'd endured, was close to
doing her in.

"Mia, this is Kate. Kate, this is Mia." Lars pulled up an extra
chair to the small table. "I'm sorry. I saw you talking and thought
you'd met."

"Just did," Kate said and slid into her chair, crossing long, brown
legs.

Mia eased down carefully and had to move her chair away from
the table to make room for the belly. She folded her hands on the

glass top and then let them drop to her lap, fearing her swollen digits would distract her, or worse, Lars.

"Yeah, Mia, you know Kate. Remember? I told you about the insanely brilliant lawyer who lived in my building?"

Kate laughed and swung a rope of hair behind her shoulder, nailing an audition for a Pantene commercial. The blue in her v-neck sweater picked up flecks of the same color in her eyes. "Give me a break, Lars. As if you aren't off-the-charts in your own field." They eyed each other with playful scrutiny.

Mia shoved back from the table and cleared her throat. "I think I'll get some tea."

Lars stood. "No, let me. Do you still like mango?" He was already moving toward the counter.

"Yes, please." Mia breathed deeply in the moment of silence. *He still knows me*, she thought. *He still knows the details.*

"How are you feeling?" Kate's voice forced Mia's eyes away from Lars's retreating back.

"Um, fine, thanks." She sucked in the flesh under her chin, going for a definition she hadn't exactly possessed since the fifth month of her pregnancy. "I'm tired, but I feel good."

Kate's grin showcased a whiplash-worthy row of white teeth. "Lars was looking at the cutest fuzzy blankets in this shop in Seattle. He said you're not finding out if it's a boy or girl?"

Mia shook her head. Her thoughts were stuck on an image of Lars standing in a Seattle baby boutique, holding up a blanket for another woman's approval.

"Mango tea, decaffeinated." Lars set the mug in front of Mia. "Kate, are you still okay with your coffee?"

"Absolutely," she said and leaning over to Mia, whispered, "It's my one indulgence. A girl can't grow up in Seattle and not appreciate a good cup of Starbucks, no matter if it's the chain that's taken over the world." She shrugged and took a slow sip.

To Mia the action looked inappropriately sexual.

"I'm working on her," Lars said, shaking his head in disapproval. "At least I've gotten her to switch completely to organic, free-trade. And you use soy milk now instead of cream, right?"

Kate nodded. "You're such a purifying influence on me, Lars."

Mia closed her eyes and drifted into a sea of hot tea, hoping when she opened her eyes again, the world would be set aright, Kate would be surfing with someone else's boyfriend in Maui, and Lars would be looking at her with the adoration of a puppy dog.

"So how was the shower?"

Mia opened her eyes to Lars's voice and found she still sat in Zuba's purgatory. "Not too great," she said, a little snippy, she thought when the words were out. "I had a fight with my mother in front of everyone."

Lars looked sympathetic. "That's horrible. Too bad we can't choose our parents, right?" He shook his head and bit into a chocolate biscotti.

"I think you're so brave," Kate said, focusing a sympathetic gaze on Mia. "To keep the baby when things with your mom are so difficult and you have no other family in town … I couldn't do what you're doing. I didn't." She shook her head. "When I was in high school, I had an unexpected pregnancy and had to abort. Thank God for modern medicine because I was *not* ready to be a mother."

Mia looked at the woman, feeling the muscles in her jaw and hands tighten to the point of burning. "I'm sorry you had to go through that," she said and looked at Lars for some response.

He swallowed some chocolate and washed it down with tea before speaking. "You are both very brave women," he said, face shrouded in solemnity. "It's a complicated era in which to be female."

Mia realized her mouth was open and she shut it quickly. It wasn't as if she'd never met a woman who'd had an abortion. In fact, much to the consternation of her mother, she did a project in high school on *Roe v. Wade* and came out firmly entrenched in the pro-choice vote. But on this day, in this space, in front of those two with a beach-ball belly among them, she felt a strange sense of betrayal. Or maybe it was unmerited provincialism, as if she had taken the less enlightened, less medicinal approach to unplanned pregnancy. She watched Kate swirl a tiny straw through her coffee and was frightened at the impulse to dunk her face into a vat of decaf with heavy cream.

As if reading her mind, Kate's eyes snapped up from her cup and she turned to Lars. "You know what, I'm an idiot. You two need time to talk and my history should not be the topic of conversation. I'll head back to the hotel and give you your privacy." She reached out to Mia and placed a hand on her arm. "It's great to meet you, Mia. I hope everything goes really smoothly these last weeks." Her fingers squeezed Mia's arm gently and she left them.

Lars watched her go. "She's amazing," he said with a look of admiration Mia thought more befitting to, say, Eleanor Roosevelt or Mahatma Gandhi. "I don't know what I would have done without her these last few months."

"You have got to be kidding me." The words left Mia's head and mouth at the same time.

Lars looked genuinely perplexed. "What did you say?"

She felt the heat of tears sting her eyes and cursed her recent readiness to weep. Blasted hormones. "Lars, are you dating her?"

"What? No," he said with a guarded surprise that told Mia he'd at least considered the possibility. "She just decided to tag along at the last minute, especially when she heard I couldn't go anywhere near your mother or the shower."

"Right." Anger had begun to pulse throughout Mia and she was grateful as she much preferred rage to tears. "So you aren't with her *yet* is what you're trying to say."

"Mia, you should lower your voice," Lars said. His eyes darted around the room.

"I really don't think I should," she said more loudly. "If our conversation is good enough to be heard by your brilliant, amazing lawyer friend, then why not the whole of Zuba's Tea Shack?" She gestured wildly at the tables peppering the room. "Heck, why don't we go retrieve Kate so she can see this firsthand too?"

Lars pushed back his chair and glared at her. "Do you want to go for a walk?"

Mia was panting, her nostrils flaring in anger. "No," she said quietly. "I do not want to go for a walk. I'm exhausted, my feet are swollen, and it's a lot of work carrying around a small human being in the front of your torso. Let's just finish this here."

Lars sighed. "If you'll promise to be reasonable. Mia," he said, his eyes imploring. "I just don't know what you expect from me."

She shook her head slowly. "And I don't know how you can

possibly be in need of a cheat sheet. You fathered a child, Lars. Typically a father raises his child alongside a mother. They become a family."

"Do you mean get married?" Lars asked. A mix of fear and disdain settled on his face. "I thought we were above all that."

"First of all, marriage is not always a cop-out. It's lasted as a human tradition because there are good, valuable reasons for it."

"Whoa," he said, holding up open palms in defense. "What happened to *my* Mia? The one who mocked her parents' marriage as something they did out of convenience and societal pressure but not because of any higher purpose? Like love?"

Mia tipped her head to one side, keeping his gaze. "I'm not saying I'd like to imitate my parents' marriage, or any marriage for that matter. I would think we'd make our own way and figure out how to build a family on our own. But yes. I want to be married."

"Wow," Lars said. "I did not see this conversation going in this direction."

"Where *did* you see it going?" She felt a lump form in her throat, suspecting she might very well need a thick skin for his answer.

"I want to be a good dad." Lars knitted his eyebrows together and spoke carefully. "I do. But I think I may have to do it long-distance for now." He looked at her and seeing no change of expression, went on. "Things are finally good for my career. In fact I'm really pleased with how it's all taking off. I've built a great community of friends in Seattle. And Kate ..." He drifted off, his cheeks pink with sudden blush. "Listen, we haven't even kissed. But I can't lie to you. I feel things for her."

Mia pulled her arms around herself, resting them on her belly shelf. She shook her head slowly, back and forth, back and forth. The blood drained out of her cheeks and her breathing felt shallow, merely necessary for survival instead of the hot indulgence she'd felt minutes earlier in the flush of her anger.

"She knew," Mia said. She looked at his hands, not wanting to connect with his gaze. "She saw all the things I didn't want to see."

"Who?"

Mia looked up at Lars. She saw a pattern of freckles on his nose and cheeks she'd never noticed before. "I'm leaving now," she said in the same voice she would have used to tell him she'd decided to change brands of deodorant. "Don't call me."

He said nothing and she thought as she stepped out into the darkness of the street that he'd shown uncharacteristic wisdom in remaining silent.

# 29

# Plan B

She made it until four that morning before breaking. Both hands formed into white fists, she pounded on the door under a yellow hallway light.

"Mom," she called through the wood. "Mom, it's me. Please. Mom."

She slumped forward, her forehead meeting the coolness of the door as she continued to pound. Silas opened his door across the way and moved toward Mia with the speed of someone a third his age.

"Okay, honey. You're okay," he said pulling her arms down and tucking her head against his shoulder with gentleness. "We'll get that mama of yours, okay? She'll hear you."

Mia stood, wrapped in the surprisingly strong arms of Silas, when Babs threw open the door. Her face was smeared with a thick covering of white night cream. She took one look at the pair before her and her eyes bugged out of bare circles empty of the mask.

"Oh, dear God, have mercy. She's in labor." Babs moved toward Mia and then backed into her apartment. "Silas, you call the ambulance. I'll grab a hot water bottle and a basin. And a clean sheet. I've seen this a million times on *General Hospital*."

Silas shook his head slowly. "Barbara Jean, your daughter is not in labor. She would like to speak with you." He kept Mia in a tight side embrace and returned Babs's gaze.

She screwed up her face in concentration. "Right now? At four o'clock in the morning?"

"Yes, baby," Silas said with the patience of a preschool teacher. "She would like to speak with you at four o'clock in the morning." He jerked his head at Mia, who was still nestled in his shoulder, clinging to the sleeves of his striped pajamas.

"Well, come in, for Pete's sake," Babs said, moving aside for Silas and Mia to shuffle into her apartment. "Why must people be so cryptic around here?" she muttered to herself as she shut the door.

Silas led Mia to Babs's couch and guided her carefully onto the cushions. He tucked a blanket around her lap, even though the apartment was none too cool in an evening of lingering September heat. Unfazed by the white goop all over her face, Silas looked at Babs and spoke with exaggerated consonants. "You two sit down now and work this thing out." His eyes spilled forth caution that would have been best accompanied by a wagging finger. "This is no time for pride or selfish ambition, in the words of the apostle Paul."

"I get it, I get it." Babs rolled her eyes and sat in a chair opposite the couch. "See you tomorrow, button."

Silas leaned over to kiss Mia on the top of her head. "You're a sweet and smart girl, Miss Mia. And you're going to be just fine." On his way out he stopped to kiss Babs's hand, avoiding a smearing of night cream on his lips. "You're not always sweet but you are smart. And I'm smitten with your sassy self anyway."

She pretended to pout as he closed the door quietly behind him. The two women sat without speaking. Mia heard the air conditioner grind up into a reluctant cycle, as if irritated to be roused again so late in the season. After a moment Babs cleared her throat. Her voice was so quiet, Mia could barely make out the words above the air-conditioning racket.

"All right. I'll say it. Mia, I'm sorry for intruding. I never should have let my mouth run with Lars. This is your life and—"

Mia's shoulders shook in deep, hard sobs.

"Oh, geez. I'm so sorry." Babs scooted next to her daughter. "Dang it. I *knew* I should have listened to Silas and gone right up tonight to make amends. I just get a little testy sometimes when he uses the Bible against me, this time with that whole 'Don't let the sun go down on your anger' thing." She'd pulled Mia to her with one arm and rocked her gently as the girl wept.

"He's leaving me," Mia said finally, blowing into a tissue with great force. "Or I guess I left him." She shook her head. "We're leaving each other."

"Oh, honey." Babs's eyes welled with tears, which splashed through her eyelashes and in muddy white streams down her cheeks. Mia stared, momentarily distracted by this rare show of emotion by her mother. The mime makeup made the image even more compelling. "I'm so, so sorry. I know how it feels to be rejected."

At the sound of the last word, Mia broke into fresh sobs. "And it's not just me he's rejecting," she said through tears. "It's his own child. His own flesh and blood! What kind of man does something like that?"

Babs shook her head. "I'm not really one to cast stones, as they say. We all make mistakes, but some of us seem to be bent on making the biggest ones. I'd know."

Mia sniffed and took in a shaky breath. "Do you mean leaving us?" She paused. "Or staying when you were miserable?"

Babs sat very still, the tears continuing to run unimpeded down her cheeks. Even with the layer of cream, weariness spoke plainly on her face. "I wasn't blameless in either." She turned her gaze to Mia, a sad smile lifting her mouth. "I'm running out of ways to apologize tonight."

Mia let her head drop onto her mother's shoulder and knew no other would fit her cheek as well. "I'm sorry too," she said. "My whole body is heavy with being sorry."

"Let's be done with that part then, all right?" Babs smoothed Mia's hair with slow, gentle strokes. "It's time to try something new."

Mia sighed, allowing the weight of her eyelids draw them down. "I don't know if I can do this by myself," she said. Her words ran together in exhaustion.

"You're not by yourself." Mia could hear the steel in her voice. "We Rathbun women can be tough old broads when necessary. We'll round up the help you need."

Mia felt sleep seeping into her. "I'm not by myself."

"No, honey. You're not alone."

Mia felt the warmth of her mother's hand rest on her head in silent blessing as her body dropped into the mercy of sleep.

• • ● • •

*Late September, Year of Your Birth*

*Dear Little One,*

*You're almost here. My due date is a week away and the doctor says you're making signs that you might not even wait that long.*

*I wanted to write you a letter before you're out of your current apartment complex and moving into mine. I worry that with all the diaper changing and breast-feeding (try not to think about it too hard) and sleep deprivation, I'll forget to tell you things you should know. Bullet points have always been helpful to me, so:*

*• You weren't exactly planned. I know, I know, this is not the way a mother is supposed to begin a letter to her baby, but I have the feeling not much of our life together will be typical.*

*• It was not my plan, but I'm overwhelmed with how perfect it was. Your grandma (who will insist you call her anything but "grandma") attributes this to God and His strange providence. We'll talk later about that.*

*• Your dad and I loved each other. Not perfectly, by any means, but you should know we did. And do, I suppose. More about that later as well.*

• *This is likely to be a grand adventure and I would beg for your patience and understanding as I've never done it before either.*

• *Babs has done it before, but still treat her with caution. For example, never, ever accept food products from her without my approval.*

• *You owe me big time for the havoc pregnancy wreaked on my formerly lovely abdominal region. Big time. Huge.*

• *Stretch marks, I've found, are nothing that can be avoided with cocoa butter or fancy lotions sold to people like Angelina Jolie and Katie Holmes (you can look up those names online). And for the record, one's skin is not the only thing stretched to breaking point with the expectation of a child.*

*This is just the primer. But I wanted you to know what I was thinking right before your debut.*

*I'll see you soon.*

*No one is more surprised than I at the ache of my love for you.*

*Mom*

# Phoenix

Mia checked the hall mirror only because years of personal hygiene had made it a habit, not out of any wishful thinking that she could do anything about what she'd find there. She tucked an escapee curl behind her ear instead of taking the time to gather it into the ponytail restraining the rest of her hair. Her eyes, normally one of her favorite features, were one minute step away from being swallowed by the pillowy nature of the rest of her face. She patted her cheeks in an effort to drum up instant color, licked her lips and tried a smile. The baby, far too large for its cramped quarters, dragged a lazy arm or leg across Mia's belly and she felt the weight of the child shift uncomfortably to one side.

"Science fiction," she said aloud and then jumped when a knock rattled the door beside her. She unhooked the chain and flipped aside the deadbolt. The open door revealed Adam, hair in an impressive though likely unintentional bouffant and bearing four grocery bags.

"Hi," he said from behind one of the bags.

"Let me help," Mia said, moving toward one of the parcels.

"Don't insult me, pregsy," he said, pushing past her toward the kitchen. "These are heavy." He stubbed his toe on the edge of the range and cried out. "Besides," he said, letting down his bags, one at a time, onto the countertop. "What kind of a manly man would I be if I let a pregnant woman do my heavy lifting?"

She leaned against the kitchen table. "You'd probably be considered something of a pansy."

"Exactly." He clapped his hands together and brushed them off, face full of pride for having navigated the precarious transit. "So now you can rest assured. I'm all the man you'd ever need." His grin spilled as much out of his eyes as out of his mouth.

Autumn had made its first crisp entrance that morning and had filled the air and trees with a breath of expectancy, priming the world for its eminent display of color and drama. Adam wore no jacket but had made a shift in his wardrobe from the ever-reliable T-shirt. He rolled up the sleeves of a soft brown corduroy shirt that matched his eyes. "Ready?"

"To birth or to help you cook?"

"Either, though the former might work better with trained professionals." He washed his hands in the sink and she handed him a towel.

"Thanks for doing this," she said. "Both for the nutritional value and for the distraction from the fact that I'm seven and a half days beyond my due date. *Seven and a half days*, if one is counting and one certainly is."

Adam set to peeling garlic. "I wish I could do more than help you put together pans of lasagna. How does it feel to be almost in labor but not yet?" He cast a sidelong glance. "Am I going to regret asking this question? What with my being a manly man and all?"

Mia set a cutting board on the table and began slicing tomatoes. "I'll clean up my response so as not to frighten the uninitiated. It feels like I'm carrying around a watermelon in my belly but that my belly is sick and tired of watermelon so it has given the responsibility to my pelvic region, which is not entirely equipped for weight-bearing exercise."

"That's enough detail, thanks," he said. "I'm getting the picture. As many tedious hours in psych lecture taught me to phrase, *what I hear you saying* is that you are uncomfortable and anxious to get the pelvic show on the road."

"Well stated, doctor." She didn't particularly like cutting tomatoes. The skin never cooperated with her cheap knives and the slices were so unwieldy after the first incisions. Juice puddled on the table surrounding the cutting board. But when a man says he'll fill a girl's freezer with homemade pasta, a girl knows when to shut up and keep cutting.

They worked in silence, washing, chopping, slicing, mincing. Mia watched the bowl of tomato chunks grow as she worked and thought about the quiet way in which her friendship with Adam had grown over the last months. When she replayed the weeks of feeling alone, desperate for Lars to return and hungry for resolution, she could see Adam's face and kind eyes on the periphery, never overstaying his welcome in her life but not more than two steps away, either. She looked at him, bent over the sink and rinsing a tall crop of leeks.

"Adam," she began and stopped, unsure of how to continue.

He looked at her above the spray of water. "What's up? Are you sick of tomatoes? They're kind of a pain, I know. Here, you take these. I'll show you how—"

She shook her head. The seriousness of her face made him reach to turn off the water. He waited for her to speak.

"I realize this might not be the greatest compliment as it's coming from a girl in my condition."

"You mean knocked up? In the family way? Inpregnito?"

"That will be sufficient." She rolled a tomato toward her and began chopping again to give her hands something to do. "So I might not be the one you'd like to hear this from but, um. I think you're—" She looked up at him, knife in hand. "I think you're one of the most beautiful human beings I've ever met. You've been so good to me." She shook her head and felt her cheeks grow hot, her eyes stinging with tears. "You're the real deal, Adam Malouf. Some girl is going to be very lucky to land you."

He looked down at the floor and seemed bothered by her words.

"Did I say too much?" she asked, flustered. "I'm sorry. And don't worry about the crying. I get emotional about everything these days—"

Suddenly he was in front of her. "You should put down your knife. Makes a guy nervous." The smile in his voice made her look up. He drew her out of her chair and into his arms. She closed her eyes and he brushed her lips with a kiss made of honey, mint, cashmere, maybe a touch of chocolate.

They pulled slowly away from each other.

He spoke first. "Don't ruin this moment by telling me you're

damaged or not a great catch or any of that other rot you spout
off with. I know you're pregnant, I know your hands and feet are
swollen, and I know you've gained more weight than whatever is
written in that ridiculous book Frankie reads all the time."

She groaned.

He drank in every millimeter of her gaze. "I know all that." He
shrugged slightly. "But I can't do anything but be floored by you.
So much so that I had to catch my breath when you walked into
your baby shower." He grinned. "Great place to pick up chicks, baby
showers."

"You're sick."

"I'm not done. You do things no one else can do and you do them
so well. Like Flor? That was amazing. And your patience with Babs,
God bless her. And the way you've carried this baby with dignity and
… courage. You're courageous, Mia."

She was crying. Her head rested on his chest and she could feel
the drumbeat of his heart. He held her, kissed her gently on the top
of her head. She could feel her eyelids swelling after crying but knew
there was little left that could scare this one away.

After a moment he cleared his throat. "Mia?"

"Mm-hm?" She closed her eyes and shifted slightly so the belly
was out to one side of their hug.

"I think you just peed on me."

Mia's eyes flew open and she jumped back in horror. "Oh,
please, no," she groaned. "My bladder can't hold anything these
days and the baby's crushing it—" She stopped, her eyes bulging at
the puddle on the floor. "I don't think that's … I think my water
just broke."

Adam turned rapid-fire toward the stove. He flipped off the
ignited burner with a vengeance and sprinted to the door. A second
later he was back, grabbing his phone off the counter. "I'll call a cab.
Do we take a cab? Or do I call an ambulance?" He wasn't looking
at Mia, who stood fixed to the spot on the floor where he'd left her.
When she didn't respond, he looked up from his rabid scrolling.
"Mia?"

"I think we call a cab," she said in an unnaturally calm voice.
"But I should probably have a towel."

"A towel!" Adam said the word much like he might have
exclaimed "Eureka!" upon finding gold in a California stream. He
raced to the linen closet and Mia heard lots of banging doors along
with one cuss word.

She took the towel he tossed at her from the doorway.

"Now do I call a cab?" His eyes were twice their normal size.

"Yes," she said, amazed at the even tone of her voice when her
pulse was setting a personal best. "And Babs. You should tell my
mom the baby's coming."

He whipped a thumbs-up behind his back as he ran out the door
and into the hallway, skipping the elevator and going straight for the
stairs.

Her gait was careful but purposed as she walked around the
apartment, retrieving her prepacked suitcase from the bedroom,
toothbrush and toiletries from the bathroom, a lightweight coat from
the front hall. She felt the first of what would be many contractions
and sat carefully on a kitchen chair. One hand on her tightening
belly, one on the back of the chair, she watched the door, tried to
breathe, and prayed for her child.

• • ● ● •

Babs stationed her face inches from Mia's. She followed her daughter's gaze to the ceiling and said in her best Delia the Yoga Teacher impression, "Beautiful. Now breeeeeeeathe."

Mia ignored her completely and let out a high-pitched whinny. "I can't do this anymore," she wailed to the nurse standing opposite Babs. "Give me drugs."

"All right," the nurse said. Mia had been staring at the woman's photo ID, which was suspended from her neck on a lanyard reading *St. Jude's—We Care.* Above large block letters proclaiming HELEN, the photo was outdated, as were the height of bangs Helen had worn the day her image was captured. "You have written in your birth plan to distrust your first three requests because you …" Helen flipped through the file on Mia's bedside table, "quote 'would like the miracle of birth to take care of itself without human intervention or unnecessary medication.'"

"I was insane!" Mia screamed. "Delusional! Living in a dream world!" She halted her tirade to scream through another contraction.

"We need an epidural. Stat!" Babs's face was white, though this was considerable improvement over the green she'd worn when stationed at the other end of the table during the last OB check. At that point she'd teetered in her stilettos and had needed Helen to escort her to a chair near the window. Now white-faced but no longer swooning, Babs turned beseeching eyes toward the nurse. "You can help her, Helen. Please put this woman out of her agony."

Helen's face remained immobile. Thirty-four years of experience

282                                  Kimberly Stuart

in labor and delivery had provided her with coping skills fit for nuclear holocaust. The two hysterical women before her weren't even registering on her Richter scale. "I'll call the anesthesiologist but I have to warn you. It might be too late." She walked calmly out of Mia's room, white shoes squeaking on the tile.

"I'm going to die," Mia moaned. Her hair splayed out in every direction on her pillow. Beads of sweat pooled on her forehead. She clung with white knuckles to either side of the hospital bed. "This is not normal. There's no way women do this every day and live—" She stopped talking to endure another contraction.

Babs stuck her face between the bedrails. "Mia, look at me." She held up her index finger. "Blow out the candle. Blow it out, like this." She demonstrated a forceful push of air aimed at her "ignited" index finger.

Mia wept and turned her head to face the wall. "In case I don't make it," she panted, "I want you to know I love you, Mom."

"I love you too, sweetheart." Babs fingers patted Mia's arm like the beak of a woodpecker. "But you're going to make it. Everyone feels like this right before the baby's out."

"You're lying." Mia's voice sounded like the scary mini-person in *The Lord of the Rings.* "You have to say that but it's not true."

A sharp knock sounded on the door and Dr. Mahoney blew in, Helen behind him. "Mia, Mrs. Rathbun, how are things going?"

"Get. It. Out," said Gollum Mia. "I don't care if you have to go in with a lasso. Get it out of my body because I'm going to die."

Babs smiled sheepishly at the doctor. "I think she's tired."

Dr. Mahoney snapped on a pair of latex gloves and positioned himself at the foot of Mia's bed. "Let's take a look." He gently pried

Mia's legs apart. After a quick check he asked, "Did you call for an epidural?" He pulled his mask down over his chin and rolled his stool backward away from the bed.

Mia nodded.

"I'm afraid that's not going to happen. You're ready to push."

"Ready to push! Ready to push!" Babs clapped her hands excitedly like a windup toy.

"Whoa, not quite yet," Helen said when she saw Mia grimace. "Give us a chance to get ready."

"Get ready?" Mia's voice was a full-on shriek. "You've had twelve hours to get ready!" In the far recesses of her mind, a small warning light blinked above a sign reading *Avoid Rude Behavior to Those Who Hold Your Life in Their Hands*. She ignored it, however, and kept glaring at every medical professional in the room.

Dr. Mahoney's face did not register any emotional response to being chastised by a ranting female. "Okay, Mia. When I say go, you push while Helen counts. When she gets to five, you can take a breather." He planted himself between the stirrups and waited. Finally he spoke. "Here's a good contraction. Okay, Mia. Push!"

She gritted her teeth and felt a relief, albeit crazed, flood her body. After hours of passive pain, at least she was able to *do* something.

"Five. Take a break." Helen almost sounded bored.

Babs was panting in the chair by Mia's head. "I don't remember any of this," she muttered to herself.

"And so explains the continuation of the human race," Helen said and snorted a quick laugh before letting her face become implacable once again.

"Here we go," Dr. Mahoney said. "Push, Mia."

She complied and felt disappointment grip her when she felt just as miserable upon the contraction's end.

"You're doing great," Dr. Mahoney said. "Don't get discouraged. You've only pushed twice and many women do this for two hours."

Mia's wail floated past her door and into the waiting room, or so reported the desk nurse after the fact.

"Push!"

Mia took a deep breath and bore down. Any sense of dignity out the window hours before, she gripped both knees to her chest and saw stars as she finished the contraction.

"Excellent," Dr. Mahoney reported from the front lines. "Do you want a mirror? The head is cresting."

"Absolutely no," Mia said, eyes squeezed shut. "No mirrors. It's bad enough that you're having to see it."

"I couldn't agree more," Babs said, shuddering.

"Suit yourself." Helen shrugged. "It's the miracle of life, right in our very midst." No inflection in her voice, just a stubborn monotone that wanted to share in the miracle.

"Here it is. Push, Mia. Hard!"

Just when Mia thought she should start looking for a bright light or a halo and wings, Dr. Mahoney hooted.

"Baby's out!"

Mia felt a titantic pressure lift off her body and she closed her eyes in gratitude.

Dr. Mahoney turned the squirming baby toward his mother and beamed. "It's a boy, Mia. You have a beautiful baby boy."

"A boy," she said softly to herself, eyes riveted on the tiny, screaming baby Helen gathered into a blanket. She watched as the nurse wiped him down and wrapped him up, handing him to her carefully.

"Hey, there, sweet boy," Mia said quietly, stroking his pink cheek with her fingers. "I'm here. Mama's right here." The boy's weeping slowed, his brow furrowed at the warmth that blanketed him. "You're okay, peanut."

She watched him watch her, mournful indigo eyes searching the shadows above him for a first look at the voice that had served as his nine-month-long lullaby.

Babs wept quietly beside the bed. "He's so perfect," she said into the hand that covered her mouth. "Only God could make something that perfect."

Mia pulled her fingers across the soft hair of her baby boy and felt the joy of ten thousand mornings fill her. The baby's eyelids dropped without ceremony and he settled into the crook of Mia's arms for a much-deserved rest. *Only God could make something that perfect.* She let the words ring in her ears like a layered peal of bells. Perfection from disaster, grace from self-punishment, beauty from ashes. She leaned to kiss her baby on his nose, offering the moment, the years that stretched in front of her, as an act of grateful worship.

# Epilogue

Mia adjusted the baby backpack and pulled Charlie's foot away from her badgered kidneys.

"It's only a couple of blocks away," she said for the fifth time.

"Bug repellent, bug repellent … I know I had some in here." Adam began throwing things out of an inappropriately large canvas duffel bag and onto the sidewalk in front of Mia's apartment.

"I'm pretty sure there are no bugs out yet." Mia squinted up into a cloudless sky and let her eyes close in the warmth that had finally permeated winter. It had been a doozy, that winter, for a variety of reasons, so the sun's glorious weekend appearance had been met with an impromptu decision to go for a picnic in the park. Adam, however, was not one for impromptu. In fact he had an uncanny ability to sap the spontaneity out of spontaneity.

"I *knew* it," he said, holding up a plastic container of OFF! wipes. "And you, you naysayer," he said, pointing the wipes at Mia. "You'll thank me when no one comes down with West Nile. Charlie, tell your mom it's always better to be safe when it comes to plagues."

Charlie had his face smashed against the back of the pack and was intent on eating a canvas loop that sat at eye level.

"Thanks, dude," Adam said, forcing Charlie's pudgy hand into a fist for a knuckle bump. "You are wise beyond your six months."

Babs burst out the front door in full regalia. A large-brimmed red straw hat topped a matching sundress, a bit optimistic for April, Mia thought. Babs had broken out the self-tanner weeks prior so her limbs looked sun-kissed and ready for the afternoon. Black patent leather flip-flops, impossibly heeled, showed off a recent pedicure.

"I'm ready!" she announced, striking a pose at the top of the stairs.

"Girl, you're always ready," Silas said with admiration when he joined her on the stairs. "How about turning a little readiness this way," he said, puckered up and leaning in for a kiss.

"Stop it," Babs said, shaking her head in feigned modesty. "Charlie is watching."

"Ain't nothing wrong with a man getting loved by his girl, am I right, little man?" Silas leaned down to give first Mia and then Charlie a peck on the cheek. "How's my family?"

"Very well, Silas," Mia said, smiling. She'd never had a stepfather, but she'd decided Silas would be a perfect fit. The wedding was scheduled for the end of the month, just before Babs returned to her seafaring duties with Silas at her side. Mia looked at her mother and noted again the way her eyes danced when in Silas's company. After many years of covering it up, Babs had shed a layer of loneliness that was carefully folded and locked away by the man who now cradled her feisty heart.

"Shall we?" Adam said. He wore a canvas hat reminiscent of Gilligan and Mia had to suppress a grin at the effect.

"Flor and Frankie are meeting us at the park," she said and fell into step with Adam behind her mother and Silas. The older couple began a leisurely stroll. Their voices were hushed, arms entwined with Silas guiding Babs and her heels around puddles in the sidewalk.

"Are you sure you don't want me to take Chaz?" Adam asked. "I feel really weird having you tote him around. You're kind of short."

Mia laughed. "Thanks. But I'm just fine. He's a whole lot lighter than the load you've got strapped to your bod."

He looked down at the picnic basket, the cooler, and the duffel, their straps and handles crisscrossed over his frame. "I hope I got everything."

She took his hand and they walked in silence. Charlie babbled to a noisy bird that perched in a tree across the street. A car splashed through a deep puddle and a little girl laughed through the open window.

"We made it through the winter," Mia said, shaking her head. "Didn't it feel like it lasted forever?"

Adam raised her hand to his mouth to brush it with a kiss. "May I never see that side of you again."

"Hey, that's not fair! I—"

Adam was laughing. "I'm just kidding." He jerked his thumb back to Charlie. "He wouldn't eat well, wouldn't sleep well, you wouldn't let me help.…"

"Not entirely true," Mia said. "You babysat so I could get my hair cut."

"Right." His tone was wry. "That occurred once every other month. What would you have done without me?"

"All right, so it took me awhile to let you help. I wanted to do it by myself. Prove that I could do it by myself."

"Takes a village, people." Adam let Charlie hold his finger in a death grip as they walked. "I'm just glad you got over yourself."

"Me, too," she said, not even bothering to argue the point. It had taken a good three months to reach the bottom of her reserves but by that time she was ready to officially denounce her pride and take any help even the postman would give her. Babs had done her best but had turned out to be useless during the night, late on the uptake before ten in the morning, and chomping at the bit to get out of the house by dinnertime. That allowed for a precious few hours of help, which Mia accepted with relief. The other sixteen hours a day were hers to deal with and she'd felt the need to do it solo. Charlie, though, packed a punch in such a small body, and Mia had finally admitted her little family would be better off welcoming the support they were offered.

They stopped at an intersection.

"Lars is coming this weekend, right?" Adam pushed the button to trigger a green crosswalk.

"Yes," she said. "Friday to Sunday." Her effort to keep the sarcasm out of her voice failed miserably. "Two and a half days to dabble in parenthood. Certainly a fair representation of what *I* do on a weekly basis."

"Now, now, single mother. Bitterness does not become you." The gentleness in Adam's chiding told her he understood better than most the precarious balance she tread.

"I'm not bitter," she said. "He's doing what he can, I suppose. He does love Charlie, in his own way. And I'd never be able to pay for good child care without his help. But I can see him visibly relieved when he boards the plane back to Seattle after each visit."

Adam squeezed her hand. "Aren't you relieved too?"

"I would be if I didn't have such a difficult relationship to tend to here."

"That's it," he said, jogging ahead a few steps into the cleared crosswalk to block her progress. "Put down the baby. Greco-Roman."

Babs heard the commotion behind her and stopped at the curb with one hand on her hip. "Children, can we make it one more block? We're almost there and you're scaring the baby."

Mia and Adam laughed at her concern as Charlie was giggling like a fiend while Mia hopped around dodging Adam's advances.

Silas chuckled and steered Babs by the elbow toward the park once again. Adam saw that they'd averted their eyes and pulled Mia toward him in a long, sweet kiss.

"You're goofy," Mia said, glancing at the cockeyed hat that topped his head.

"And yet you can't get enough," he said and kissed her again. He pulled away. "When will you marry me and let me make an honest woman out of you?"

She shook her head. "We just met." She waited for an uproar and wasn't disappointed.

"Just met?" he said. "We've known each other for years! Since you first came into the store and I started nursing my unrequited love! And I was there for all of Charlie's pregnancy—"

"Not technically. Not for the very beginning, for example."

"I'm choosing not to visualize that." He continued over Mia's giggling. "I brought you food, I calmed you in times of chicken-less-ness, I called the cab for the hospital."

"Dr. Finkelstein cautions her patients against moving too fast."

Adam groaned. "You mean the woman who can't ever see you because she's busy with Glitter the dog?"

"Sparkles."

"You're holding Sparkles and Friend's opinions higher than mine?" His voice cracked with a forgotten adolescent charm.

"Actually I fired her."

"Suh-weet. Really?"

"No. One can't really fire one's therapist. I just told her I wouldn't need to see her anymore."

Adam grinned. "Glitter will be so happy to have the undivided attention. Plus now you can put my education to good use and pay *me* for psychoanalysis. I'm the good guy here, remember? I've never once been unfaithful to you with a terrier."

"I know." She stood on her tiptoe to kiss his cheek. "You've been a rock star. And I've always wanted to marry a rock star."

He smiled and they began walking again. "You *would* be a great rock star wife. Hot, a little trashy, big knockers."

"Wait until I'm done breast-feeding. You'll rue those words."

Charlie laughed at something very funny to the infant mind; his timing was impeccable.

"Good man," Adam said and blew a raspberry on Charlie's chunky leg. "Already acknowledging the value of an hourglass figure."

Mia rolled her eyes but felt happiness permeate her body, her mind, the movement of her legs onto the soft bike path entering the park. She took a deep breath of daffodil-drenched air and lifted a silent prayer of gratitude to God. Even in the bleak afternoons of December, January, February, when her heart was dangerously black with resentment toward Lars, toward her circumstances, even toward the baby that sucked her dry with his need for her, she'd felt underneath the layers of discontent an abiding and stubborn love reaching out to pull her in. She'd felt the heaviness of her journey lifted by people who stood committed to her and to her little family. The women from Ebenezer, who'd filled her apartment with home-cooked meals for eight full weeks after Charlie's birth, clucking about his beauty and wrapping her in strong arms for a prayer of blessing each time before they'd leave. Silas, who'd sneak upstairs on his own and push her out of her apartment so she could go for a walk to "clear her mind." Babs, who'd shown a different, tenacious mother love for her and for Charlie in the way she held them, cared for them, put them to sleep in beds that were never made any more. Frankie and Flor, who'd joined forces and given her in-home pedicures and demanded a monthly movie night, just the girls and Charlie.

Babs and Silas reached Frankie and Flor and gathered the girls in a large embrace. They turned en masse and waved like fools at the cargo strapped to Mia's back.

"There's Flor, Charlie," she said, waving back. "And Aunt Frankie and Nana Babs and Pop … Look at all the people who love you."

Charlie kicked in wild agreement, anxious to greet his adoring posse. Adam ran ahead to set the picnic table and Mia followed him with her eyes. She smiled as she approached, filled again with the strange beauty that comes from being loved by a man who knows himself and the girl of his affections well but chooses to build a life together anyway. Light filled the park and Mia allowed joy to sink into any parched and broken surfaces still living within her. She opened her arms to the bevy of hands reaching for her son, reaching for her, pulling them both into the bottomless embrace of family.

## ... a little more ...

When a delightful concert comes to an end,

the orchestra might offer an encore.

When a fine meal comes to an end,

it's always nice to savor a bit of dessert.

When a great story comes to an end,

we think you may want to linger.

And so, we offer ...

AfterWords—just a little something more after you

have finished a David C. Cook novel.

We invite you to stay awhile in the story.

Thanks for reading!

Turn the page for ...

- **Excerpts from the private journals of Barbara "Babs" Rathbun**
  - **Announcing with Great Joy ...**
  - **Adam's Begrudgingly Vegetarian Portabello Burgers**

# Excerpts from the private journals of Barbara "Babs" Rathbun

January 1

*Happy New Year! Could I possibly have a better job? I spent last night counting down to the brand-new year on the upper deck, next to the topless area that, thankfully, was not in use due to the hour. Though I must say I've seen plenty of those people only minimally interested in the sun and mostly interested in the parade, if you know what I'm saying. Last night I danced with not one but three doctors, one of whom is recently single and from SPAIN. He showed me how they eat one grape for every chime that sounds at midnight. Muy interesante. Unfortunately, he (Miguel? Manuel? Something like that) had to catch an early flight out of port to get back to saving the world, one surgery at a time. I certainly did not stand in his way. Where would all of us be without professionals like him?!*

February 12

*Having a very difficult time getting a hold of my daughter, who appears to be stuck in the late nineties with regards to her emotional maturity. I've already written at length about her similarly troubling FASHION time warp and will not take more time on the subject here. To date: twelve phone calls, ten answering-machine messages, two postcards, all unanswered. Considering taking more drastic measures.*

Date Unknown

*Mia is pregnant by that wretch of a Scandinavian. I'm nearly beside myself with horror and grief. I never should have let her watch that sex ed. video in sixth grade. My work experience has been called upon without pause; there's something so comforting to people in having a sunny disposition in the face of crisis. Just this morning, as I was picking up Mia's mail, her neighbor, a very nice black man who might be related to Barack Obama, said I looked like the face of sweetness itself. I smiled a winner smile to show my gratitude but had to wipe away tears on my way back up to Mia's place. Goes to show: The show must go on but the actress leads a lonely life.*

*Listened to Barbara Streisand the rest of the morning.*

May 21

*Wazzup wazzup wazzup! I'm hip to the hop with urban culture and putting down ROOTS in Chi-town. This is a city that explodes with high adventure and new experiences, not the least of which is soul food. Silas and I have visited three of his favorite restaurants. At Sugar Snap's, I became fast friends with our waitress, Shanelle, who has invited me to her house to teach me how to braid hair. She swears it doesn't matter that my last cut left me with no longer than two inches of length. I was forced to believe her. I mean, remember when Oprah showed up one day—just like that— with long and perfectly coiffed curls? If she can do it in Chicago, so can I! Peace out.*

June 3

*Mia is not far enough along to be acting so miserable. She absolutely wigged today when I surprised her by cleaning out her closet. Apparently waffle-print henleys are still all the rage among tree-huggers. She insisted on keeping ALL NINE.*

June 30

*Chicago has lost its luster. The heat today will reach a scorching 101 degrees, no breeze, 92% humidity. WHY oh WHY did I quit my job?!?!*

July 15

*Sweet Silas brought me a bouquet of baby's breath today. Told me it reminded him of me, beautiful and delicate but undervalued by those who need my help. That man made me cry, I tell you.*

August, doesn't matter the exact day.

*Hot, hot, hot, miserably miserable. I refuse to take public transportation just on the sweat principle. Even children seem tired out by summer. Were there not Lake Michigan, I think the entire city would go mad. I tried discussing the lunacy of living here with Mia, but she was not particularly receptive. Must be the final trimester. That and the swelling.*

September 30

*Mia's due date, come and almost gone. I'm so nervous, I've taken to giving free manicures to all the women in my building. Warned Silas tonight that when I'm finished with Mrs. Whittinghouse on the second floor (a prospect that gives me the willies, I must admit), he's next. He threatened to bring Mia over to the hospital himself and have them induce.*

October 8

*Charles River Rathbun! (Skjørland tacked on for the moment—it will pass).*

*Absolutely, perfectly beautiful. Mia's eyes, hair, and serious countenance. Lars's tendency for drama. All in all, the best possible introduction to being a Nana. Let the spoiling begin!*

Announcing with Great Joy . . .

Charles River Rathbun-Skjørland
8 pounds, 1 ounce, 22 inches

In honor of Charlie's birth, please
consider giving a donation to
your local food pantry.

This announcement printed with soy ink on 100% recycled paper.

# Adam's Begrudgingly Vegetarian Portabello Burgers

## (or Keeping the Peace While Madly in Love with a Non-Meat Eater)

4 Asiago bagels from your favorite bagel shop
4 large portabello caps

Sauce:
Soy sauce, sake or white wine, lemon juice

Garnish:
Romaine leaves
Sliced white cheddar, Pecorino Romano, or in a pinch, Swiss
Dill-infused mayo

1. Slice bagels and spread with butter. Set aside.

2. Brush mushroom caps with olive oil. Sprinkle with kosher salt and freshly ground pepper to taste.

3. Fire up the grill and slap on the mushrooms, trying not to think about how much better a fillet would be. Grill 2 minutes or so on each side. During the last minute add the bagels to toast. Watch the bread carefully or this step could end badly.

4. Meanwhile (or before you start, depending on how adept you are at multitasking), pour into a small saucepan ~1/3 c. soy sauce, ~1/3 c. sake or white wine, and some fresh lemon juice. Please don't press me on exact measurements; you'll know if it's wrong and then you just doctor it up. Let this concoction reduce for 10 minutes or so.

5. Mayo: Chop up some fresh dill or smoosh some dried dill in your hands. Add to mayo and mix. I also add a splash of lemon juice, salt, and pepper. Again, exact measurements are not really the issue here.

6. Assemble sandwiches. Bagel first, then mushroom, reduced wine sauce, romaine, cheese if desired, and a spread of mayo.

7. Present to vegetarian love interest with nonchalance, a smile, and the promise of a chocolate dessert. Make this enough times and she won't even mind that her mushroom shares a grill with your steak.

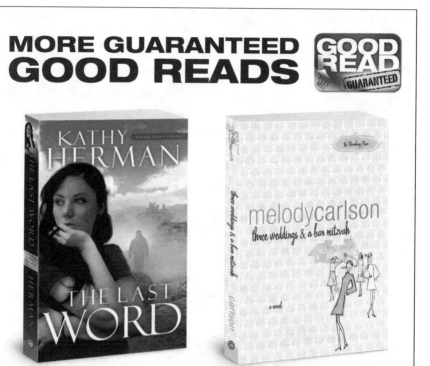

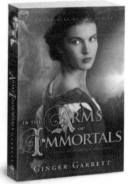